VIGILANCE

KEN LOZITO

ACOUSTICAL BOOKS LLC

Published by Acoustical Books, LLC

KenLozito.com

Cover design by Jeff Brown

IF YOU WOULD LIKE TO BE NOTIFIED WHEN MY NEXT BOOK IS RELEASED VISIT

WWW.KENLOZITO.COM

ISBN: 978-1-945223-29-7

1

CONNOR WALKED across the airfield of the CDF base at Sanctuary. There was a small hangar across the way where the Falcon Fighters Series 7 were kept. Their dark, sleek bodies had stub wings and powerful rear engines designed for atmospheric flight. He'd just recertified his flight status and was now qualified to fly one of them. Technically, no one could just take one of the Falcon Fighters, but Connor was a general in the CDF, and rank did have its privileges. He couldn't imagine any general in the NA Alliance military using a fighter for personal transport, but those in the CDF tended to be much more versatile, and he was qualified to fly the ship.

Diaz called out behind him, and Connor stopped as his friend jogged to catch up. Diaz was wearing the blue CDF uniform with captain's bars on the side. His stocky frame bulged against the smart fabric of his uniform, and Connor could hear him exhaling loudly as he ran.

When Connor rejoined the CDF, there'd been a number of former soldiers who expressed interest in rejoining as well. Some of those soldiers served on a part-time basis while others had become fully active. In response to this recent resurgence, a reserve force for the CDF had been created. Reserves were an old tradition in Earth's militaries that allowed former soldiers to maintain a less active role but provided a cushion of readily available soldiers that offset the time it would take to train civilians. Many of the reservists had come from the Recovery Institute at Sanctuary that Connor had founded a few years earlier to help soldiers reacclimate to colonial life.

Diaz caught up to him and sighed explosively. "I really need to up my cardio. I shouldn't be this out of breath."

Connor resumed his pace. "Well, you *have* been spending a lot of time at the family restaurant."

Diaz smiled. "I love cooking, but my replacement chef is more than up to the task."

Connor arched an eyebrow toward him as a comment hung on the edge of his lips.

Diaz waved him off. "Don't give me that crap. I'm on active duty, and I'm here by your side."

Connor closed his mouth and they were silent for a moment. Six months ago, they'd gotten a wake-up call regarding what the NEIIS had been dealing with before the collapse of their civilization—an interdimensional invasion force that they knew painfully little about. Connor couldn't sit idly by and let others deal with it, especially not when he knew he could help, and Lenora fully supported his decision. Connor had stationed himself at the CDF base at Sanctuary so he could be close to his family, and he made a point of being part of his baby girl's life. He refused to let the military take over like it had before.

"Where we going?" Diaz asked.

"I thought I'd take one of the Falcons for a short trip."

Diaz looked at the sleek form of the Falcon and blew out a long whistle of appreciation. It was a two-person fighter that was designed to provide air support for ground forces, as well as stinger operations for blindsiding the enemy. It was also extremely fast, and Connor needed every bit of that speed to make his meeting for the Colonial Defense Committee.

"I thought you weren't due to be in Sierra until this afternoon?"

"You're right, but I need to go somewhere else first. There's a ..." Connor paused. He'd been about to say an old friend, but that wasn't entirely accurate. Sure, the person he was meeting had been his friend once but not anymore. Not for a long time. "... an old acquaintance I need to see."

They reached the Falcon Fighter, and the officer in charge escorted them to the pad. The Falcon had sleek lines, with the cockpit in front of the engines. The canopy opened to reveal two pilots' chairs next to each other. A gray synthetic fabric covered the SmartCushion that would contour to their bodies for maximum comfort and support.

They climbed inside and Connor brought the flight systems online. When the watchtower transmitted clearance, he engaged the engines. The Falcon's repulser engines pushed the attack aircraft off the ground, and Connor eased it forward out of the hangar. They quickly ascended several thousand feet, after which Connor engaged the mains and the Falcon sped away. Despite the inertia dampeners, they both felt the kick of the powerful engines as they raced over the New Earth landscape. Diaz chuckled in appreciation. They headed north, and Connor set a course away from any of the colonial settlements.

"Thanks for coming with me," Connor said.

Diaz eyed him warily. "No problem. Who are we meeting way out here?"

"Samson."

Diaz cursed under his breath. "Not again. The last time— Are you crazy?"

Connor shrugged. "I need him."

"I don't think he cares. He threatened to kill you if you came looking for him again."

"It's been a few years, and a lot has changed. He's the only one left who hasn't..."

They were both silent for a few moments. Samson was one of the few surviving members of the Ghost Platoon. When they'd been brought out of stasis on the *Ark* more than ten years earlier, not every member of the Spec Ops platoon Connor had led for the North American Alliance Military had embraced becoming a colonist. None of them welcomed the idea, but eventually they'd all come around, with the exception of Samson. He'd had a rough time adapting to colonial living, and even though he'd been in the CDF helping to train the infantry and Spec Ops platoons, he'd never embraced the colony. Less than a year after being brought out of stasis, he left and headed out to the New Earth frontier. Connor assumed Samson had died, but he'd found him a few years ago while they were searching for NEIIS bunkers. Samson had been roaming the continent.

"Besides, he might actually talk to you," Connor said.

"I haven't seen or talked to him since he left. I doubt he'd even remember who I am."

Connor sighed. "That's just it. He doesn't forget...anything."

"I think we should just leave him alone. He never wanted to be part of the colony."

Connor glanced at Diaz. "You can say it—he blames me for his being here. But we need his help."

"Why?"

"When we created the Colonial Defense Force, we designed it to meet an enemy that was coming from space. Our infantry is extremely capable, but you were there. The threat we're facing now is different. Samson was a heavy-weapons expert, and before that he was part of a force recon team. I can try and train troops to do the job, but sometimes there's no substitute for experience, even for someone who's been out of it for over ten years. Samson would be a real asset if I can convince him to return to the colony and the CDF."

The Falcon Fighter sped along, consuming kilometers as the minutes ticked by.

"If you wanted him to come back with you, why did we take this ship? There's no room for a third person in here," Diaz said.

"I just want to ask the question. He's lived apart from people for so long that he might need to warm up to the idea. Regardless, I owe him. I can't give up on him."

"Connor, there's loyalty, but maybe you should let this go. Samson might be better off on his own. If he wanted to come back, he would've."

Connor nodded. "You might be right. Actually, you probably *are* right, but I still need to try. Also, you don't know Samson like I do."

The remainder of the trip was silent as they flew over an old mountain range. A mist lay over the land like a crippled storm cloud, sluggish and dense in some places, thinner in others. They were three thousand kilometers from Sanctuary when Connor slowed their velocity as they approached their destination and scanned for colonial energy signatures. Samson might like to live apart from the colony, but there were some technological accoutrements that Connor knew he'd used. A colonial comlink registered on the scanner output, and Connor flew toward it. An alert appeared on the heads-up display, showing a large pack of ryklars that were just over a klick from them, but otherwise there were no other predators around.

Connor set the fighter down in an open area near a grove of New Earth trees that were similar to pines but with sap that released a pungent odor in the spring. They climbed out of the airship, and Connor deployed a couple of recon drones. He'd powered down the fighter's systems, and the area was quiet except for the cool breeze that still had a bit of winter in it. The wind kicked up and the foliage shifted around them. Connor retrieved an AR-71 assault rifle and handed one to Diaz. No one went beyond colonial settlements unarmed, and now that Connor was back in the CDF, he had access to military-grade weapons. He kept the weapon in standby with the safety on, having no intention of using it. Diaz checked his and gave Connor a nod.

"So we're just going to walk in there and what? Start yelling out to him?" Diaz asked.

Connor noticed the slightly elevated tone from his friend. "You seem a bit nervous. You can wait by the ship if you want."

"Give me a break. I'm fine. I just want to get this over with," Diaz said and walked ahead of him. He turned back. "You know we could've brought a squad with us. Might've been better."

Connor smiled and took the lead.

A fog seemed to encroach upon the surrounding area, but they found Samson's camp easily enough. There was a firepit in the middle of the camp, and the charred remains of the previous night's fire glistened in the damp air. On the other side of the camp, about twenty feet off the ground, was a cabin. Its wooden construction looked well supported. The planks of aged wood were a tawny gray, and Connor wondered how long Samson had lived there. He called out a few times, but there was no reply.

"He's probably not here," Diaz said and walked toward a table. There were several tools on the table, and Diaz fingered them idly as he glanced at Samson's abode. "How does he get up there?" he asked, gesturing toward the cabin.

Connor had just glanced up at the structure, searching for a ladder, when Diaz cried out and fell to the ground as if something had kicked his feet out from under him. Then his friend was dragged toward a tree and hoisted high into the air. There was a snap-hiss as webbing burst from a hidden trap and plastered Diaz to the tree. Connor quickly looked down and saw a metallic cord slithering toward *his* feet, too, so he leaped toward the firepit and the trap missed him. He fired a few rounds at it, and it retracted to its source. At least Samson hadn't set his traps to persist.

Diaz swore. "That son of a— Get me down from here! I'm gonna—" He scowled, looking around for Samson. Connor grinned. He couldn't help himself, and Diaz's gaze swooped toward him. "Don't you dare laugh at me!" he shouted as he strained against the webbing, but it held him firmly in place. His rifle was on the ground. "Did you know about this?"

Connor shook his head. "How would I know?"

Diaz shook his head and muttered something about grabbing his knife. "You can help me get down, you know, instead of standing there doing nothing."

"I thought I'd take a few pictures and send them to the boys back home."

"Dammit, Connor! I'm gonna kick your ass when I get outta here."

Connor carefully walked toward where Diaz was trapped and stopped. He peered around the camp, looking for other traps, then inhaled and shouted, "I just want to talk to you. Then we'll go."

An arrow flew past Connor's head and buried itself into a tree. Connor squatted down and brought his rifle up, engaging the multipurpose protection suit system he wore over his uniform, even though he knew it had been a warning shot. Samson hadn't really been aiming for him, or he wouldn't have missed. Connor scanned the surrounding forest, looking for a heat signature, but didn't find any. He engaged the ryklar protocols on the recon drone and adjusted the setting for humans.

Connor turned away from Diaz. "You missed."

An arrow struck Connor's body and bounced off the MPS, which was more than up to the task of repelling such a primitive weapon. The recon drone alerted him to Samson's location just in time for him to hear heavy footfalls moving away from them.

Connor reached for the combat knife on his belt and tossed it up to Diaz, who just barely managed to catch it. Then he ran away from the camp, following Samson.

He caught a glimpse of Samson's hulking form farther along the path. Glancing up, he saw a rotting tree limb ahead, so he brought up his AR-71 and squeezed off a few rounds. The limb fell to the ground, tripping the former Ghost, and Connor caught up to him, quickly blocking the man's path.

Samson wore a long coat of ryklar skins, which looked to have been stitched together to cover his large frame. It was the ryklar skins that had prevented him from being detected on infrared.

Samson stood up, towering over Connor, and pulled the hood from his head. Years of roughing it on the New Earth frontier had hardened him. His thick brows pushed forward, and his menacing gaze was almost feral.

"I just want to talk," Connor said, holding his hands up to show that he meant no harm.

Samson lunged forward with a growl, tackling Connor to the ground, but Connor managed to scramble away just as Samson slammed his fist down onto the ground where he'd been only a moment before. Connor stood up and kicked the big man in the stomach. It felt like his boot had struck a boulder.

Samson grunted as he regained his feet, and Connor pointed his rifle at him.

"Go ahead. Shoot me," Samson said in a deep voice, calling Connor's bluff.

Connor stepped back and let go of his rifle. The auto-tether snatched it to his back, securing it in place. "Don't make me do this."

The big man lunged forward, and Connor sidestepped, shoving away Samson's powerful hands while kicking him in the rump—more of a sting to Samson's pride than anything else. Samson spun around and charged again, and Connor had no choice but to grapple with the former Ghost. Samson wrapped his arms around Connor's body, trying to squeeze the life from him, but the MPS became a hardened shell, protecting Connor from harm. He slammed his hands onto Samson's ears and then hammered his fists on the man's face, but Samson growled and heaved Connor around as a wild animal would. Connor pressed his hands on both sides of the man's throat and squeezed, seeking to cut off the circulation from his carotids, but Samson continued to squeeze Connor's body in a bear hug.

"You'll lose consciousness before you break my back. Let me go," Connor said.

Seeing that his efforts had no effect on Connor, Samson dropped him to his feet and punched him square in the face. The MPS didn't cover Connor's face, and there was a white explosion of pain through his cheek. The force of the blow made Connor stumble, but he was ready for Samson's next strike. He pulled Samson off-balance and hopped onto his back, putting him in a choke hold.

"You could make this easy," Connor said, straining to hold the big man.

Samson growled, but he started to sway on his feet, fighting to remain conscious. He stopped struggling and held up his hands. Connor didn't let go.

"All right," Samson said, finally. "I'll talk, but then you'll get outta here and leave me be."

Connor let go and landed on his feet. Samson turned toward him, and for a moment Connor thought he'd strike again.

"Let's head back to the camp. I need to get Diaz out of the tree," Connor said.

Samson grunted and strode back toward the camp. His strides were lengthy, but Connor was able to keep up with him. When they got back to camp, Diaz was busy cutting through the webbing that held him to the tree.

Samson pulled up his sleeve, revealing a PDA strapped to his wrist, and operated the interface. The tension in the webbing retracted, and Diaz swung away from the tree as he was lowered to the ground.

Diaz came to his feet and snatched his rifle off the ground. "You know, I oughta shoot you."

Connor got between them, and Diaz glared at him. "Get out of the way. Just let me shoot him in the leg."

"You came uninvited," Samson said.

Diaz shook his head, scowling. "It wasn't funny in training, and it's not funny now."

"If you'd learned better, you wouldn't have been stuck on that tree," Samson replied.

"Oh really," Diaz said, pointing his rifle at the cabin.

"That's enough!" Connor shouted before Diaz started shooting. "Go back to the ship."

Diaz glared at Connor for a moment. "This was a waste of time," he said and started to leave, but he suddenly turned around and flung a little glowing sphere toward Samson. A small, focused, concussive blast knocked Samson to the ground, and Diaz laughed as he walked away.

Samson lay on the ground for a few moments, gasping, and then laughed. Connor walked over and extended his hand, but Samson ignored it and stood up on his own.

"I've been keeping track of you," Connor said. "You move around quite a bit."

"What do you want, Colonel?" Samson asked, addressing Connor by his old NA Alliance military rank.

Connor regarded him for a moment. "Neither of us are who we once were."

Samson looked at Connor's uniform. "Just because you convinced a bunch of colonists to call you 'general' doesn't mean you are one."

"They can call me whatever they want. I only care about getting the job done, which is to protect these people."

"Well, don't let me stop you."

"It's not that simple. I need your help. I need your skillset, your know-how, your experience."

Samson shook his head. "You trained them. The Vemus are gone. Yeah, that's right. I heard about the war you fought. If the CDF was good enough for that, then they're good enough for whatever else you've got in mind."

Connor told Samson about the NEIIS and what they'd discovered.

"A new threat to the colony," Samson said. "You think that's gonna get me to come back with you? Put on a uniform? Follow orders?"

"I thought it might. I've seen this enemy. They're different from the Vemus. More dangerous. I need the best, and that means you."

Samson crossed his thick arms. "Based on what you just said, you know hardly anything about what you're facing."

"You're right. We need to do reconnaissance and find out everything we can about them because one day they're going to come here, and if we're not ready, then that's it for all of us. And that includes you. Sooner or later you've got to come back to the colony."

Samson sneered. "I never wanted this colony or these people. I don't care if they all die."

Connor regarded him for a moment. "I know that's not true. You can fool the others but not me. I know you care if innocent people die. Everyone we left behind—"

Samson's arms dropped to his sides as he stepped toward Connor. "Say their names," he hissed.

Connor met his gaze. "I don't have to. I have my own list of names, and I think of them every day, but I've moved on and you can, too. Or you can stay out here, bitter and detached from everything, trying to convince yourself that this is what you want. Dying alone isn't all it's cracked up to be. Wil and Kasey would tell you that."

"Wil and Kasey died following you."

Connor balled his hands into fists. His knuckles yearned to punch something, hard, but he clamped down on his anger. "They died trying to protect the colony. This is our *home* now." Samson opened his mouth to reply, but Connor shut him down. "There's a place for you in the CDF if you want. Even if you don't, you can still come back to any of the cities. Stop this before it's too late."

Samson's frown deepened, and he looked away.

"I don't expect you to come now, so I'll leave this comlink with you. Its broadcast range is much greater than the one you're carrying." Connor tossed the comlink toward Samson, and he caught it more out of reflex than desire. "You should come back before it's too late. You're dressed in ryklar skins like some kind of animal. You're better than that. Stop blaming me and everyone else for what happened."

They were quiet for a few moments and the fog couldn't decide whether it would swallow them up or not.

"You're not the only one left, you know. Tiegan and Sawyer are both still alive. They live in Delphi, and they have families."

"I *had* a family," Samson said. He inhaled deeply through his nose and sighed, then turned around and walked back into the woods.

So did I.

Connor watched him go as the fog quickly swallowed his old friend. At least he'd taken the comlink. The new tracker in it could accurately pinpoint Samson's location to within two meters. Just in case.

2

CONNOR WALKED BACK to the ship and found Diaz waiting for him. He'd cleaned himself up but still looked to be seething.

Diaz looked away from Connor and shook his head. "Was that about what you'd expected to happen?"

Connor glanced back the way he'd come for a moment. "Wouldn't you throw a drowning man a lifeline?"

Diaz pinched his lips together and furrowed his brow. "Sometimes they can't be saved no matter what you do," he said and opened the hatch to enter the ship.

"I still had to try."

Diaz sighed. "I know you did. Even if he did come and join the CDF, would you want a guy like that guarding your back?"

Connor climbed into the cockpit and strapped himself in, then brought up the Falcon's systems. Samson had guarded his back for years before they'd ended up on New Earth, but maybe Diaz was right and the man was too far gone.

Diaz blew out a breath. "Look at him out there. He's watching us. Do you see him in that tree?"

Connor looked to where Diaz gestured and saw Samson

looking back at them. The gray hair on the ryklar skins was a natural camouflage, but there was no mistaking Samson's dark-skinned head. Connor brought up the comlink interface on his internal heads-up display, hoping Samson would initiate a link.

He didn't.

"I guess he just wanted to make sure we left," Diaz said.

Connor nodded and engaged the flight controls. He set a course for Sierra and the flight time appeared on the Falcon's heads-up display. After running his fingers over his cheek and feeling a bruise forming there, he reached into the side compartment for the first-aid kit and applied some healing gel. The tenderness immediately subsided. It wouldn't look good for him to show up to his meeting with the Colonial Defense Committee sporting a bright shiner on his cheek.

"This has to be the last time, Connor."

"Yeah, I think you're right."

"You're lucky you were wearing that MPS. I didn't even know you had one on."

"It's a habit now, and the CDF engineers have made some upgrades to Noah's design," Connor said.

Diaz was silent for a few moments. "It's a real shame what happened to that kid. He didn't deserve it."

"None of them deserved it," Connor said a bit roughly.

Diaz took the hint that Connor didn't want to talk anymore and looked out at the canopy. Thirty minutes later they were making their final approach to the CDF base at Sierra.

The capital of the colony was where it had all begun. As the first settlement on the planet, it had become one of the primary cities that all the colonists called home, although there was talk about the governor's office moving to one of the other cities—either New Haven or Delphi, not Sanctuary. Although Sanctuary was a small city in its own right, there was never any mention of the governor moving there. Connor supposed it would all come down to the results of the next election, which was more than a year away.

Connor landed the Falcon Fighter on the landing pad and climbed out. Diaz followed him.

General Nathan Hayes met them in the hangar. "Nice ride. How'd she handle?"

"Handles like a dream. You should take one out sometime," Connor replied.

Diaz left them, saying he had to go check on an equipment transfer that was slated to go to Sanctuary. As Connor walked with Nathan to a rover that was waiting to take them to the capitol building, he glanced at a nearby squad of soldiers gearing up for a training mission.

"Don't do that," Nathan warned. "Don't come here looking to pilfer more of my soldiers."

Connor arched an eyebrow toward him. "I thought they were *our* soldiers."

Nathan shrugged and tilted his head to the side for a moment. "They are, but you keep transferring the good ones to your Spec Ops platoons."

"Since you brought it up, there *are* a couple of soldiers I was thinking of talking to while I was here."

"The answer is no, Connor. I'm not okaying any further transfers. Not until we build up our ranks a little bit more."

Connor felt a small smile raise his lips. Had he really transferred so many troops around that Nathan was watching out for it now? More than likely, several platoon leaders had voiced their concerns over the loss of capable soldiers. That was as close as they got to an outright complaint.

"I thought the reserves would help out with that, but..." Connor's voice trailed off. He'd been about to echo what he'd intended to say to the Defense Committee but then gave Nathan a guilty nod.

"I know," Nathan said. "Not an unreasonable request on the committee's part to have more facts and data before they allocate resources for even more of our defense initiatives."

"You see," Connor said, pointing his finger at Nathan, "that's why I prefer *you* to handle these types of meetings. Before you, Franklin used to deal with the political side of things."

"Who do you think *I* used to go to for advice? Regardless, Franklin has enough on his plate," Nathan said.

The fact that Franklin Mallory's son Lars was a wanted man had hit him pretty hard, and he'd been putting in long hours trying to find his son. Lars hadn't worked alone, but it was frustratingly difficult to weed out the rogue element that Connor and a few others suspected had spawned out of the Colonial Intelligence Bureau. Even though they'd been looking for the past six months, they were no closer to finding Lars or anyone he'd been working with. Lars had been well taught to cover his tracks, and Connor was reminded of that fact every time he visited Noah in the hospital.

Noah was in a coma due to severe head trauma inflicted from a fall during an encounter with Lars. Dr. Ashley Quinn had said that Noah was lucky to be alive, but the state he was in didn't really qualify as being alive in Connor's mind.

"It's important that you work together with the current government," Nathan said.

"I've been entirely transparent with them since rejoining the CDF."

"It's not that simple. You need to win them over, build bridges, or whatever metaphor you prefer. There are divisions within the colony and a great deal of fear. And there are some people who'll use that to push their own agenda. We can't be like that."

Connor nodded. "I understand, and it's one of the reasons I came here in person to meet with the committee."

He brought up his schedule for the day. It was entirely blocked out for the Colonial Defense Committee meeting, along with most of the next day. The meetings were necessary, but Connor had always been an active man and meetings weren't his idea of "active." Nevertheless, he was scheduled to give a full briefing and a status report of their state of readiness.

This wasn't the first time Nathan had fervently suggested that Connor try to work *with* certain political figures he was more likely to bump heads *against*. Lenora translated that as being "diplomatic," and she'd said as much that morning before he left, except she'd used the much simpler version—"play nice." Despite her words, the first thing he'd done was to get into a fight with Samson, but hopefully the rest of his day wouldn't be as eventful. They needed to get the colonial leaders on board with the preparedness plan he had in mind for the CDF.

Even so, thinking of his family had made him smile as he remembered the softness of his baby girl's forehead when he'd kissed her goodbye that morning. Lauren was six months old now, and Connor felt a paternal sense of pride that grew stronger with each day that passed.

"Nathan, there's something I can't remember about you. What was your skillset that qualified you for the Ark Program?"

Nathan smiled and then grinned. "Human Resources and Logistics. It wasn't until I met you that I learned how to blow things up and all the other interesting things I do now. And although I do miss commanding a warship, Sean has taken to that role quite well."

Connor nodded. "Sean does well at almost every task we give him. I'd have him involved in these meetings, but he's doing important work with the fleet."

"He's still a little rough around the edges when it comes to the more delicate side of command. That will come with age and experience."

Connor grinned. "Yeah, he's a little too straightforward right now. Diplomacy was never my strong suit either, but there's no way around it. We need to go in there and convince them of the priority of a threat we can't completely quantify. I spent years doing this in preparation for the Vemus."

"This is different," Nathan said. "The NEIIS we've brought out of stasis are well aware of the threat we're facing, which will give us support in the eyes of the committee."

"Hopefully."

3

Phoenix Station - Interior Star System Orbit. 110 Million Kilometers from New Earth.

Colonel Sean Quinn presided over Fleet Engagement Simulation Review number nine-seven-four. Since taking command of the Battle Group Trident of the CDF fleet, he'd been focusing his efforts on multi-ship engagements with a hostile attack force. His battle group was comprised of two heavy cruisers and eight destroyer-class vessels. They'd now added a freighter that had been converted into a carrier vessel capable of holding multiple squadrons of Talon-V space fighters. His battle group was the CDF Fleet's only offensive strike force until the second battle group was finished at the lunar shipyards where massive construction efforts were ongoing.

During the past six months, there'd been an extensive review of Sean's actions when he'd engaged enemy ships in the alternate universe. According to recent translations, the NEIIS referred to the enemy as the Krake, although this was a shortened version of the word. Since the NEIIS revival effort had been underway, they'd also learned what the NEIIS called themselves—Ovarrow, or something like it as this was the closest translation they had to date. Sean still referred to them as the NEIIS, as did most of the colonists. He was aware of diplomatic efforts to change that, but it didn't matter to him what they called the Krake or the Ovarrow. Each species had a role to play. The Krake were the enemy, and they had to find a way to defeat them, although Sean wasn't arrogant enough to believe that this was all riding on his shoulders. It was a team effort. However, the purpose of his battle group was to be a direct-action force capable of performing reconnaissance on the enemy and then formulating a strategy to engage them. At least this time he'd be facing them with more firepower than just one heavy cruiser.

"Colonel Quinn, the Simulation Review is ready," Gabriel said. The *Vigilant's* AI's naturally-modulated baritone voice came over the speakers in the conference room.

Sean glanced around at the small group of officers in attendance. Major Lester Brody, his former XO on the *Vigilant*, gave him a nod. Brody was now in command of the heavy cruiser *Douglass*. The *Douglass* had been named for Colonel Kasey Douglass, who'd given his life in defense of the colony. Sean remembered Kasey as a close friend of Connor's. Kasey had been Connor's second in command when they'd both been part of the Ghost Platoon for the NA Alliance Military. Many of the former Ghosts had given their lives to defend the colony. They were professional soldiers whom the CDF aspired to emulate.

"Proceed," Sean said.

The holoscreen showed a mock fleet engagement with Krake forces. Gabriel was given a certain degree of latitude to predict the abilities of the enemy forces based on the analysis of previous engagements six months ago. Gabriel also took input from senior tactical officers who had been part of the engagement, as well as seasoned veterans who'd served during the Vemus War.

The Krake ships were capable of speeds much greater than

anything in the CDF fleet. Sean doubted they'd make any serious breakthroughs in propulsion anytime soon, so they needed another way to nullify the Krake's speed advantage. Further analysis of Krake fleet tactics indicated a reliance on radically advanced combat drones. Krake combat drones were highly maneuverable and were capable of burning through the battle-steel hulls of the heavy cruisers. There'd been proposals for adding additional layers of armor to the ships, but the effectiveness of that tactic had been called into question. Colonial scientists had estimated that additional armor would provide very little protection against a Krake combat drone. The colonial government had decided, based on Connor's recommendation, that it was better to put resources into building new ships while looking for ways to augment their defenses against the Krake drones. The enemy drones were immune to point-defense lasers and grasers. The only weapon capable of disabling the drones was the high-density armament used in mag cannons. The velocity at which mag cannons fired projectiles, in combination with the materials used to create them, allowed them to disable Krake combat drones before they had a chance to melt down the hulls of the CDF ships, and CDF engineers had been tasked with finding ways to augment the mag cannon's capabilities of taking out the combat drones before they could reach their ships. Additional mag cannons with multiple range and armament capabilities had been added to the *Vigilant* and the *Douglass*. What these changes hopefully bought Sean's battle group was time to engage the enemy fleet and possibly defeat them, but there was a significant risk that Krake forces carried enough combat drones to saturate his ship's defenses. The result of this analysis had been the inclusion of the eight destroyer-class ships that were part of his battle group. Defense of the battle group was reliant upon the group as a whole. Offensive capabilities had been included as well, but this had given rise to the need for Talon-V space fighters.

"Hold simulation," Brody said.

The battle simulation on the holoscreen stopped, and Brody looked at Sean.

"Thank you," Sean said and addressed the other officers. "In this simulation, we're utilizing the three classes of Talon-V space fighters. Gabriel, highlight the different class of Talon-Vs and proceed the simulation at ten times normal speed."

Talon-V space fighters were a light attack craft that had three primary configurations available when constructed. The Stormer-class Talon V had extensive armor plating at the prow, allowing it to punch a hole into a ship so a boarding party could get inside.

"Colonel Quinn, it appears that the Lancer class is more effective with Stingers on wing duty. Perhaps we could leverage the Stormers—Storm class Talon Vs—as well?" Lieutenant Russo asked.

Sean smiled inwardly. Russo was his senior tactical officer aboard the *Vigilant*. There were other tactical officers present in the conference room, but most remained silent unless called upon. They were there to learn and strategize.

"That is correct, Lieutenant Russo. The Talon-Vs make for an agile strike force capable of multiple mission objectives. This was one of the primary drivers for our acquisition of the freighter *Nimitz* and the decision to turn it into a carrier," Sean said.

"How many soldiers can the Storm class hold?" Colonel Savannah Cross asked.

"Thirty soldiers in Nexstar combat suits per ship, so not the ultimate troop carrier vessel, but if we get enough of them into an enemy ship then they become a viable solution," Sean said and brought up the specs for the different classes of Talon-V space fighters. "The Lancer class has a crew of three and carries a mixed armament of grasers and revolver missile tubes. It has defense capabilities of counter missiles and point-defense laser clusters, while the Stinger class is a highly maneuverable, single-occupant fighter with three forward-facing cannons. We stripped out some of the heavier armament to allow for additional engine capabilities, as well as armament for the cannons."

Savannah nodded appreciatively. "Yes, I see it now. What about the development of our own combat drones? The HADES V missile is a multistage combat drone that delivers a heavy payload."

"The HADES Vs are highly capable, but there're only three stages to them, and to add any more would make them unwieldy. They were more effective at engaging Vemus forces, which were based on the NA Alliance military. During our conflict with the Krake, they learned to target the HADES Vs. However, when we detonated their payload, it momentarily sent their combat drones into disarray," Sean replied.

"There's also the limitation of controlling our combat drones. The farther they get from our ships, the more reliant we must be on the combat computers onboard. They're not autonomous," Gabriel said.

Sean nodded. "There is work being done to enhance our combat drone capabilities, but you're correct to acknowledge the limitation that distance has in our communication capabilities."

He glanced at the other officers who were watching the simulation and reflected once again on how effective these strategy sessions were at fueling ingenuity. They all wanted to come up with a strategy or tactic that would allow them to neutralize the enemy fleet, but Sean didn't think there would be any single tactic that would swing the odds in their favor. No magic bullets. There needed to be an accumulation of many efforts and developments in order for that to happen.

The simulation finished and showed that despite a forty-percent loss of the CDF battle group's capability, they were able to hold their own against a superior Krake force. Sean knew better than to use this as justification for engaging the enemy in a frontal assault, even if it were possible, but it was a step in the right direction. CDF commanders were on edge, given the capabilities of the Krake, and this was one of the reasons Sean advocated getting everybody off the bridges of their ships and into the same room to hash out some effective strategies. Besides being an effective team-building exercise, it was also part of Sean's standing orders to rotate the tactical officers who would be called upon to provide firing solutions when they did engage the enemy.

The meeting ended and Sean dismissed the officers. Lester and Savannah stayed behind.

"I think we're getting more effective," Brody said.

"Yes, we're getting better at defeating the simulation, but ultimately, we don't know what else the Krake can do," Sean said and glanced up. "I'm not discounting your efforts, Gabriel."

"Understood, Colonel, and I agree with your assessment. Perhaps we should shift our focus to more reconnaissance-based scenarios."

"I'm sure that would help, but I noticed that there were no scientific advisors at this review," Savannah said.

"They're focusing on the construction of the space gate based on the prototype we found near Sagan. We'll be meeting with them for a status update. There are multiple projects associated with those efforts. The current theory is that the NEIIS had stumbled onto something that not even the Krake were able to do."

Brody nodded. "They teleported part of their city to another planet."

"Yes, but the evidence indicated that the structures were heavily altered, so I don't think we're teleporting anywhere anytime soon, but they did say there were other ways of using what the NEIIS stumbled upon," Sean said.

"I've been around more than a few NEIIS structures on New

Earth, particularly at Sanctuary," Savannah replied. "The estimation is that the NEIIS were not a spacefaring race."

"No, they weren't, but they think the NEIIS stole technology from the Krake during their war with them."

There was no end to theoretical insights into how the NEIIS and the collapse of their civilization resulted in advances that should have been beyond their capabilities, but it was a puzzle that the colonists continued to work on.

"The real mystery is why the Krake haven't come here yet," Sean said.

Brody shrugged. "We *did* disable the gateway on the planet, which is what they seemed to have used."

"At some point in the NEIIS history, the Krake made it to our universe. If they did it once, then they can do it again. Only this time they know we're here," Sean said.

"We have no idea why the Krake travel to multiple universes. It's hard to understand an enemy if we don't know what their motivations are," Savannah said.

It was all speculation, and Sean didn't have a good answer for it. None of them did. He couldn't afford to get consumed by what he didn't know, yet there was nothing wrong with being aware of it.

"We still have a job to do, and I'm glad the Krake haven't come here yet," Sean said, and the others nodded their agreement.

If the Krake came to their universe, Sean suspected it would be with a significant fighting force. And given what the enemy had no doubt learned about the CDF, there was the possibility that it would be an overwhelming force. They needed to get the space gates working so Sean could lead a force through to do reconnaissance of their own.

4

———

CONNOR WAS NEVER one for lengthy meetings, but sometimes they were necessary. In preparation for the Vemus War, the colonial government had established a defense committee whose members included the governor, mayors, and various colonial leaders, including Field Ops and Security. Tobias Quinn had been smart to do this in the beginning as they were bringing colonists out of stasis.

Connor hadn't thought about Tobias in a long time. He'd died during the Vemus War, but Connor missed him. They'd been at odds on certain issues, but they'd always been working toward the same goals. He sighed inwardly and glanced around the large conference room. Everyone in the room wanted to survive, but it seemed like there were too many groups preoccupied with their own goals. Connor supposed he shouldn't have been surprised by this development as the colony matured. They'd worked together preparing for the Vemus invasion, but what they were facing now was completely different.

He glanced at Governor Wolf, who was flanked by her advisors, Bob Mullins and Kurt Johnson. Connor didn't like either of the two men, but as Lenora liked to point out to him, he only needed to work with them. Johnson reached a pudgy hand toward a glass of water and lifted it to his mouth as his bulging stomach pressed against the fabric of his shirt. Connor was quite sure that if he and Johnson were being chased by a ryklar, he was sure to survive because Johnson would be the ryklar's next meal.

Seated next to Johnson was Meredith Cain, the head of the Colonial Intelligence Bureau. Meredith was a bit of an enigma to Connor. She was an older woman, but Connor didn't know her actual age. Prolonging treatments had allowed humans to live for nearly two hundred years. He'd heard that she was an organizational mastermind, especially with disseminating important information to the right people. The success of the Colonial Intelligence Bureau was only made possible by its cooperation with the CDF and Field Ops and Security. Connor had clashed with them more than once during their involvement with the Office of NEIIS Investigation as they searched for NEIIS stasis pods.

Connor's lips twisted into a small frown. Was there anyone in this room that he hadn't been at odds with at one time or another? He saw Nathan Hayes glance at him with a wry smile, leaving Connor to wonder if Nathan had guessed his thoughts. He looked away from Nathan and saw Damon Mills sitting nearby. He hardly looked a day older than when Connor had first met him ten years ago, but he still had a bald head and a stocky frame. The main holoscreen showed individual vidcom links for people who couldn't be at the meeting in person, including Nathan's wife, Savannah Cross, and Colonel Celeste Belenét. The Lunar Base commander had unflinchingly attacked Krake forces as they emerged into their universe. She'd done her duty, following established protocols to the letter.

Mullins cleared his throat. "I'd like us to move on to our next order of business," he said and gestured with a swiping motion to clear away the presentations on the main holoscreen.

Nathan stood up. "NEIIS revival sites are within capacity. We're working at improving communications with them by utilizing field experts outside of the CDF. There has been a recent development in that the NEIIS actually call themselves the Ovarrow."

"Is that the name of a particular faction, or the name they call their own species?" Governor Wolf asked.

"It's a species name, Governor," Nathan said and then proceeded to give them a detailed update. "Some of the NEIIS who were brought out of stasis have suffered from severe cellular degeneration. This presents itself in the rapid shutdown of internal organs that ultimately leads to their deaths."

There was a quiet intake of breath by the other committee members in the room.

"Is there anything we can do to help?" Governor Wolf asked.

She *seemed* sincere enough, but Connor couldn't be sure if she really was. *Someone* had ordered Lars Mallory to exploit the NEIIS in stasis. They'd gleaned some intelligence from the interrogation sessions Noah had uncovered, and it was likely that the person responsible for leading that effort was sitting in this room. He just didn't know who it was.

"CDF medical staff have been trying to help the NEIIS afflicted with this, but it's not enough. Beyond the physiological differences, which, quite honestly, I'm not qualified to speak about, they are an alien race. We must proceed cautiously or risk making things worse for the NEIIS we're trying to help. What I'd like is more help from the colonial R&D labs. We need a way to determine whether the NEIIS inside the stasis pods are afflicted with this condition of cellular degeneration before we wake them."

Governor Wolf seemed to consider this for a moment. "We can

absolutely help with that," she said and glanced at a man on the holoscreen. "Darius, are the NEIIS aware of this post-stasis complication?"

"It's unclear whether they were aware of the issue before going into stasis. I do have my team working with local experts, but communicating with the NEIIS is challenging."

"Governor," Connor said and waited for her to look at him. "The stasis pods Lenora and I found did vary in construction. It seemed that the foundation for the technology was similar but not necessarily how they were built. Perhaps we can narrow it down by the types of pods that were used."

Johnson inhaled explosively. "You *would* know quite a bit about the stasis pods they used, particularly how to destroy them."

Connor met the pudgy advisor's gaze. "I've already given my testimony about the events that took place at the NEIIS military bunker," he said with a special emphasis on the word "military." He glanced back at Governor Wolf. "It's important to remember that the NEIIS were part of a collapsing civilization. They were by no means innocent, and they fought to survive by any means necessary, including making their planet inhospitable to an invading force. I think that in addition to what Nathan has requested, we should also have the recovery teams look for signs of deliberate tampering with the stasis pods."

Wolf leaned back in her chair and rubbed the knuckles of her fists on her chin, lightly tapping them for a moment. "I recognize that you, General Gates, are quite knowledgeable about the NEIIS based on your work in recent years, and I'm familiar with the protocols followed by the Office of NEIIS Investigations," she said and glanced at Mullins. "We might have to change that name now that we know what they call themselves. Anyway, I'd like to know who would tamper with the stasis pods." Several people started to speak at once, but Governor Wolf looked at Connor. "What do you think?"

Connor took a moment to gather his thoughts. "General Hayes is more involved with the NEIIS than I am, and without concrete evidence, my opinion is purely speculation."

Wolf nodded. "I understand that, and no one here is going to hold you to your speculation. But I'm willing to wager that your own interaction with the NEIIS has given you a keener insight into them."

Memories of the military bunker came to the forefront of Connor's mind—Siloc trapping him there and fighting other NEIIS to escape. He'd almost died. It had taken him weeks to recover. "Siloc was from just one faction of the NEIIS society. We know the NEIIS fought wars among themselves. I don't think it's a great leap of logic to think *they* might've sabotaged the stasis pods of competing factions, if it came down to it."

Johnson sighed heavily. "To say a species merely wants to survive and worked toward those ends doesn't help us. We need concrete evidence."

Connor shrugged and looked back at Governor Wolf. "The NEIIS are just one part of the obstacles we face. We can all agree on what motivated the NEIIS to do the things they did in response to a threat from another universe."

"This again," Johnson said. "Let me guess—you want us to prepare for an invasion. Devote copious amounts of resources to a threat that might not ever manifest."

Connor rubbed his knuckles, imagining punching Johnson right in his pudgy little face. Instead, he smiled. "I am one and zero for predicting a danger to the colony in the form of an invasion force. Do you really want to bet against me on this?"

Johnson narrowed his gaze and turned toward Wolf.

Governor Wolf frowned and held up her hand to Johnson before looking at Connor. "I'm not denying that you discovered a big piece of the mystery concerning the NEIIS, but we can't know for sure whether these invaders can even get here. The archway was destroyed, and no others have been found in spite of an extensive search effort."

"The arch wasn't completely destroyed," Nathan said. "We've been working at rebuilding a gateway of our own, both here on the planet and at Phoenix Station."

"I'm aware of both of those projects, but it was my understanding that there was still quite a bit of work to do," Governor Wolf said.

"Governor," Mullins said, "I've been opposed to these projects since the beginning. If we re-create the gateways, what's to stop the invading force from using them to come to our world?" he asked, casting an accusatory glance at Connor.

Wolf pressed her lips together. "We've been through this before, Bob."

"I know, but we should stop them—"

"They've come here before," Connor said, interrupting Mullins. "On their forward-operating base, they were trying to make contact with other universes. There was a whole list of them. The operations at the base were one of established efficiency. They won't stop. So the question isn't whether these invaders will come to New Earth, but what we'll do when they come here."

Mullins shook his head, and Johnson crossed his arms.

"My next question is for the CDF leaders in this room," Wolf said. "I cannot fault General Gates for believing what he does. He's seen a threat to this colony, and he'll work to his utmost to mitigate this threat. However, a military is not an independent entity. The CDF is an extension of the colonial government—an elected government. I've had other political leaders admit to me that there is a significant risk..." she paused with a slight frown. "...*concern* is a better word, that the CDF has become nothing more than a bully, operating independently of what the government wants. My question to the two ranking CDF officers in this room, General Gates and General Hayes, is that if I were to give the order to abandon these projects, is that an order you would follow?"

Connor didn't look at Nathan. If he had, or if Nathan had looked at him, it would have been seen as some sort of collusion. "If the consensus of this committee was to abandon the gateway projects, then we would follow those orders. Depending on the evidence gathered, we might work to sway the committee to do what we believe is best for the colony, but you're right: a civilian government controls the military."

"I would echo the same sentiments as General Gates, Governor Wolf," Nathan said.

Connor tapped his fingertips on the conference table. "I just want to be completely transparent with the committee. The best way forward for us is to gather more intelligence. We are accomplishing this by working with the NEIIS, but it's not enough. The NEIIS lost their war with the Krake. They lost their world and almost their entire civilization. We have the ability to take this beyond what the NEIIS ever accomplished, but to do that we need to rebuild these gateways and use them to learn all we can about these invaders. After we've gathered more intelligence, then we can make a decision as a group. That's my intent. I don't want to fight another war, but I also won't sit here and tell you that if we ignore this problem, it will simply go away."

"Thank you, General Gates and General Hayes," Governor Wolf said. "You've given us much to think about. I think this is a good time for us to break for the day."

The committee members took their cue to pack up their belongings and leave the conference room.

"Governor Wolf, I'd like to have a word with you, if you wouldn't mind," Connor said. He saw that Mullins and Johnson acted as if they would wait behind with her. "Alone, if that's all right."

Mullins' face became an entertaining shade of red, but

Governor Wolf gestured for them to go. Once the room was empty, she watched Connor expectantly.

"I thought it might be best if you and I had an honest discussion," Connor said.

Governor Wolf leaned forward. "I thought we were already being honest."

"I know your advisors don't trust me, and I know the fact that I've rejoined the CDF hasn't been met with a lot of enthusiasm, but none of that is going to keep me from doing my job. I just want you to know that you can trust me. I'm not working to undermine your authority."

Governor Wolf pursed her lips for a moment. "Connor, you're straight as an arrow. I don't have to guess what you're thinking or what your intentions are. They are as clear as day. But others in the committee are rightfully cautious of you. There's history here that's working against you, particularly regarding the Parish administration and his removal from office. I don't mean to bring up things from the past, but there has been a precedent set. Parish was outspoken in his politics concerning... well, you, in particular. But the Vemus War began, and he was proved wrong."

"Parish tried to have me killed. It happened right before the war began."

Wolf's mouth opened slightly, and her eyes widened in surprise. "I had no idea he'd done that."

"Not many people do, but that was why Tobias and I removed Parish from office. It was necessary at the time."

Wolf shook her head and sighed. "Sometimes things aren't always black and white. Not with our responsibilities. The reason there's so much mistrust where you're concerned is because you represent a rogue element in the colony. The effects of this have taken the form of unintentional consequences."

Connor crossed his arms in front of his chest and pressed his lips together. "You mean Lars Mallory."

"Precisely, but him and a few others are the ones we know about. What about the others we *don't* know about?" She walked toward the window, gazing out of it at the colonial monument to Old Earth. She turned and looked at Connor. "I'm not your enemy or an obstacle for you to overcome. Neither is my administration."

"Your advisors leave something to be desired," Connor said dryly.

Governor Wolf smiled, and it actually took years off her face. "They're good at their jobs and serve a necessary function. Just like you do."

Connor exhaled out of his nose and tilted his head to the side. "The gateways are reaching the testing phase. We've done all this work. Are you really going to shut us down?"

Governor Wolf seemed to consider Connor's question for a few moments. "Did you know hornet nests can be built in the span of a few days? Then, when the season changes, they can go dormant while a dedicated few remain in hibernation. My biggest concern with these gateways is that we will be kicking a hornet's nest."

"I understand, and I have the same concerns myself."

"Yes, I believe you do."

"We'll take precautions. The protocols we'll follow will be presented to you. We'll involve you and your office, and also the rest of the committee as much as possible, but this is a CDF project," Connor said.

Wolf nodded. "All right, I won't stand in your way. I agree with your assessment that we definitely need to know more about what you discovered six months ago."

Connor felt the edges of his lips begin to relax with relief, but then he frowned. "Had you already decided that before we spoke or during the meeting?"

Governor Wolf smiled again but didn't reply.

5

THE NOONDAY SUN shone so brightly in the clear blue skies that New Earth's rings blended with the horizon in the distance as Dash walked through the entrance to Sanctuary's medical center. For the past few months, he'd been dividing his time between helping with the NEIIS revival efforts and trying to find Lars Mallory, but he hadn't made much headway with hunting for the colony's foremost fugitive, and most of his time was taken up working with the NEIIS. His knowledge of the NEIIS ruins and language was heavily relied upon.

He'd hitched a ride on a supply run to Sanctuary and would be returning to the CDF base near New Haven in a few hours. He could've checked on Noah remotely and had done so in the past. Noah had taught him how to circumvent secure systems, and the medical center was easily accessible now. He received a daily report on who accessed Noah's room and medical records, and he knew he wasn't the only one. In the months following Noah's injury, Dash had periodically returned, hoping to see some indication of progress toward recovery.

Dash waved at the person who sat at the reception desk that

day, all of whom knew him by name, and took the hall on the right toward Noah's room. The long-term care facility wasn't much bigger than a few rooms since most ailments that affected the colonists could be quickly healed. There were rare cases when a person spent up to a week recovering at the medical center, but any length of time beyond that was almost nonexistent.

He turned the corner and saw that the door to Noah's room was open. Slowing his approach, he heard Lenora and Dr. Ashley Quinn speaking inside. After thinking about hovering outside and listening in on their conversation, he decided against it, gave a soft knock at the door, and walked in.

"How's he doing?" Dash asked, looking at the steady rise and fall of Noah's chest. There was a breathing apparatus with tubes connected to Noah's head. The bruising on his face had all healed, but Noah remained in a coma.

Lenora gave him a hug and Ashley spoke a friendly greeting.

"There's been no change in his status. Just some minor brain activity one would have in a deep sleep. There have been only two instances of brain activity like that happening, but it's something," Dr. Quinn said.

Dash exhaled and gave a single nod. He'd wanted to hunt down Lars Mallory, but Connor asked him not to. He'd told him to trust that Field Operations would do everything they could to capture Lars. Dash didn't like it, but he'd learned to trust Connor's judgment, which didn't mean he didn't keep a lookout for Lars Mallory. He utilized the skills Noah had taught him to check security systems, looking for signs of tampering, but Lars had become a ghost these past six months.

"Isn't there something else we can do?" Dash said, then quickly clamped his mouth shut and shook his head. "I'm sorry."

"Don't be sorry. I understand how you feel," Dr. Quinn said. "We can heal the body quite well and fast, but the brain is a different matter entirely. By all accounts, his brain is healed as far as we can tell. The actual tissues and fibers that make up the brain are intact, and there's no damage from the blunt force trauma Noah experienced."

"Why doesn't he wake up then?" Dash asked.

"Noah's brain is healed, but there is scarring, and there might be bruising that we don't have the ability to detect. Even if the tissue repairs itself in certain pathways in the brain, it doesn't mean everything will be as it was before," Dr. Quinn said.

"Are you saying he won't ever wake up?"

"No," Lenora said. "The human brain is one of the most complex organs, and even now we're still learning more about it."

"In this case, time is the best medicine, Mr. DeWitt. Noah will wake up when he's ready," Dr. Quinn said.

Dash glanced at the bed, reliving the moment Noah had fallen off the cliff and his body had crashed to the ground far below. "I'm sorry to keep asking these questions. I guess you get them a lot."

Dr. Quinn smiled. "I'm used to it. I think it's good that people come to visit Noah. There've been theories that say that it helps, that they know you come to see them."

"It's not surprising," Lenora said. "Noah was one of the early risers in the Ark."

"Early risers" was a reference to those among the first groups awakened from stasis when the Ark reached New Earth over twelve years earlier. "I remember when Sanctuary was just a small forward-operating research base with a skeleton crew. We had Noah going to all the FORBs back then to help set up communications systems and our monitoring equipment."

The comlink chimed on Dash's PDA and he answered it because he saw Tommy Lockwood's identification.

"Darius Cohen's assistant is looking for you," Tommy said.

"Why?"

"They want confirmation of the new translation protocols."

"That's easy; they work," Dash replied.

Lenora came over to his side and looked at the holoscreen on Dash's PDA.

"Dr. Bishop, I had no idea you were there."

"Hello, Mr. Lockwood. What's going on?" Lenora asked.

"Whenever the NEIIS gather in groups it makes the CDF soldiers on watch nervous, and several NEIIS are requesting to return to their territories. We think they want to be more involved with the efforts to bring their people out of stasis," Tommy said.

"Understood. I'll be back there as soon as I can. The supply run isn't returning for a few more hours though," Dash said.

"You can take one of the research center's C-cats," Lenora said.

Dash glanced at Lenora for a moment and then looked back at Tommy. "You heard Dr. Bishop. Tell Darius I'll be back in about an hour then."

The comlink closed and Dash looked back at Lenora and Dr. Quinn. "I guess that's my cue to leave."

"Just make sure you register with the research center that the C-cat you're taking has been authorized," Lenora said with a smile.

Dash grinned. "Come on, I haven't borrowed a C-cat in a long time."

He left the medical center and headed toward the Colonial Research Institute at Sanctuary. After a brief check-in with the vehicle depot, he walked out to the C-cat landing pads. C-cats were civilian aerial transport vehicles commonly used by the colonists. He approached the C-cat, which was a smaller model that was capable of transporting only four people at a time. He saw that the storage hatch was open, and someone was loading it.

"Excuse me, I've been cleared to take this one," Dash said.

A hand reached up and closed the storage hatch, and his eyes widened as Merissa Sabine's hazel eyes regarded him for a moment. "No time to stop in for a visit?"

She had her long, dark hair tied back and tucked behind her ears.

"I was going to, but I was at the medical center and then got called back to the research base. Otherwise, I would have."

He walked around to the front of the C-cat and stopped in front of her, unsure whether to say anything else. Merissa stepped toward him and gave him a kiss on the cheek. He caught the brief scent of the shampoo she'd used to wash her hair, and the memory of it tugged at him.

"It's good to see you."

Merissa smiled. "Oh, you'll be seeing a lot more of me. I'm coming with you to New Haven."

Dash frowned. "Why?" he asked and quickly followed that with, "I didn't mean it like that. It's just that you've either been here or at Sierra."

She seemed to enjoy watching him flounder for a moment. "Why does anybody go to the research site at New Haven? The NEIIS. They want somebody on hand with expertise in planetary scientific studies."

He nodded in understanding. She was one of the first people to put forth the theory explaining a radical ice age that had impacted New Earth. He smiled at her. "In that case, I'll be glad for the company."

"I thought so," Merissa said and climbed into the C-cat where she immediately began bringing up the flight control systems. Dash snorted to himself after accepting the fact that he would be a passenger. He looked at the pretty girl sitting inside and thought there could be worse ways to spend the hour it would take to return to New Haven.

6

CONNOR WALKED into the large C-cat that had just launched from the landing pad at the roof of the colonial government building at Sierra. He was on his way to the CDF base near New Haven where they were attempting to rebuild their own version of the arch the Krake had used for interdimensional travel. Six months ago, he might have grinned at a thought like that. Not so much now. Scientific theory had become a reality, and with it came all the unintentional consequences one could dream up.

As he walked up the aisle, he saw Kurt Johnson adjusting his seat belt, and Connor suppressed a scowl that threatened to show on his face.

"General Gates, thank you for letting me and my assistant accompany you to the test site. I'm quite eager to observe the test of the arch," Johnson said.

It wasn't as if Connor had much of a choice—the spirit of cooperation and all that.

"Not a problem. I'm happy to have you along. I think it's important for the Defense Committee members to come out and personally experience our work. You'll find there's a big difference between a holoscreen in a conference room and seeing it firsthand."

Johnson nodded, causing his jowls to vibrate even after he stopped nodding. "Agreed. I think it will be enlightening for us all."

"You'll have to excuse me. I have an important call to make," Connor said, and continued up the aisle. He reached a seating area that gave him a bit of privacy from the others on the ship and noted that the flight time would be forty-five minutes, which was practically a snail's pace in comparison to how fast he'd arrived at Sierra.

Diaz looked up at him and then glanced back down the aisle to where Johnson was speaking with his assistant. "You know," Diaz said softly with a hint of mischief, "I'm pretty sure we can do a low-altitude airdrop for that part of the cabin. What do you say? Just a little check of the emergency systems or something like that?"

A small smile lifted Connor's lips. "As tempting as that is, I'm pretty sure he'd see right through it. No, we need to cooperate and bring them into the fold."

"No fun, but I get it."

Connor sat down and brought up his personal holoscreen, opening a comlink to Sanctuary. A few moments later he saw his wife's smiling face as she answered his call while holding Lauren. Lenora pointed at the camera in the wallscreen of their home at Sanctuary, and a broad smile stretched across his face at the sight of their six-month-old daughter. "Hi there."

Lauren, recognizing her father's voice, looked at the wallscreen and made a cooing sound.

"I'm surprised to find you home," Connor said.

"Not for long. I'm on my way back to the Research Institute," Lenora said. "Oh, before I forget, Ashley told me something interesting today."

"Oh yeah? What's that?"

"You're not going to believe this, but there was a time when babies didn't sleep through the night. They'd only sleep a few hours at a time and parents had to get up to feed them. Can you imagine how much sleep deprivation that would cause?" Lenora said and then arched an eyebrow. "We don't all have military-grade implants that allow us to get by with two hours of sleep."

Connor frowned in thought. "Every few hours... How long did that last?"

Lenora kissed Lauren's cheek. "Sometimes a year or even longer."

"I guess we're lucky."

"Yeah, it would be hard to imagine life without a sleep regulator, and thankfully, the nutritional content of our food is better than it was back then so babies can go longer between feedings. Anyway, how'd it go with the Defense Committee?"

Connor told her about the meeting and his conversation with Governor Wolf. "It might be a few days before I get home."

"We'll be here. Ashley's going to watch Lauren for a little while," Lenora said and held up Lauren's arm to wave at the camera before the comlink was closed.

Raising children on the colony was quite a bit different from what Connor remembered back on Earth when he'd had his son. The colony experienced childrearing as a community effort rather than relying solely upon a child's parents. Cultural adjustments such as this encouraged population growth, and while Connor had been a bit skeptical in the beginning, Diaz had assured him that it was quite normal—and he would know since he had five children.

Connor spent the remainder of the flight going through his messages and taking care of various things on his ever-growing list of things to do. When the high-priority items had been addressed, he accessed the flight systems and opened the forward cameras on his holoscreen.

Diaz glanced over as a large CDF base sprawled onto the landscape they were heading towards. They were over fifty kilometers away from New Haven, but it was important that the base was located in close proximity to the NEIIS city that had been discovered at the bottom of the lake. A small community of researchers and support personnel resided within the confines of the base. At the center of it all was a dome-shaped structure, which was where they were rebuilding the arch gateway. They'd retrieved pieces of the original arch from the lake, but they'd made the new gateway much smaller. If they *did* get it to work, they wouldn't be sending a fleet of ships through it anytime soon, but a significant ground force could go through it just fine.

The ship landed and the passengers left through the exits. A small squad of soldiers waited for Connor, and he spotted a familiar face.

"It's good to have you back, General Gates," Flint said.

"It's nice to be back. Is there anything to report, Captain Flint?"

"Dr. Volker and his team say they're ready to begin their tests as soon as you arrive. I've assembled our response teams and defense installations inside the dome."

"I'm sure Volker can't wait."

"He's bursting with enthusiasm, General."

Connor had reinstated Carl Flint to the CDF, with a promotion to the rank of captain, and then put him in charge of a Spec Ops platoon that trained at the base. When they got the gateway to work, it would be Flint who would lead the first platoon to the other side. He was the right man for the job since he'd already seen what would be waiting for them there. Flint had been taken captive by the Krake and survived. His knowledge of them and his ability to lead made him the obvious choice.

Ground transport took them to the interior of the CDF base, and they went through the security checkpoints that took them into the central dome. Connor thought he heard Johnson huffing from all the walking. He glanced at the man and saw beads of sweat along his brow, but Johnson gestured for them to keep going.

They walked to the command center, which provided a bird's-eye view of the dome's interior. On one side were the remnant pieces of the arch that they'd been able to recover from the lake. On the other side was their prototype—a smaller version of the arch—that was six meters tall and fifteen meters across at the base.

Dr. Volker greeted them. "I see you brought a few extra people."

"Representatives from the Colonial Defense Committee are here to observe the test, if you wouldn't mind giving them a brief overview of the project," Connor said.

Dr. Volker's gaze took in the group, and he smiled broadly. The man positively loved having an audience. "I assume you are all somewhat familiar with the work going on here. We're attempting to reverse engineer what the Krake built on this planet hundreds of years ago. In fact, it's not actually clear when the arch was built, but there were enough components left intact that we felt we could make a real effort at recreating it."

"Excuse me," Johnson said, "but is this arch related to the space gate found on Sagan?"

Volker nodded. "Yes, it is. The NEIIS were attempting to build their own gateway on the planet based on technology we believe they stole from the Krake. It's unclear, and we're still working with the NEIIS that come out of stasis to understand exactly what happened. However, we think they stumbled onto something else during one of their experiments, and part of their research facility ended up on another planet in the star system. How did this happen?" Volker asked and let a few moments pass before continuing. "We've reviewed the evidence gathered, and while the buildings appeared somewhat intact, that's difficult to determine because the atmosphere on Sagan is so much different."

"Are you saying the NEIIS stumbled upon some way to teleport an object from here to another planet?" Johnson asked.

"Not exactly, or I should say not safely. However, the discovery has spawned other research projects, one of which is ready to be tested as well."

"That research project is being managed at Phoenix Station," Connor said.

"I'd like to hear more about this other research project," Johnson said.

Volker glanced at Connor, who gave him a nod that wasn't lost on Johnson.

"Instantaneous communication across vast distances has been theorized for hundreds of years, but we've never really been able to make it work. Our communications arrays are all based on the limitation of the speed of light. If we send a transmission to Phoenix Station, for example, there's a six-minute lag before we get a reply. What we've discovered from our analysis of the arch is that the NEIIS had added components to it, probably after the ice age had begun. We think that the Krake forces must not have been here when they tried this or were at least not in control of the arch. We're really not sure, but they did attach extra components in an effort to tie in another arch that we haven't located yet. It would take too long for me to go into specifics, but the potential is there for what the research scientists have been calling 'subspace communications,'" Volker said.

Johnson nodded and his eyes were wide with anticipation, almost like a hunger at the thought of getting a new toy to play with. "And who is overseeing this project?"

"The lead scientist on Phoenix Station is Dr. Oriana Evans, who is also overseeing the space gate. She was the scientist to first determine that the CDF heavy cruiser, *Vigilant*, was in an alternate universe."

Johnson repeated the name of the scientist in charge and made a note of it. "Brilliant. Thank you for sharing that. Please proceed."

Connor was already aware of the efforts with subspace communication going on at Phoenix Station. He also knew the technology wasn't entirely predictable at this point, but they needed to leverage any advantage they could.

Dr. Volker looked at Connor. "General Gates, we require your authorization to proceed."

Connor glanced out the window toward the arch they'd built. For a few moments, he hesitated, thinking that perhaps they *should* wait. But the moment passed, and he looked back at Dr. Volker. "Authorization given," Connor said and transmitted his official authorization to the computer systems on the base.

7

CONNOR GLANCED at Flint and gave a jerk of his head toward the door. Flint nodded and left to be with his team by the arch.

"Dr. Volker, please confirm the ready status of your teams and monitoring stations," Connor said. He looked at Johnson and the other civilians. "You are free to observe from here, or you can move to the observatory next door to us."

Johnson stayed behind with several members of his staff while the others went to the observatory.

"Lieutenant Rogers, what's our status?" Connor asked.

Lieutenant Rogers sat at a workstation with a trio of holoscreens. "We have every kind of sensor pointed at the gateway, General. Four infantry squads have gathered in full combat suits and are supported by heavy weapons. The Hephaestus failsafe is online."

"Understood," Connor said.

The Hephaestus failsafe was an insurance policy to protect them against the gateway. The materials the Krake used to construct their arch were highly resistant to all but the most powerful weapons. Connor didn't want to rely on blowing up their own military base, so he'd challenged engineers to come up with a different option for them to disable the arch. The failsafe utilized focused sound waves that would shatter key supports, forcing the arch to break apart into intact pieces. There was a hundred meters of open space behind the arch, so the damage to the CDF base would be minimal if they had to engage the failsafe, although using it could set their efforts back months.

A few minutes later, Connor received confirmation from Flint that his backup squad was at the gateway.

"Dr. Volker, are the science teams ready?"

A scientist of Asian descent spoke quietly to Dr. Volker, and he turned back toward Connor. "We're ready, General Gates."

Connor looked at the arch. "Very well. Lieutenant Rogers, you're clear for arch-activation protocols."

"Yes, General. Proceeding with arch-activation protocols."

The arch was forty meters from the command center, and Connor felt his brows push forward as he watched. He glanced at the CDF soldiers gathered near it. They were well trained, and he was confident they were up to the task of dealing with anything that could potentially come through the arch. But this thought was immediately followed by the nagging questions of whether they'd taken enough precautions. Were they ready for this?

"Here we go again," Diaz said, speaking quietly so only Connor could hear.

Connor gave a slight nod.

He peered at the area in the middle of the arch and saw it begin to shimmer as if a mist was forming. Then there were slight ripples before the shimmer returned.

"The arch is active, but we're not getting any readings through it from our sensors," Lieutenant Rogers said.

Connor opened the comlink to Flint. "Send the recon drone through, Captain."

A video feed appeared on the main holoscreen that showed the recon drone heading toward the arch. A secondary feed showed what the cameras and sensors on the recon drone detected as it approached the arch. The hazy mist became more defined as the recon drone closed in, and then the area in front of the drone changed to inky blackness. Connor glanced at the other video feeds. The power draw to the arch remained constant. After a few seconds, the mist appeared again, and he watched as the drone sped toward the event horizon. Every observer found themselves holding their collective breath as the drone flew through—and all the data feeds from it were cut off.

Connor waited a few moments to see if they could re-establish contact.

"General Gates, I'm receiving some kind of signal," Lieutenant Rogers said. "I'm not sure what this is. It's strange—garbled, or it's not a signal at all."

The arch shut down and an alert appeared on the main holoscreen.

Power failure.

"Flint, confirm that the power has been cut off to the arch," Connor said.

There were a few murmurs in the command center and then Flint replied. "The power is off, General. Did you guys turn it off at your end?"

Connor glanced at Lieutenant Rogers, and she shook her head. "That's a negative, Captain. Secure the area and let the engineers check the arch."

The comlink closed and Connor walked over to Dr. Volker. "Were you able to detect this signal?"

Dr. Volker peered at his personal holoscreen and looked up at Connor. "Yes, Lieutenant Rogers is correct, but we're not sure exactly what it is. Here, I'll show you."

Connor looked at the holoscreen. It showed a burst of some

kind, but the system was unable to determine what the signal actually was.

"We'll need some time, General Gates."

Connor nodded and saw Johnson coming toward him.

"A bit underwhelming, I thought," Johnson said. "Why did the power cut out?"

"We're not sure. The first step is to check our equipment to make sure it's functioning properly. After that, they'll go over all the data gathered from our sensors, including the signal," Connor said.

Johnson frowned. "I thought they said it wasn't the signal."

"They don't know what it is exactly, and they'll need some time to work on it."

"What happened to the recon drone?"

Dr. Volker joined them. "There is ample evidence to suggest that the drone did successfully transition to another universe."

"That's good news, right?" Johnson asked.

Connor shook his head. "Not necessarily. We know it's not here, but we don't know where it is, which means we're a long way from sending anybody through that thing until we can figure out why the power was cut off. It also looked like there was some kind of interference."

Johnson looked at the arch and compressed his lips. "So what happens now?"

"We'll give them some time to analyze the data, like I said before, but I think we need to talk to the NEIIS. Reveal to them what we're trying to do here," Connor said.

Johnson frowned in consternation. "Any dealings with the NEIIS are diplomatic issues. You'll need permission from Governor Wolf."

Connor knew what he had to do, but for some reason having Johnson say it to him was irritating. He couldn't let it show, however, and he was a beacon of cooperation. "Of course," he said simply, and Johnson looked almost stunned. "Before I do, I'm going to have a look at the arch myself and talk to the engineers working on it. Want to come with me?" Connor asked.

Johnson blanched and then shook his head. "I appreciate that, General Gates, but I'll remain here and speak with Dr. Volker a little bit more."

Connor suppressed a chuckle. He knew there wasn't a shred of courage in Johnson's spine. The man was like a spider with his fingers involved in many different things, but when it came to getting his hands dirty, he faltered.

Connor headed for the door. He ordered Lieutenant Rogers to inform him of any discoveries and to follow confidential protocols. He'd added that last bit for Johnson's benefit. The advisor wouldn't have direct access to the results of the data analysis until Connor had reviewed it. He'd worked with Dr. Volker for the past few months, and while Connor agreed with Sean's assessment of the man—that he was unsuited to serve aboard a warship—he was quite capable at running research projects on the ground.

Connor nodded to Diaz and they left the command center. He used his neural implants to craft a preliminary report to send to Governor Wolf, informing her of the status of the test. He was sure Johnson would be doing something similar, but in the spirit of cooperation, he was willing to play along.

8

THE VALKYRIE CLASS III combat shuttle made its way toward Phoenix Station, and Sean glanced at the mammoth space station on the shuttle's main holoscreen. Combat shuttles had no windows due to the structural weakness they'd impose on a machine designed for war.

The CDF had salvaged the wreckage from the original space station and rebuilt it after the Vemus War. Fortunately, Phoenix Station had significant armament and manufacturing capabilities to sustain itself almost indefinitely. The station was the colony's first line of defense against an invasion force and functioned as the control hub for the missile platforms maintained throughout the star system.

"Colonel Quinn," Sergeant Malone said from the pilot's seat, "Captain Halsey from the *Vigilant* would like to speak to you."

Sean acknowledged the comlink on his personal holodisplay and Halsey's face appeared. "Miss me already, Halsey?"

"You're not my type, Colonel," Halsey said with a smile. "We've had a resupply ship from Phoenix Station, and there's some equipment I wasn't aware of that's to be installed ASAP. I'm contacting you to confirm. Sending over the details right now. There—you should have it."

A sub window appeared on the holoscreen, and Sean read it. "They look legit to me."

"The orders do, but am I reading this right? Colonial subspace communications equipment?"

"No, it's an elaborate joke the CDF brass put together for your entertainment," Sean said, giving him an exasperated look. "The orders are clear."

"No, I understand that, Colonel. I just thought this equipment was still in the testing phase, and now they're deploying it to not just the *Vigilant*, but to the rest of the battle group as well."

"The preliminary tests must've been successful enough to make this happen, which means you need to get it installed and learn how to use it."

"Don't worry, Colonel, I'll have our new toy up and running by the time you get back from the station."

"Halsey," Sean said before the comlink closed, "just... make sure you read the manual first. We're the pride of the CDF fleet, and it wouldn't do for us to install our new equipment backwards."

Halsey saluted. "Don't worry, Colonel. My crackpot team of engineers are all over this project. In fact, I'll have them tear out the existing comms array because we won't need it anymore."

Sean grinned. "Better keep the old equipment, just in case. After all, it's had hundreds of years of proven reliability."

Halsey feigned disappointment. "Understood, Colonel. Thanks for confirming. Halsey out."

The combat shuttle landed in one of the main hangar bays.

"Colonel, what time will you be returning?" Sergeant Malone asked.

"It might be awhile. After you get the shuttle squared away, you should have the remainder of the day," Sean replied.

He stepped off the shuttle and was greeted by Lieutenant Jordan.

"Welcome to Phoenix Station, Colonel Quinn. If you'll follow me, I'll take you to Colonel Cross's office."

This was far from his first visit to Phoenix Station, but Savannah must have wanted to meet with him right away if she sent someone like Lieutenant Jordan. The man's impeccable uniform and almost precise movements left Sean wondering if he'd ever relaxed a day in his life.

Colonel Savannah Cross had taken over command of Phoenix Station eight months ago. She was married to General Nathan Hayes, and they had a son who was almost two years old now. Sean frowned in thought, trying to recall their son's name, but he couldn't remember and his jaw clenched. Officially, it wasn't imperative to remember details like that, but he felt that he *should* know it.

"Oliver," Sean said quietly.

Jordan glanced back at him. "I'm sorry, Colonel Quinn. Did you say something?"

Sean shook his head. "Just thinking out loud. I was trying to remember... never mind, it's not important."

Lieutenant Jordan left Sean outside the offices of the station commander. Inside, a young woman sat at the reception desk, and Sean told her who he was there to see. About a minute later he was cleared to proceed, and he walked into the station commander's office.

Colonel Cross stood up from behind her desk and smiled. She wasn't alone. A CDF officer stood at attention off to the side and hadn't looked in his direction when he entered the room.

"Colonel Quinn," Savannah said. "Welcome."

The office was a vision of someone who kept everything in her life in order—from the tidy desk to the wall art to the plants that breathed life into the space. It was a sanctuary of sorts, but a little too orderly for Sean's liking. He saluted Colonel Cross. Though they were the same rank, she'd held it longer than Sean and therefore had seniority.

She returned Sean's salute and gestured toward the officer standing at attention. "This is Major Vanessa Shelton."

Sean walked towards the desk and looked at the Major. She was of average height, with dark skin and hair. Her brown eyes flicked toward him for an instant.

"Reporting for duty, Colonel Quinn," Shelton said.

Sean frowned. He'd heard that name before but couldn't quite remember where. Why was he having so much trouble with names today? He looked at Savannah.

"Major Shelton is your new XO. Her orders came in from COMCENT this morning," Savannah said. She made a passing motion toward Sean, and the orders appeared on his internal heads-up display.

"I thought I had a list of candidates to interview while I was here," Sean said and looked at Major Shelton. Her service record appeared, and he scanned through it quickly. "It says here that you're the commander of the destroyer *Talbot*. Is that correct, Major Shelton?"

"Yes, Colonel. And prior to my position on the *Talbot*, I served under General Hayes on Lunar Base."

Sean nodded. Now he knew where he'd heard that name before. He read more of her service record.

"Do you still want a list of candidates, Colonel Quinn?" Savannah asked.

Sean pressed his lips together, making a show of considering. "That depends on how Major Shelton answers this next question. What is the purpose of Phoenix Station?"

Shelton briefly frowned in concentration. "Phoenix Station is the first line of defense from a hostile force outside this star system. However, in light of recent events, this station can act as a trojan horse should a Krake invasion force attack New Earth. Beyond that, Phoenix Station also serves as an R&D facility that has been tasked with reengineering space gates."

Her answer was concise, and Sean liked that, but he wasn't about to let her off the hook that easily. "You have command of a warship, a destroyer no less. Why make the jump to the XO of a heavy cruiser? Was commanding the *Talbot* not enough for you?"

"I stand by my record on the *Talbot*, Colonel. While in command, combat readiness and safety drills have increased in efficiency by over seventeen percent. I'm aware you have a list of qualified candidates for the XO position on the *Vigilant*," Major Shelton said and looked at Sean. "I'm sure they are all fine officers and could execute their duties on your ship with alacrity, but none of them have my experience. They didn't serve on Lunar Base during the Vemus invasion. They didn't help plan the counterattack while the Vemus invaded New Earth. Now there's a new enemy that we will more than likely be facing in the near future. My experience alone puts me at the top of that list of yours, Colonel."

She held Sean's gaze for a moment and then resumed her stand at attention. Her biostatistics appeared on Sean's internal heads-up display, and they were all in the normal ranges. Her confident tone wasn't a pompous boast.

Sean knew full well the role that Lunar Base had played in the Vemus War. He let a pregnant pause pass before he said anything. "Very well, Major Shelton, report to the *Vigilant*. I have no doubt that with your excellent service record, it won't take you much time to become familiar with the ship. Once you get aboard, I want you to check in on Captain Halsey's work. He's the lead engineer and is installing our new subspace communication systems."

Major Shelton gave him a salute. "Thank you, Colonel Quinn. I won't let you down."

After Major Shelton left, Sean heard Savannah let out a breath. "Sometimes you're just like him."

Sean smiled. "Like who?" he asked innocently.

They could drop the formalities now that they were alone.

"Connor."

Sean nodded. "I suppose. Shelton certainly seems sure of herself. I agree with everything she said, but I could also tell that she really wanted the job."

"It's a good fit for you, I think. It's one reason Nathan recommended her."

"How is Oliver? Is he here with you on the station?" Sean asked.

She smiled. "Yes, he is, but I'll be taking him back to New Earth next week."

Sean caught the hint of remorse in her tone. "It must be hard being away."

Savannah regarded him knowingly. "We make it work. As you no doubt know, senior officers are in short supply. Would you want to take over Phoenix Station?"

The question wasn't a serious one, and Sean knew that. "I'd prefer to stay with my current command."

Savannah smiled. "You've gotten a real taste for commanding a ship. I can see it in your eyes. You wouldn't let it go easily, would you?"

"That wouldn't be my first choice. I'll go where I'm needed, but right now commanding the *Vigilant* and the battle group is probably the best place for me."

Savannah reached inside her desk and pulled out a bottle of honey-brown liquid. She put two glasses on her desk and poured. "Single-cask bourbon. Nathan's influence, I'm afraid." She handed one to Sean. "I agree with you, but more importantly, so do Connor and Nathan."

Sean raised his glass and drank the bourbon. It was warm and smooth as it blazed a path down to his stomach. "This is really good."

"I'm glad you think so. We've started a distillery back home—a bit of a side project—and it took us awhile to find the right kind of wood. We could have used synthetics to create the kind of oak we needed, but we wanted to try something different."

Sean finished his bourbon and set his empty glass on the desk. "If you have a few bottles to spare, I'd love to take some back to the ship with me."

Savannah smiled and then finished hers as well. "I think I can make that happen." She looked at him for a moment as if considering her next question. "There's something that... something I've always wanted to know."

"All right, ask me."

"You knew I was hiding my pregnancy. I'm just wondering when you first figured it out."

She was referring to the end of the Vemus War when Connor had sent her back to New Earth, citing CDF regulations.

"I didn't know you were pregnant at the time; I just thought you were hiding something. After the attempt on Connor's life, I made it a point to keep my eye on anyone who might pose a significant threat to him. He almost died on my watch, and it had become second nature for me to look after him."

Savannah nodded. "Fair enough. And for the record, Connor was right to send me back to New Earth. I didn't agree with him at the time, and it took me awhile to understand," she said, and her gaze slid to the picture of her son on the desk.

There was a chime from Savannah's assistant.

"You and I are scheduled for a meeting with the engineers regarding the status of the space gates, and we have the demonstration of our new subspace communication systems," Savannah said.

"Good. I have a few things I'd like to suggest to the engineers. More like a request," Sean said.

He glanced down at the bourbon almost wistfully, imagining the glorious taste of another two fingers' worth of the stuff.

"You really did like it. I almost thought you were just being polite," Savannah said.

Sean shrugged. They left her office, and on their way out, Savannah asked her assistant to send a case of bourbon to the *Vigilant*. Sean thanked her, and they left.

9

As Sean walked through the hallways to the meeting, he noticed something about the people living on Phoenix Station. There was a sense of normalcy on the station that he hadn't seen aboard his ship or on any of the other ships in his battle group. Phoenix Station was first and foremost a military installation, but there had been accommodations made for the increasing civilian presence. There were also civilians aboard his warship, but he had more control over who was allowed there, and he made sure they understood the importance of their work. Perhaps he was being a bit unfair, but it was a warning sign that shined brightly in the depths of his mind. He was sure it hadn't been there in the months following their brief engagement with the Krake, but it did worry him. It wasn't best practice to keep one's subordinates wound up too tightly, but there was a risk that the threat to the colony wasn't as readily apparent as it really was. The Krake were real, and they would have to work to mitigate this threat. He remembered Connor struggling with this when there was hardly a hint of the Vemus coming to attack them.

He glanced at Savannah and wondered if he should say

something to her. He didn't want to offend her because this was her command, and she should run it as she saw fit. Perhaps he should leave it alone. Colonel Cross was more than up to the task.

Spending years in Spec Ops had ingrained certain habits into Sean that he doubted would ever go away—habits like evaluating the room, knowing where the exits were, and the general mood of the people there. They entered the conference room, and the people inside were much more serious than the people he'd seen throughout the rest of Phoenix Station. There were a few CDF officers in the room, as well as several science teams. He saw Oriana on the other side of the room. Her back was to him, but there was no mistaking her tall, slender form. Her velvety black hair rested on her shoulders. She laughed and placed her hand on the shoulder of the man next to her as she handed him a tablet computer. It was a small, harmless gesture, but Sean's eyes tightened just the same. The man turned and saw Savannah, then immediately started walking over to them.

Sean finally recognized the man—Dr. Nicholas Grant. He was a lead engineer on the space gates. He was tall, with chiseled features and a pronounced chin. He had that annoyingly perfect hair that wasn't too short or too long and just enough to snatch the attention of more than a few women in the room. He smiled, showing a perfect set of teeth that made the dimple on his chin more pronounced.

"I believe you know Colonel Sean Quinn," Savannah said.

Grant stuck his hand out, and Sean shook it, receiving a firm handshake in return. "Colonel Quinn, I bet you're anxious for the status of our space gate reengineering efforts."

"I'm not the only one. This a high-priority effort, which is why I authorized the temporary use of my science officers."

"Yes, and I'm thankful that you did. Their help has been instrumental in getting us this far," Grant said.

Sean looked at Savannah. "Excellent. Let's get started."

He took a seat at the conference table and gave a quick raise of an eyebrow in greeting to a few familiar faces. Oriana sat down not far away and gave him a wave.

A wave?

Oriana had divided her time between serving on the *Vigilant* and at Phoenix Station, which Sean supported wholeheartedly. It was thanks to her that they'd been able to return home after their encounter with the Krake. She was a brilliant scientist and had great instincts when faced with the unknown.

A wave?

He must have let his disappointment show because the smile on her face faltered and then her expression became one of distant professionalism.

Dr. Grant stood up and asked for their attention. "Time is a valuable commodity, so we need to get started. Thanks to Dr. Evans," Grant said, gesturing toward Oriana, "we've had a major breakthrough with the Space Gate Initiative, and we're on the cusp of being able to test the gate. We're confident that we've worked out the issues we've been having with it."

"There was a recent test on New Earth that wasn't so successful. How is the space gate here different?" Sean asked.

"I'm glad you asked," Grant said. "What we've discovered here is that the NEIIS were attempting to reverse engineer the arch on the planet. While doing so, they stumbled upon a lot of other things, to put it mildly. So part of the reverse engineering effort was already done for us. We're simply assembling the pieces and... perfecting it a bit, if you will. In essence, we're using everything we've learned up until this point—knowledge gained from studying the NEIIS themselves and the systems they left behind. Also, our own substantial technological base."

"Have you run preliminary tests?" Savannah asked.

"Not yet, but we've run simulations based on the new data," Grant said and looked at Sean. "The data from the test you referred to, Colonel Quinn, looks promising. They're making progress."

"So there's no actual proof that it works yet. Just simulations," Sean said.

"I understand your skepticism. Our next step is running a physical test."

"Understood. What about the power requirements for the space gate?" Sean asked.

"It's within our current capabilities. Actually, more to your point, the reactors aboard a heavy cruiser warship are more than up to the task of operating the space gate. Again, this is a theory, and I know you would want to test it to prove it."

Sean nodded. "No, that's fine. I'm glad you had an answer."

Grant smiled as if he'd spent hours practicing the perfect smile in the mirror. "Not me, Colonel Quinn. Dr. Evans anticipated your questions."

Sean glanced at Oriana, as did the others, and she nodded at Grant. "My time on the *Vigilant* has given me more of a perspective on the importance of this project and how it needs to fit the particular requirements of the CDF."

She turned her gaze toward Sean, and there was a slight arch of her eyebrow.

"Indeed, we've missed you," Sean said. He looked at Grant. "I have an additional request for your team regarding the space gate, assuming that it works."

"My team is at your disposal," Grant said.

"We need to make it mobile."

The confident look on Dr. Grant's face faltered. "I'm afraid I'm not following you, Colonel Quinn."

"It's all fine and good if we can make the space gate work here, but the intent is to send ships through it. What we need is to give our ships a way to get themselves back home."

Dr. Grant frowned for a moment, considering. "I've reviewed

all the reports on the archway and the space gates. It seems that the Krake leave them at stationary positions."

"I am aware of how the Krake utilize the space gates, and that's not what I asked. I'm asking that we take this a step further," Sean said and then looked at Oriana.

"I'm not sure it's possible," Grant said.

Sean didn't look at him but kept his gaze on Oriana. He could tell when she was focusing her mind on a problem. "Do you believe the same, Dr. Evans?"

"I would need time to consider, but I wouldn't say it's impossible. Not yet anyway," Oriana said.

Sean looked at the others around the room. "It's critical that we get the space gate to work, but it's just as important to keep in mind how we'll be using them, the conditions under which we'll be called to use them. And the fact that we haven't seen the Krake use them in such a way doesn't mean they haven't. Dr. Grant could be correct that it's impossible, but we cannot rule it out. The next step after making this work is to be able to bring our own gate with us when we send ships through to a parallel universe, even if it's only possible to be used by a heavy cruiser." Sean looked at Savannah. "My battle group has two heavy cruisers, as well as eight destroyers and a converted freighter for a carrier. We're meant to recon the enemy and engage them if we need to."

Savannah rested her knuckles on her bottom lip for a moment. "It's a good suggestion. I agree we need to pursue this."

Sean looked back at Dr. Grant. "Just to be clear, I want a mobile space gate solution. Meaning that when we use it to take our battle group through, I want to be able to take the gate with us to be opened from another area. A repeatable solution, if you will. This would be a tactical advantage if you could get it to work."

Grant nodded. "I think I understand now, Colonel. We'll see what we can come up with," he said and gestured at the science teams.

Sean thanked him.

"Okay, we're ready for our demonstration, which is the new subspace communication systems. We'll be opening a channel to Lunar Base, which will also have a link to the CDF base on New Earth. Please direct your attention to the central holoscreen."

The holoscreen flickered, and then they saw the command center on Lunar Base.

"Hello, this is Colonel Belenét, Lunar Base actual."

Savannah stood up. "Hello, Lunar Base. This is Colonel Cross, Phoenix Station actual."

There was a round of applause. The communication had no latency at all. Sean was impressed. Using their existing communication systems, this type of interaction would have had a twelve-minute lapse, meaning that was the amount of time it would take for the signal to reach Lunar Base.

A second window appeared on the holoscreen, and Sean saw Connor and Nathan appear. They both greeted everyone.

"Excellent work," Connor said. "Is there any—"

The holoscreen window showing Connor and Nathan went dark, as did the one on Lunar Base.

Sean looked at Dr. Grant, who was busy checking the systems. He had a finger to his ear and was speaking to somebody on a personal comlink. Grant looked up at everyone with a guilty smile. "It looks like we've hit some form of hiccup. The connection was lost, but you did see that it worked, at least in part."

It had worked for about thirty seconds before it cut out.

"We understand this is new technology," Savannah said. "Try to figure out what the problem is, and we'll take it from there. In the meantime, we'll deploy subspace communication systems to Colonel Quinn's battle group. They'll do extensive field testing with it and provide you with feedback."

They took a break. Sean tried not to take too much delight in Dr. Grant's agitation, but he couldn't help it.

Oriana walked over to him. "You seem to be enjoying yourself."

Sean shrugged. "I'd like to take a few moments to reflect on the stumbling of one of the greatest minds in our colony."

Oriana let out a small laugh and glanced around to see if anyone had overheard them.

"Seriously though, are you ready to come back to the *Vigilant*?" Sean asked.

"I'm not sure. There's a lot of work to be done with the space gates. I was going to propose that you replace me."

Sean felt his jaw tighten. *She's not coming back.* He smoothed his features. "You know there's no replacement for you."

Oriana snorted and smiled, eyes twinkling. "Flattery is not going to get you anywhere with me. You should know that by now."

"It couldn't hurt."

"So when did you come up with the request to bring the space gates with the ship?"

Sean tilted his head and pursed his lips for a moment. "Honestly, maybe an hour ago. We were running through tactical simulations of our engagement with the Krake. The space gate represents a single point of failure. We can't afford to be stranded."

"I understand that, but if we made it part of the ship and that ship got destroyed, you'd still be stranded."

"Possibly. So we need to be able to transfer the gate between ships, or at least the heavy cruisers. I'm sure you'll come up with something."

Oriana shook her head in exasperation. "It's not that easy, you know."

"Brilliance never is, or so I'm told—I think by *you*, actually."

Oriana regarded him for a moment as they each experienced the unspoken connection between them. Neither one of them had broached the subject or been anything other than friendly professionals. They worked well together, and he didn't want her to stay at Phoenix Station. He'd been about to say as much when Dr. Grant came over.

"Well, that was embarrassing," Grant said.

"Like you said, this is new," Sean said. "I'd heard the theory before, but it's still surprising that we're able to establish a link through subspace. There were quite a few people thinking we'd be able to *travel* through subspace soon," Sean said.

"There are still people wanting us to focus on that, but the NEIIS really did stumble upon it by accident, and it's not safe. The little evidence we have suggests that it physically altered anything that went through. We were able to establish a link only because we were able to build a receiver. The signal does get altered, but it's like dialing in a broad spectrum of signals. Once you get it right, the connection establishes itself."

"Yeah, but we need it to work for longer than thirty seconds," Sean said.

Grant nodded and looked at Oriana. "We have a lot of data to go through, as well as prep work for the space gate test."

In one sentence Sean felt like a third wheel, as if he were intruding upon them. "Go ahead. I'll follow up with you later," he said to Oriana.

10

CONNOR HAD NEVER BEEN to Camp Alpha. It was located in a secluded spot away from any colonial settlement, and he thought it had been a FORB at one time. Colonial HAB units had been built for civilians and the extensive CDF presence. The NEIIS were cordoned off, and their HAB units were replicas of the smaller circular shelters that had been found on the continent. The camp was more of a compound, with perimeter fencing in designated areas for the NEIIS to use.

"We didn't escape entirely unscathed," Diaz said, gesturing toward Johnson and his staff as they exited the vehicle.

Connor had given Governor Wolf an update and received approval to go to the revival camp and ask the NEIIS for help. As they were leaving, Johnson had caught up to them and announced his intention to accompany them.

"I guess he's keeping an eye on me."

Diaz nodded. "Probably."

Connor shrugged. "Either that or— no, it's that. Doesn't matter, though. We still have a job to do."

They went to central processing and were met by Major Alexis Brooks, who was in charge of running the base.

"General Gates, welcome to Camp Alpha. I'll take you to Darius Cohen," Brooks said.

If Johnson was annoyed by the lack of deference given to him, he didn't show it. They followed Major Brooks as she escorted them through central processing toward the civilian wing of the camp.

As Connor walked through the area, there were more than a few people who noticed. They must not have expected to see him since Nathan was the one in charge of running things there.

Diaz raised his arms and smiled. "I know you weren't expecting to see me here, but that's just the way it is. For those of you who don't know what I'm talking about, ask around. I'm the owner of the Salty Soldier in Sanctuary, creator of such delicious meals that your mouth will water just thinking about it," he said and gave Connor a wink. "You'll die—"

"I'm going to die if you keep going on," Connor said, and Diaz waved at the onlookers.

"They loved me. A few of them are curious now. They'll be in touch; you'll see."

Brooks led them to the far side of an open work area with the heading Diplomatic Relations on the wall nearby. There was a group of people gathered, and Connor recognized one of them.

"Is that who I think it is?" Diaz asked.

Dash waved to Connor, and the man he was speaking with turned toward him.

"General Gates. It's nice to meet you in person. I'm Darius Cohen."

Darius had short blond hair and a friendly face. "I was surprised to learn you were coming here."

"I'm afraid circumstances made it a necessity."

Darius nodded. "I understand. Governor Wolf has brought me up to speed. She said you'd like to ask the NEIIS a few questions."

"That's the long and short of it," Connor said and nodded a greeting to Dash.

"I'm not one for delaying. If you want to talk to the NEIIS, or the Ovarrow as they call themselves, then let's get to it," Darius said.

Connor gestured ahead of him. "After you then."

Darius took the lead and Connor walked next to him. Johnson threaded his way to walk behind them. Connor heard Diaz make a comment to Dash, who chuckled softly.

"So I'll tell you how this will work. There are almost a hundred NEIIS who have been brought out of stasis, but they are in various stages of health."

"What sort of health issues are they having?" Johnson asked.

"As far as we can tell, it's some sort of cellular degradation as a result of being in stasis. After careful examination of the pods, it seems that the NEIIS went into stasis before they'd perfected the technology, meaning it wasn't entirely safe."

"You mean they went into stasis knowing that there would be complications when they came out of it?"

"That's what we think," Darius said.

"It's not surprising," Connor said. "They were desperate. There's a mounting pile of evidence that indicates just how desperate the NEIIS were. But you said the complications don't affect all of them. Were there different stasis pods? The ones that I've seen mostly looked the same."

"By outward appearances, they do look the same," Darius confirmed. "However, it was the internal components and materials used to maintain stasis—a state of cryo-sleep, if you will —that we believe is one of the problems."

"How many of them are sick?" Connor asked.

"Almost half of them," Darius said.

"What?" Johnson said. "Half of them are dying?"

Darius shook his head. "Goodness, no. There are different degrees to which the cellular degradation afflicts them, but fifteen of them are dying. They're simply beyond our ability to help. We're limited in what we can do for them because their physiology is so much different than ours."

"What are you doing to help them?" Johnson asked.

Connor almost thought Johnson sounded concerned, but he didn't believe it.

"We've revived some of their scientists, and we're attempting to communicate with them about the issue."

"Do the health issues affect all the NEIIS factions or just some of them?" Connor asked.

"We hardly have enough of a sample from each faction to make that determination. As you already know, there are factions we're not bringing out of stasis at this time, and I will say that this has not gone unnoticed by the NEIIS."

The current protocol was to avoid reviving NEIIS from the military faction they'd identified during Connor's interaction with Siloc. They were dangerous, but Connor knew it was only a matter of time before they would have to deal with it.

"What do you mean that it hasn't gone unnoticed?" Connor asked.

"We do have basic communication capabilities with them, but it's through a translator of their written language. As we brought them out of stasis, they were naturally curious as to who we were but also about what had happened to the rest of them."

Connor nodded and could see that that was a logical reaction.

"Will we all be going out among the NEIIS?" Johnson asked.

Darius shook his head. "No. We've done it before, and it causes a major disruption among them sometimes—only large groups, I might add. They're a bit territorial at times. There are several... I'm not sure if 'leaders' is the right word, but there are some of them who are more amicable to communicating with us than others. We have a way to signal them and they will come to talk to us."

"A signal? What sort of signal?" Johnson asked.

"Signal was probably the wrong word," Darius said. "We have a designated meeting area that we show up to. It's important that they have their own space."

Connor pressed his lips together for a moment. All of these accommodations sounded good, but the NEIIS were an intelligent species. They'd no doubt realized that there were restrictions on what they could do. A prison was still a prison no matter how accommodating this camp was for them.

Darius led them to a room that had multiple large holoscreens showing the NEIIS camp. NEIIS were humanoid in shape. They walked on two legs and had two arms, but that was where the similarities ended. Their skin was a few shades of brown, almost pebbled, like that of a reptile. Pointy protrusions stemmed from their shoulders and elbows, but it varied among individuals. They had long arms and large hands, which sported four thick fingers with stubby black nails sturdy enough to be considered claws. The movement of their arms as they walked gave them a natural head bob as they moved. They had thick brow lines on either side of their heads, and their hook-shaped nostrils were at the same level as their dark eyes. The curvature of their wide mouths made them all appear as if they had deep frown lines.

"We do have a couple of teams out among the NEIIS right now," Darius said. He guided them to a door that led outside and stopped. "The fewer of us to go, the better. If we all go out there in a large group, it's intimidating, and it hinders open communication. I'll be going, and so will Mr. DeWitt, as his skills are needed for the translator. Anyone else besides you, General Gates, joining us?"

"You said the fewer of us, the better, so it'll just be me," Connor said.

"Surely one more person can't make that much of a difference," Johnson said.

Connor looked at Johnson. "What do you want to ask them?"

Johnson frowned. "I just wanted to observe."

Connor gestured toward the phalanx of nearly identical workstations around the room. "This is where you observe."

Johnson's gaze narrowed, but he didn't push the issue. Diaz looked as if he was going to protest, but Connor gave him a warning glance. It wasn't as if he was going to be in any danger. There was sufficient protection around.

Darius opened the door and led them through. They followed the fenced-off path to an open space that looked like a waiting area with a few long benches in the middle.

Connor glanced to the side and saw that a few of the NEIIS were watching them. "Do they have access to this area?"

Dash shook his head. "When they choose to talk to us, they go to their designated area, and we go inside."

Connor didn't like it, but the tone Dash used indicated that it was a normal occurrence. He made a mental note to speak with Nathan about that later.

The NEIIS watched them with curiosity. Connor noticed that Darius didn't wave at them or speak to them at all. In fact, he just went about his business with an occasional glance in their direction.

"So what made you decide to be the diplomatic lead here?" Connor asked.

They walked to one side of the open area and two of the NEIIS walked to the other side.

Darius looked at him with a smile. "It's the chance of a lifetime. I get to interact with an alien society. Learn their social behavior."

"Raylore and Jory have come to talk to us," Dash said.

Connor raised an eyebrow. "Are those their names?"

"It's based off the translator, but when they speak their names, it doesn't sound anything like that, so we're working with a best guess. It's definitely a self-designation," Dash said.

Darius opened the security gate to the NEIIS waiting area and the gate on the NEIIS side closed. Darius walked through and Dash followed with Connor. The last time Connor had been this close to any NEIIS, he'd been fighting for his life.

The two NEIIS watched Connor while Dash brought up the holoscreen. There were two interfaces that came up on either side, and one of the NEIIS—Jory, Connor thought—stepped up to it. Raylore stayed by the door.

"A new face," Jory said. The NEIIS didn't make a sound but entered the information using the interface.

Darius introduced Connor and told Jory that Connor would like to ask him a few questions.

Connor stepped up to the holoscreen and connected to it via his implants. He then put up an image of the underwater arch. Jory flinched, but Raylore merely watched.

"You can speak to the interface and it will translate for you as best as it can," Dash said.

Connor nodded and uploaded another image that was an NEIIS symbol. This one had a glowing emblem with a few wavy lines underneath it. Raylore shifted his feet. Connor had the arch and the emblem next to each other. "Do you know how this works?" he asked, pointing to the arch.

Jory took a step back and glanced at Raylore.

Connor added a third image of the arch they'd built.

Jory was becoming increasingly upset, but Raylore was almost rigid. He made a few grunting sounds. He strode to the interface and began inputting his message, then paused before finishing it to look at Connor. "It is forbidden."

"We need to know more about it," Connor said.

"It is forbidden," Raylore repeated.

Connor decided to try a different approach. It was time the

NEIIS understood the stakes. He uploaded an image of the Krake base camp filled with soldiers. The image had come from the recon drone Connor used when he'd been in the alternate universe. "We need to know how the arch works because of them."

Jory banged on the gate and it opened to the NEIIS area. He hastened through and waited. Raylore regarded Connor in a way that sparked a memory of Siloc. He'd seen that look many times during their brief encounter. It was one of suspicion.

Raylore looked at Darius. "No bargain."

The NEIIS walked away from them and none of the others approached the area for more than a few seconds in order to catch a glimpse of the images on the holoscreen.

Connor looked at Darius. "Are they always this uncooperative?"

"General Gates, I feel I need to remind you that the NEIIS are not being held hostage. You asked the question and they gave you an answer. Give them some time. They've been through a lot."

Connor walked toward the NEIIS gate. He needed answers and he needed them now. A comlink registered itself on Connor's internal heads-up display. It was Dr. Volker.

"Connor, I hope I didn't get you at a bad time. We've done some analysis on the signal, and we think it's colonial based, but we're still having trouble deciphering it. I thought you'd like to know as soon as possible."

"A colonial signal..."

"We're still working on it, I assure you."

Connor closed the comlink.

"Pardon, General, but we couldn't help overhearing. You've detected a signal?" Darius asked.

"We ran a test with the arch in that picture. We think a gateway was opened and we received some sort of signal. Dr. Volker was informing me that they believe it's colonial based. It's one of ours, but they're having issues deciphering it."

"Connor, Tommy Lockwood is here. I bet he could help," Dash said.

Connor found himself wishing Noah was there. The signal would have been deciphered by now. "I think that's a good idea. Let's go see him."

"Before we do that, there's something I'd like to say," Darius said, and Connor nodded. "Diplomacy isn't your strong suit, I can tell. You're frustrated that the NEIIS didn't simply answer your questions, but that's not really how this works. Especially with a subject that's so troubling to them. Communication takes time among people; now imagine trying to do this with another species. We'll speak with them again, and perhaps there will be a different outcome, but I must caution you. You need to think of this as dealing with a foreign nation. We need to give them something if we want their cooperation."

"What do they want?" Connor asked, preferring to cut to the chase.

Darius smiled. "I think that question would have more of an impact on them if it came from you. We have a few ideas, which I'm happy to share with you, but it's important that they communicate their wants and needs to you. That way you establish a relationship."

Connor frowned in thought for a moment. "That's why Raylore said it wasn't part of the bargain?"

He felt a growing appreciation for Darius Cohen's advice, but the situation with the NEIIS was too fragile. How long would they be content to stay at the camp before they demanded to be released?

11

THEY WENT BACK into the observatory, and Connor reached out to Carl Flint for a status update on the arch.

"They don't know why the power was interrupted," Flint said. "It's not a failure because technically there was power available. Did you get anywhere with the NEIIS?"

"Not yet. Do me a favor and send me a copy of the signal they detected."

"Yes, sir. Sending it over now."

Connor received the data and forwarded it to Lockwood for analysis. He looked at Dash. "I sent it to Lockwood. Would you mind bringing him up to speed?"

"I'm on it," Dash said and walked over to a small breakout room where Lockwood was working.

Kurt Johnson came to Connor's side. "Do you really think this tech specialist is going to be able to help with the signal analysis?"

Connor nodded. "Thomas Lockwood is extremely intelligent. It's one of the reasons Noah Barker recruited him."

Johnson nearly winced at the mention of Noah's name. "It's

terrible what happened to him. It's been six months and he's still in a coma."

Something in Johnson's reaction made Connor suspicious. "There's still enough brain activity to indicate that he's alive. The doctors agree that we'll just have to wait."

Johnson nodded and waited for Connor to continue.

"Regarding whether Lockwood can help, sometimes putting the right people on a task can make all the difference. Noah proved that to me time and time again. They just have a different way of looking at a problem, and where other people get stumped, they're able to work through."

Johnson looked unconvinced. "Yes, well let's hope."

Connor didn't reply, and Diaz came over. "I just listened to a short lecture from a guy named Pip on how we shouldn't be quick to judge the NEIIS. He said I was being ethnocentric."

"That must have been very hard for you."

"At first I thought he was trying to insult me. I think he thought I was going to hit him."

"Did you?" Johnson asked.

Diaz frowned. "What do you think I am?"

Johnson shrugged.

"It's hard not to judge the NEIIS. We've seen what they did to their planet and to each other," Connor said.

Johnson looked at him. "Do you think we're superior to them?"

"That's easy," Diaz said. "Yes."

Johnson glanced at Diaz before turning his gaze back to Connor.

"We'll see," Connor said.

The door to the breakout room opened and Dash and Lockwood came out. They walked directly to Connor.

"It's a colonial signal. It's John's signal," Lockwood said. His eyes were gleaming with excitement. "The ID matches that for John Rollins. He's there."

Johnson cleared his throat. "You think you've managed to decipher the signal in twenty minutes when the R&D folks at the CDF base haven't been able to do it in almost twenty-four hours?"

Lockwood frowned, his cheeks becoming red.

"Why don't you show us what you have, and then we can decide whether your interpretation of the signal is valid," Connor said.

Lockwood nodded and Dash gestured toward the nearby holoscreen.

"So the signal was detected during the test of the archway. It appears to be chaotic, but then I got to thinking. The signal came from another universe, which I don't know that much about. I just know it's different. I was thinking that perhaps..." Lockwood paused for a moment and grabbed a nearby coffee mug. He held it up in his hand. "In this universe, the coffee mug is here. Right side up. It looks like a mug. But if it came from another universe, it could be completely different. It could be upside down and perhaps inside out. So I wrote up a quick interpreter program that broke down the pieces of the signal and fit them back together."

"And what did you find?" Johnson asked.

Lockwood gestured toward the holoscreen, which now showed a partial communication signal.

Connor frowned. "Is that all there is? It looks incomplete."

Lockwood nodded. "It's almost like we're looking at a recording of a message. Like a recording of a recording." He frowned for a moment. "Like an echo."

Johnson shook his head. "Yes...like an echo. I understand that, but what does it say?"

"Nothing. It's just a distress signal," Lockwood said.

Connor frowned and he saw Diaz give him a nod.

Johnson caught it and looked at Connor. "What am I missing? Even if this was true, how would a distress signal come from the alternate universe?"

Connor looked at Lockwood. "Thank you, Tommy. Good work," he said and then turned back to Johnson. "Rollins was a combat engineer in the CDF. He'd certainly have the skills to set up a distress signal. We left him behind and haven't been able to determine whether he'd been killed. There was another person, too. His name was Taylor, but I'm not sure what his skillset was."

"But," Diaz said, "our arch is over fifty kilometers from the original site. That range is beyond any personal distress signal."

Johnson's gaze flicked toward Diaz for a moment. "I also recall reading that the atmosphere was toxic. Isn't that right?"

Connor shook his head. "Nothing that would kill you, but you wouldn't enjoy it. Rollins could've escaped, but he also knew the archway here was at the same location. He might've counted on that."

Johnson narrowed his gaze. "You think he's still alive?"

"Until there's evidence to the contrary," Connor replied.

"This doesn't change anything," Johnson said, gesturing toward the holoscreen.

"This changes everything. We left people behind, and they need our help. We need to get back to them ASAP," Connor said.

"You don't have the authority to do any of that. Governor Wolf needs to hear about this, as well as the rest of the Defense Committee," Johnson said.

Connor drew in a deep breath but knew that Johnson was right, at least in part. "Why don't you go update her? Tommy, can you take him somewhere private where he can speak with the governor?"

Lockwood nodded. "I can take you. Please, follow me."

Johnson regarded Connor for a moment as if he wasn't quite sure whether to leave or not, but ultimately he followed Lockwood toward the breakout room.

Diaz leaned toward Connor. "Smooth, but I think you only bought yourself a little bit of time."

"A little bit of time is probably all we'll need," Connor said and gestured for Dash to come closer. "Can you take me back inside the NEIIS settlement?"

"I can, but we'll need Darius to come with us," Dash said.

Connor glanced over at Darius Cohen who stood a short distance off, speaking with several members of his staff. Connor thought about sneaking into the NEIIS settlement to get what he needed, but the more rational part of his brain won over in the end.

"All right," Connor said.

Dash led them over to Darius. "They want to go back in."

Darius raised his eyebrows in surprise.

"The signal from the alternate universe is from survivors we left there. I need the NEIIS's help in order to get back there. They need to tell me what they know about the Krake and about the archways," Connor said.

"Going back now will be highly disruptive," Darius said and held up his hand. "I understand the importance of this, but we can't just go barging in there."

"What if we walk among them and ask their permission to speak with them? If they don't want to talk to us, we won't make them," Connor said.

Darius considered this for a few moments, but Connor knew he wouldn't refuse. If anything, the diplomat thrived on civil interaction.

"We can take a small group in there, but you cannot be armed," Darius said.

"Like hell, we won't," Diaz said.

"We go unarmed so as not to present a threat to them," Darius said.

"What if they threaten us?" Diaz asked and then looked at Connor. "They weren't there the last time when we were surrounded by a bunch of these..." He let the thought go unfinished.

"We can't go completely unprotected. Stun batons should be acceptable. Would you agree with that?" Connor asked.

Darius pressed his lips together for a moment. "How many people are we talking about here?"

Connor glanced in the direction that Lockwood had taken Johnson. "Just four of us right now."

Darius looked at them and arched an eyebrow toward Diaz.

"Diaz comes with us," Connor said.

"All right, we'll do this your way," Darius said.

Connor caught the unspoken message that if anything went wrong, it would be his fault. He could live with that, and he gestured for Darius to lead the way. He needed to get out there quickly without Johnson breathing down his neck.

"YEAH, THIS IS A REAL GOOD IDEA," Diaz groused.

They'd entered the NEIIS common area a few minutes earlier. Darius led them, walking at a leisurely pace, and Connor kept pace with him. The NEIIS kept their distance.

"What's the plan if we do get their help?" Diaz asked.

"One step at a time. Depends on what we can learn," Connor said.

He didn't like being unarmed. Despite all the outward show of treating the NEIIS like refugees, this place felt more like a prison camp. The NEIIS couldn't come and go as they pleased, and they knew it. There was an underlying resentment in their gaze.

"How long will they stay here?" Connor asked.

Darius turned toward Connor and was about to answer when a group approached them. Dash brought up the translator, and Raylore threaded his way to the front of the group.

"Why have you returned?" Raylore asked.

Connor walked up to the second interface. "I would like permission to speak to the Ovarrow," he said using the name of the species that the NEIIS called themselves.

Raylore looked at Connor as if he were taking in his appearance. He looked at the nearest NEIIS and made a few sounds that seemed like a quick, high-pitched chattering to Connor's ears. He doubted he'd ever be able to understand their language. More NEIIS walked toward them and waited. Even Darius seemed surprised by this. He gave Connor an encouraging nod.

Connor looked at Dash.

"Just go ahead and speak. The translator will do its best to interpret what you say," Dash said.

Connor nodded and looked at Raylore. "I need your help. The Krake have some of us prisoner," he said and gestured toward himself and the others. He hoped the meaning was clear. "We need the archway to work in order to rescue them." He paused and the NEIIS seemed to do their best equivalent of human muttering among the small crowd. Connor brought up the image of the archway they were building. "Our gateway doesn't work right. You've built one before. We've seen it. We need to understand how it works."

Connor brought up another image of the partial NEIIS settlement they'd found on Sagan. Raylore seemed to study the image, and the deep brows on the sides of his head went almost rigid for a moment.

"We know you were trying to re-create the archway. We know you fought a war with the Krake. And we know you were defeated."

Some of the NEIIS backed away a few steps, but Raylore continued to watch Connor. There were several others that also didn't show any signs of fear at what Connor was showing them.

"The Krake know we're here," Connor continued. "It's only a matter of time before they come back."

Raylore's thick fingers navigated swiftly through the NEIIS interface. "This is why we need the Mekaal."

Connor frowned and glanced at Dash, who shook his head slightly. "Who are the Mekaal?"

"Protectors," Raylore said.

Another symbol appeared on the holoscreen. It was of three intertwining triangles, and Connor's chest tightened. The protectors were the NEIIS military.

His first instinct was to refuse, but he knew he couldn't. He felt the others watching him, and Darius was on the verge of saying something. Connor held up his hand and Darius became still. The gesture wasn't lost on Raylore. Connor gestured for the NEIIS to continue.

"We want more of the Ovarrow brought out of stasis," Raylore said.

Connor looked around at the remaining NEIIS and gestured toward one that looked sickly. "Some of you are not well when you come out of stasis. We are trying to help you. This is why we haven't brought more of you out."

"We are aware of the sickness," Raylore said.

Connor's eyes widened. Had the NEIIS been aware of the risks going into stasis, or was Raylore acknowledging Connor's statement? If they'd known the risks and done it anyway, then the NEIIS might have been even more desperate than he'd initially thought. He looked at Dash and Darius and saw that they hadn't known about this. They must've suspected it, though, because they didn't look as surprised as Connor felt.

"I know of a place that our mechanics worked on using Krake technology. This is what you seek," Raylore said.

Darius leaned in toward Connor. "You're bargaining with them."

Connor nodded and looked back at Raylore. "What do you want? Do you want to be free? Do you want to leave?" Connor said and gestured to the area beyond the perimeter fence.

"Prisoners. We are prisoners," Raylore replied.

Connor considered for a moment. He was the one bargaining, and the colony would have to live with whatever deal he made with the NEIIS.

"You are not prisoners. We're trying to help you," Connor said.

"Where did you come from?"

Connor pointed above them. "We came from far away. I need to know if you'll help us."

Raylore looked at the sky and then back at Connor. "Are you a soldier or protector?"

Connor met the NEIIS's gaze. "I'm both."

Raylore seemed to consider this for a moment. "The Krake are coming."

Connor nodded. "Yes, they are."

Raylore tapped a few more symbols on the interface. "They are always coming."

The NEIIS's shoulders slumped, and Connor felt as if he were looking at someone who'd learned that the conflict they'd hope to escape would never end.

"If we work together, maybe we can stop them," Connor said.

"We need the Mekaal and our mechanics," Raylore said.

Connor glanced at Dash. "Mechanics?"

"The translation is imperfect. He probably means their technicians or their engineers. The equivalent," Dash said.

Connor turned back to Raylore. "Can you tell us where your mechanics worked on the Krake technology?"

Raylore gave a look Connor couldn't mistake, and it confirmed that he had what Connor needed. He remembered Siloc having that same look when he'd held Connor's PDA.

"We can show you. We will travel with you there," Raylore said.

Connor frowned and glanced at the other NEIIS nearby.

"General Gates," Darius said, "we have no authorization to allow the NEIIS to leave this area."

"Maybe not, but we'll get it after the fact," Connor said.

Diaz glanced up at the sky and frowned. "What is that?"

The NEIIS looked up at the sky as well.

"Darius, I need to know if you're with me," Connor said.

"I'm not sure what you mean."

"I'm taking some of the NEIIS out of here. The protocol states that I need you as my diplomatic liaison."

Darius's eyes widened and he looked at Dash.

"It's how he does things," Dash confirmed.

Connor turned toward Raylore. "You have a deal. We'll bring more of your people out of stasis, including the Mekaal, and help you establish your own settlement. In return, you'll help us with the archway and fighting the Krake."

Raylore waited a few moments for the translation to finish and then looked at Connor. "This is acceptable."

The troop carriers from the CDF base landed just beyond the perimeter fencing. Connor had transmitted his authorization for their approach to the base commander.

"You know Johnson isn't going to like this," Diaz said.

Connor smiled. "He'll be fine. Where we're going, there's lots of walking, so it's better if he stays." He looked at Dash. "We need to make the translator mobile. Is there something you can do to help?"

"Of course. I think I can adapt the PDA interface for the NEIIS to wear and use. We can link them all up and be able to communicate with each other," Dash said.

"Good," Connor said. "I hope this is something you can do on the fly because we're leaving right now."

Dash glanced at the troop carriers, catching Connor's meaning, and nodded.

Connor turned back toward Raylore. "How many of you want to come?"

He hadn't planned on taking the NEIIS anywhere, but he had little choice. Darius had been right. This was a negotiation between two independent groups, regardless of the fact that one of those groups was being held in isolation. He didn't want to think of it as a prison—not if the NEIIS would someday be their allies. Now more than ever, they had to get the archway to work. The distress signal from Rollins was deeply troubling. Rollins must have found a way to survive for the past six months. It was too long. If Rollins had been captured, the Krake would know more about the CDF and the colony by now.

Once they had their heading, he would need to contact the colonial government before they began accusing him of keeping them out of the loop. Johnson would have a field day with this, but Connor didn't care. He wasn't about to bring the governor's advisor on a field mission. He'd indulged the little man enough for now.

13

SEAN STOOD in the command center at Phoenix Station. It was a large, open area with nearly identical workstations staffed by a mix of CDF and civilian personnel. Panels and consoles flickered, giving the area an odd radiance.

It had taken Dr. Grant and his team almost two days to prepare for the physical test of the space gate. Apparently, being on the cusp of a new discovery meant that actual testing required thorough safety checks and confirmation that equipment was functioning within specified parameters. Sean was being too hard on the man, and he knew it.

Major Shelton had sent him an update, informing him that the new subspace communication systems had been successfully installed on the *Vigilant* and the rest of the battle group. Shelton had requested permission to begin testing the new communications capabilities to determine whether its performance on Phoenix Station had been an anomaly or if it was the norm. Sean authorized the test. So far, Shelton had proven to be proactive and quite capable.

Since this was a live physical test of the space gate, the actual gate machines had been moved farther away from the station. Reverse engineering them had opened the doors for new methods of producing energy. The gate machines were metallic cubes that acted as massive conductors capable of amplifying the energy put into them, creating a field that allowed them to transition to another universe. If it worked right, they'd also be able to return home.

The gate machines were equipped with maneuvering thrusters, which would allow them to maintain their positions while the gate was open. Dr. Grant had warned against using the nomenclature of "gate" in regards to what they were doing. They weren't opening a gate; they were transitioning through universes.

"Colonel Quinn," Lieutenant Cleaver said from the tactical workstation, "Talon-V stingers are in position at a minimum safe distance from the space gate."

"Understood," Sean said and looked at Savannah. "Our observers are in position."

"Dr. Grant," Savannah said, "we are ready to begin the test."

The main holoscreen showed a live video feed of the space gate.

"Thank you, Colonel Cross. Sending the startup sequence and coordinates. It will take a few minutes for everything to get up and running," Grant said.

Sean glanced at the auxiliary workstation where Oriana sat and walked over to her. "Tell me again why we think this will work?"

"Because the prototypes were in working condition when we found them. You want to know why we should expect our space gate to work when they're having issues getting the arch to work back home?" Oriana said.

"The thought had crossed my mind."

"There are a lot of things on a planet that can interfere with what we're doing here."

"Like what?"

"New Earth has a powerful magnetic field that is even stronger than what we had on Earth. We think it's because the iron core is a bit bigger. There are more reasons, but operating as we are out here simplifies things in terms of interference," Oriana said.

Sean looked at the main holoscreen and saw that they were almost ready to begin. "Let's hope so."

The main holoscreen was divided into multiple sub-windows showing different video feeds and sensor data from the space gate. The only things they could visually observe were the glowing points for the alignment indicators on the gate machines.

"The space gate is up, and power is holding steady," Grant said.

Sean peered at the space between the gate machines and opened the comlink to the squadron commander. "Lieutenant Polanco, can you confirm what you see?"

"It looks like we put a frame around a window, sir. No discernible difference beyond the gate. Scanners aren't showing anything out of the ordinary either," Polanco replied.

"Understood. Stand by," Sean said and looked at tactical. "Release the probe."

"Explorer probe online, Colonel," Lieutenant Cleaver said.

"Send it through," Sean said.

The command was straightforward, but Sean knew that the probe was operating within a strict set of protocols. Once it went through the gate, it was to hold its position. They watched as the probe closed in on the space gate. Speed and telemetry data were consistent. The probe passed through the gate and all data feeds from the probe flatlined.

"Total loss of communication with the Explorer probe," Specialist Erickson said from the comms workstation.

"The same here. We only have visual," Lieutenant Cleaver said.

Sean noticed that Grant was smiling and offering congratulations to his staff. It seemed a bit premature.

"Comms, confirm visual status of the probe with Lieutenant Polanco and the other Talon-V pilots near the gate. I want to know if the pilots positioned behind the gate can see the probe," Sean said.

His orders were confirmed, and he could hear Erickson speaking with the pilots.

"Wouldn't they see the same thing we're seeing here?" Oriana asked.

"Probably, but I want it confirmed. I don't like that we've lost comms with it."

Savannah joined him. "Looks like it's working."

The space gate had been active for over ten minutes, which was longer than the arch was reported active on New Earth.

"Colonel Quinn," Specialist Erickson said, "I have confirmation from the Talon-V pilots that they have visual evidence of the probe, but the pilots on the other side of the gate do not."

Dr. Grant came over to them, grinning as if they'd shared a joke. "Colonel Quinn, I thought you'd be happier. We did it!"

Sean ignored him. "Tactical, send a command to the probe to return along its previous trajectory."

"Yes, Colonel," Lieutenant Cleaver said.

Dr. Grant frowned. "We've lost all data feeds. Why would you think a command is going to make it through?"

Sean saw Oriana look at him for a moment, considering. She understood, at least.

"Because all we know is that *we're* cut off from the probe and not the other way around," Oriana said.

Sean tilted his head to the side as a small salute to her.

"Good thinking," Savannah said.

"Indeed," Grant said and watched the main holoscreen.

A few minutes passed, and it was hard for them to tell whether the probe was coming back. Until it did. Once the probe was back through the gate, the data feeds that had been flatlining sprang to life with new information.

Sean smiled. "Now we can call it a successful test. All you have to do now is make it mobile."

Grant frowned. "There are maneuvering thrusters on them—"

"No, I want to be able to bring the gate machine with us when we go through it."

"I don't think it's possible."

"We won't know unless we try," Sean said. He paused for a moment. "The gateway is still up. Can the gate machines make the gateway open more?"

"As long as they maintain the alignment, the gateway should remain intact... again, in theory," Grant said.

Both Sean and Savannah watched him expectantly and he went back to his staff.

"Nothing drastic, Dr. Grant. Just a nudge now," Sean said.

Oriana went to speak with several of her colleagues off to the side. The data showed that the gate machines had moved with no adverse effects on the gateway.

"Excellent," Savannah said. "Begin the space gate shutdown sequence."

A few minutes later, Grant confirmed. "Space gate is offline."

"Tactical, I want you to send the Explorer probe back through the gate," Sean said.

Lieutenant Cleaver confirmed the order and they watched as the probe went back through the space gate. This time, all the Talon-V pilots confirmed that they could see the probe. There were no residual effects from the space gate. They'd retrieved the probe and were bringing it back to Phoenix Station for analysis.

Sean looked at Savannah. "So once anything goes through, it's one-way communication, but at least the probe was able to come back through the gate. I was hoping this wouldn't be entirely one way."

"There is that. I don't understand why it works that way though."

Sean glanced at Dr. Grant. "We're not the only ones."

14

THE SUBSPACE COMMUNICATION system had worked for a whole five minutes before it cut out in the middle of General Hayes' question. Sean watched as Grant excused himself from the meeting room, saying he'd be back in a few minutes.

Brody cleared his throat. "I was just reading the preliminary reports on the space gate. They indicate that the power consumption remains consistent once it's established, even after we increased the size of the gate. I thought that was interesting."

Savannah frowned and glanced at Sean. "What don't you like about Grant?"

It was just the three of them there so they could speak plainly.

"He's too quick to celebrate. I'm sure he's a brilliant scientist," Sean said, giving a slight tilt of his head. "He must be if you have him here, but it's as if he'd never encountered anything remotely like Murphy's Law."

"What's that?" Brody asked.

"If something can go wrong, it will," Sean answered.

Savanna smirked. "Are you getting cynical in your old age?"

Sean smiled and shook his head. "No, I just believe in being a little more thorough before I declare something a success."

"Dr. Evans seems thorough enough, but who else would you put on this project? Is there anyone else you can think of who could help?"

Sean felt his eyes tighten. He knew whose help he would've liked to have, but Noah was still in a coma at Sanctuary, and nothing had changed regarding his recovery. He looked at Savannah and shook his head. "No one who's available. I think the team we've got here will have to suffice."

A few minutes later Dr. Grant returned.

"Still working on analyzing the problem, but it's the same as before. The issue is that once the connection is made, the polarity of the signal changes and becomes a different signal altogether. Hence, we lose it entirely. It's almost as if we need an infinite number of receivers so that when that occurs, we don't have a loss of signal like we do now."

"The five-minute time window is consistent with what we've seen among the battle group," Brody confirmed.

"I appreciate that," Grant said and took a sip of his coffee. "I think it's important to remember that this is a new field of science that's never been discovered before."

Sean leaned forward and rested his elbows on the table. "No one is blaming you, but please accept this small bit of constructive criticism: I would hold off from declaring anything a success at the onset."

"Don't you worry; I've learned my lesson," Grant replied.

Sean wasn't convinced that he'd learned anything, thinking Grant had been a little bit too quick with his response.

"Looks like we'll have to do this briefing the old-fashioned way. We received a data burst from COMCENT," Savannah said.

A holoscreen appeared in the middle of the conference table and a video message from General Hayes began to play.

"I guess you're still working out the kinks to the subspace communication systems. That is to be expected. Meanwhile, we've had a number of new developments here at home that I think you should be aware of. The testing of the arch at our base near New Haven wasn't a complete failure. We received a signal and were able to decipher it. The signal was a distress beacon associated with John Rollins' identification. For those of you who are not aware, Rollins was with General Gates when he went to the alternate universe. He was one of the people declared MIA, but now there's evidence that he has somehow survived in a hostile environment. General Gates is working with the NEIIS to find their research location in hopes of gaining the information necessary to make the gate work. I reviewed your report on the space gate functionality and the successful test. I think for every success we have, more questions are raised. Foremost is why all communications were lost when you sent the probe through the gateway, but here on the planet, we opened a gateway for a brief amount of time and received the signal through it. Some of this doesn't add up, but I believe we'll find answers in the end. Given what I've just told you, I think we should seriously consider sending a recon team through the space gate at Phoenix Station. I will wait for your response."

The message finished and the holoscreen turned off.

Sean stood up and took a deep breath. "We need to use the gate."

"Don't you think this is a little premature?" Grant asked.

"It's not ideal, but if we always waited for the ideal, we might never do anything."

"But we haven't done as you asked. We haven't made the space gate mobile."

Sean locked eyes with Savannah for a moment. "It would be nice to have, but it's not a necessity. It's a point in space that we can pinpoint pretty accurately. So we'll need to establish protocols for activating the space gate from Phoenix Station."

"This is reckless," Grant said and looked at Savannah. "Colonel Cross, you have to agree with me."

"Using the space gate does have a certain degree of risk, particularly to this station, but what you're forgetting is that this station was designed for battle," Savannah said.

Grant took a moment to look at all of them. "Am I the only one who sees this? We don't know... We're only seeing one side of this. We open that gateway and do what, exactly? Send another probe and hope it will make it back with some data so we know the people we send through will survive?"

"We also don't know how our gateway appears to anyone on the other side of it. We could be sending a shining beacon to the Krake," Sean replied. "You're not saying anything we haven't already discussed. The point you're missing is that we have to go."

"I don't understand why it has to be right now."

"For one, we left people behind. They might still be alive. If it were you, wouldn't you want us to come there to rescue you?" Sean said and paused for a moment. "On the practical side, it means that the Krake have learned something about us, and we need to do our own reconnaissance. Only then can we understand the real threat the Krake represent. That's why we have to go."

Grant sighed heavily and looked at Savannah.

"Colonel Quinn and I are in agreement. I'll send our proposal for COMCENT to review," Savannah said.

Grant frowned for a moment. "So who makes the final decision? Is it General Hayes and General Gates? Or is it the Colonial Defense Force Committee?"

"The Defense Committee could block the decision, but they won't. They've been briefed and understand what's at stake and the need for learning what we can about the Krake," Sean replied.

Grant's shoulders slumped. "I'm sorry, I just feel like this is all happening so fast. We've only just gotten the space gate to work."

"We appreciate all your efforts. Please continue with your work," Savannah said.

Grant stood up and turned to Sean. "I promise I'll do the best I can. If you'll excuse me, I think there's more to be done before you go."

He left the room.

"I think he finally realized what you were trying to do, or at least what's at stake," Brody said.

"If it helps him focus, I'll take it," Sean said.

A comlink text message appeared on his internal heads-up display. It was from Oriana, and she wanted to speak to him privately at her lab.

"How soon can the battle group be ready to leave?" Savannah asked.

"We've been resupplying since we've been here, but I know there are some outstanding repairs on the destroyers. Probably fifteen hours. That would be the soonest we can be ready," Sean said.

"Right, we'll tell them twenty-four hours just in case Murphy shows up," Savannah said with a wry grin.

"I'll return to the *Douglass* and meet with the ship commanders," Brody said.

Sean looked at Savannah. "I have some things to take care of, and then I'll head to the *Vigilant*."

"Good. I'm going to meet with Andrew Foster, who's heading up manufacturing. I just had a thought that as we build more space gates, we could deploy them at predefined coordinates in the system. That way you wouldn't be reliant upon the one here at Phoenix Station," Savannah said.

Sean nodded. "Having more than one door would be a good thing."

He left the meeting room and headed to Oriana's lab. He'd

replied to her initial comlink text, so she was expecting him. Inside the engineering lab, long work tables ran the length of the room, but there was only one well-lit area to the right side.

Oriana was alone. She turned toward him and smiled. "For normal people, it's dinner time. Most people like to eat."

Food would have been nice to have, but it would have to wait. "That explains why you're still here, freak."

Oriana's expression went from slightly amused to annoyed in the span of a heartbeat. "Honestly, sometimes I don't understand how you've risen so high in the CDF ranks."

"I excelled at charm school. Why did you want to see me?"

Oriana gestured toward a virtual model of the space gate machines. "I think I have a way to make them mobile. You said you wanted a way to take a gate with you."

Sean rubbed the bottom of his chin, which had the beginnings of a beard. He needed to shave. "All right, you have my attention. Show me what you've got."

"I have to warn you that it could be dangerous. In fact, I haven't proposed this to Dr. Grant yet."

"You say that like it's a bad thing. You're worth a hundred Dr. Grants."

"The reason is," Oriana said, ignoring his comment, "in order to test it we could lose the space gate." She entered a few commands on the holo-interface and a representation of Sean's battle group appeared. "The battle group has two heavy cruisers that are capable of powering the space gate. We send the battle group through as planned, but the last ship to go through must be a heavy cruiser. It will be the one that brings the space gate machines through with it. What we observed in the test was that once the space gate machines are powered on, expanding the gateway doesn't increase the power requirements all that much. So I thought that if we attach the gate machines to the cruiser while using their thrusters, it might get them through the gateway. My theory is that we have the thrusters maintain the alignment and perform a roll maneuver. Using a tether to attach it to the hull of the *Vigilant,* it could pull the individual components through the gateway. Once the components are through, the gateway will be closed. You can think of it as pulling your shirt off and your clothes being inside out."

Sean watched the three-dimensional model showing a simulation of her theory. He frowned in thought for a few moments. She was right; this was risky. "Have you done the calculations—"

"Yes, I have. There is little risk to the ship, but—"

"The only risk is in losing the space gate itself. I get it," Sean said and rubbed his chin again. "What made you think of this? I mean, even trying it this way is way out of the box."

Oriana's full lips opened for a moment and then she pressed them together. "It's silly."

Sean smiled. "Well, now I have to know."

"I heard a snippet of a conversation. They were talking about how tired they were and that they just wanted to go to bed and pull the covers over their heads. So it got me thinking, what if we could do something similar with the space gate machines? The critical component is that they maintain the alignment; otherwise, we lose the gateway. We can maintain the alignment even as the gateway machines themselves go through the gateway."

Sean nodded. "And there's no risk of any backlash of energy or something like that? I don't want to risk Phoenix Station for this."

"We can move the space gate away from Phoenix Station to minimize the risk."

Sean made a show of looking back at the holoscreen for a few moments. "Assuming this works, I'll need a team of experts who understand the space gates better than anyone else. I just happen to have an opening on my ship. Can you make any recommendations on who would best fill that slot?"

Oriana shook her head, but he saw the slight curvature of her lips.

"Come on," Sean said, "you're not really gonna stay behind. The best use of your skills is out there." He'd almost said "with me" but didn't want to push his luck.

Oriana's eyes gleamed. "You speak so highly of my skills. I'm flattered."

"I'm being honest."

She stepped closer to him. "Are you?"

Sean felt the heat rise in his chest. "Wait a minute. What are you doing?"

Oriana took another step closer, and now she was less than a foot away from him. "I'm just wondering how long you can maintain your concentration."

Sean saw the slight flush of her cheeks and felt himself begin to lean in. He stopped. "You're testing me."

She smiled and backed away.

"I thought we'd been through this."

Oriana feigned ignorance. "There's nobody here, and we're not on the bridge of your ship."

"No, you're right, we're not. However, if I was inclined to push this to the limit," Sean said, gesturing toward her, "I certainly wouldn't pick an engineering lab to make my move."

Oriana tilted her head to the side and Sean wondered whether he'd been a fool not to have taken a shot.

"The job offer still stands," Sean said.

Oriana rolled her eyes. "I never officially transferred off the *Vigilant*. So unless you're kicking me off the ship..."

Sean had been so busy for the last few days that he hadn't actually checked. "Oh, in that case then you need to get back to the ship."

Oriana laughed. Just then, the doors to the lab opened and a group of engineers walked in.

15

THREE TROOP CARRIERS flew across the New Earth landscape with several Hellcats flying escort, and Connor was convinced they'd brought sufficient firepower to deal with any issues they might come across in their search for the NEIIS research facility. He hadn't expected that twelve of the NEIIS would be coming with them, but once Raylore put the word out to the others, they'd had more volunteers than they could bring with them. Connor decided to split the NEIIS volunteers into two groups on two different troop carriers. Darius Cohen brought Brenda Collins, one of his colleagues, to act as a liaison for the second group. Connor didn't know her, but he was comfortable with the fact that Carl Flint was on that ship with his Spec Ops team.

Darius and Raylore walked over to where Connor stood. The NEIIS kept looking around at the interior of the ship, his gaze lingering on the equipment they'd brought with them. It was difficult for Connor to gauge the level of curiosity of the NEIIS. Most of them were reserved, as if they were anxious about revealing their thoughts. They seemed to defer to Raylore, with the exception of Jory, who spoke to Dash away from the others.

Jory was from a different NEIIS faction than the others. His brown skin had streaks of tan, and the protrusions on his shoulders and elbows, even the ridges on the sides of his head, were less pronounced than the others, which Connor thought could be attributed to Jory's younger age.

The NEIIS were no strangers to mechanized methods of transportation, but he wasn't sure they'd had anything like CDF troop carriers or their Hellcats. Siloc had kidnapped him using an old glider. Most of the NEIIS machines they'd found among the ruins were in a state of extreme disrepair. The only exception was the stasis pods they'd found, which were hermetically sealed in vaults protected from the elements.

Connor brought up a holographic map of the planet and centered the view of the massive supercontinent that was New Earth's primary landmass. He looked at Raylore. "I brought you with us, and now you need to tell us where we need to go."

The mobile translator Dash had put together translated Connor's words into the NEIIS text equivalent, and a series of symbols appeared. They really needed a phonetic translator so they could at least speak to one another, but it wasn't ready.

Raylore stepped closer to the holoscreen and pointed to a region on the map. As one of the NEIIS's thick, elongated fingers came close to the holoscreen, it zoomed in on the area. Raylore pulled his hand back for a moment and peered at the screen. Then he adjusted where he was pointing and tapped another area. A triangular waypoint indicator appeared on the map where Raylore had specified.

"Thanks," Connor said. The waypoint was almost on the other side of the continent.

"That's eleven thousand kilometers away," Diaz said. "Is there anything that's closer?"

Raylore took a few moments to read the message and then gestured once again to the area he'd indicated before. "The research center was part of the old —. It's the only place I know of that would have what you need to make the arch work."

The translator inserted a dash for words that it wasn't sure how to translate. The area hadn't been explored by the colonists beyond the brief round of surveyor probes used to provide a general map of the continent. Colonists tended to stay on their side of the continent.

Connor opened the comlink to the pilot. "Coordinates have been sent. Circulate them to the other ships for me, please."

He looked at Darius. "This is going to take us a little while to get to."

"I understand," Darius replied.

"Do they understand?"

A few moments later Raylore nodded. The gesture was a little bit awkward, but the NEIIS must have seen colonists utilizing it.

"I'd like to know more about where we're going," Connor said.

Raylore told them about the various republics the factions of the NEIIS civilization had been part of. Some republics rose to power while others fell, similar to the nations of Earth's history. The wars the NEIIS fought among themselves escalated to global conflicts. It was during this time in their history that the Krake appeared. Their intimate knowledge of the NEIIS indicated that they'd been watching them and perhaps even manipulating them for years. The Krake even had the ability to disguise themselves as NEIIS, which Connor hadn't been surprised to hear given what he'd seen of the Krake. They had similar but not identical body types, almost as if they were two distinct lines on the same branch of the evolutionary tree.

Raylore paused in his narrative, and Connor merely waited for him to continue. The NEIIS nearby watched as Raylore shared more of their history.

"When did you begin fighting the Krake?" Connor asked.

"There were some republics that partnered with them, and

they had an advantage over the other republics for a time," Raylore explained. "But eventually, we observed a pattern with the Krake partnerships. They only lasted for a certain amount of time, and then they always shifted their focus onto the most powerful republics. They'd build up republics, only to topple them by supporting a different group. There were some of us who thought the Krake were taking these actions purely out of curiosity. They were powerful. In order to survive, an underground resistance was formed, drawing upon multiple republics. We escalated our tactics and strategies against each other."

Diaz blew out a breath and looked at Connor. "They fought among themselves, and the Krake used them," he said, shaking his head. Then he looked at Raylore. "How long did your wars last?"

Raylore gave the NEIIS equivalent of a frown, as if the question had never occurred to him. "There has always been war."

Connor glanced at the other NEIIS nearby. Their appearance was so different from humans that he wondered if it was influencing his opinion of them. Grim lines showed along the ridges of their brows, as if they'd evolved only to struggle to survive. And now they'd been brought out of stasis to an alien species that had taken up residence on their planet. Humanity was no stranger to fighting wars, but there had been long periods of peace as well. Fighting wars that constantly whittled down the entire population was unheard of on Earth. The history of the NEIIS was one of brutality and survival, but they weren't innocent, and Connor wondered how they could find a common ground to form an alliance with them—something beyond a common enemy. They needed the NEIIS knowledge of the Krake. He had to understand the enemy if there was to be any chance of defeating them. The NEIIS hadn't fought one single war; they'd fought many of them for perhaps hundreds of years. If what Raylore had said was true, then fighting a war was the only way the NEIIS knew how to deal with their problems. They might've been manipulated into it, and they might not have had a choice, but they would never be innocent. How long would it be before the NEIIS wanted their planet back?

Connor looked at Darius. "Have you heard accounts like this before?"

"Not with so much detail. The general consensus from the other NEIIS we've interviewed after bringing them out of stasis was that they fought wars. I don't have to tell you about that. Based on the archaeological record, the NEIIS are as prone to violence as we are. Perhaps even more so," Darius said.

Connor looked back at Raylore and regarded him for a few moments. "The Krake are our enemies as well. Do you think we'd be able to stop them if we fought together?"

"I am not a protector."

Protector was the NEIIS way of referring to their military. "Do you think we can stop the Krake?"

Raylore looked at him for a long moment. "We've tried, but they keep coming back. Stasis was our supreme effort to outlast them. We believed that they would lose interest in our planet if all of the Ovarrow were gone."

Connor didn't ask his question again. He had the answer. Raylore didn't think they could defeat the Krake.

Raylore returned to the other NEIIS, and Connor turned off the translator.

"I don't think any of that helped. Do you still think we can trust them?" Diaz asked.

Connor shook his head. "We need them, but everything in my gut tells me not to trust them." He glanced at Darius. "I know this isn't diplomatic, but this isn't going to be easy. Things have changed."

Dash had joined them and heard the last bits of their conversation. He looked concerned. "What's changed? We knew they fought wars."

"War might be the only thing they know. They didn't go into stasis with peaceful intentions. They went to stasis to endure and possibly fight another war when they came out. Now we show up and start living on their planet. On top of that, the Krake are not gone," Connor said and looked at Darius. "Has your office done psych evaluations on the NEIIS?"

"We have video records of all our interactions with them, but it's difficult to determine their thoughts and intentions without our own biases interfering. They are an alien race, and there's a high probability that we might misinterpret something," Darius said, raising a hand in front of his chest. "I'm not saying I disagree with anything you said. They're not a happy bunch, but my understanding is that we need this alliance with them to learn what we can about the Krake."

"Glean intelligence from them—yes. But should we keep bringing more of them out of stasis?" Diaz asked.

"What would you propose we do? We can't put them down like animals, nor can we simply let them go. Alliances are about building bridges. It's not all black and white," Darius replied.

Diaz looked at Connor. "That's all fine and good, but there is a very real possibility that we might be fighting a war with them someday."

"You might be right. It's something that's been discussed before, at least between Nathan and me, but it doesn't change anything. If this place that Raylore is taking us has what we need to get our arch to work properly, then this is what we have to do," Connor said.

"They're not all like him," Dash said.

"What are they like?"

"You can tell they've been through a lot, even before they went into stasis, but this cellular degenerative disease is a more immediate threat to them than the Krake. Even though this was a militaristic society, they can't all be devoted to their Republic. I've spoken with many of them, and I think at the end of the day they'd just prefer to be left alone. If we can help them with that, there might not be any problems for a long time," Dash said.

Diaz shook his head. "I don't care. I don't trust them, and I never will."

Connor knew that once Diaz made up his mind, there was very little anyone could do to change it. The thing was that he agreed with both Diaz and Dash. He looked at the young man. "I want you to continue to develop those relationships. Get to know them because it might make a difference in how we proceed. Just remember that they aren't like us, so you need to keep your guard up. Do you know what I mean?"

Dash nodded.

The troop carrier's intercom system came online. "General Gates, we're closing in on our destination."

"Understood. I'll be right there," Connor said and looked at Darius. "We need Raylore and the others again. I'll put a live video feed on this holoscreen for him so he can pinpoint where exactly we need to go."

"I'll go get them," Darius replied and left.

Diaz looked around at the CDF soldiers nearby and then back at Connor. "I think we brought enough soldiers with us."

"Better than just a few of us trekking across the landscape ourselves. Come on, let's go to the front."

They headed up to the cockpit where Lieutenant Wes Andrews piloted their troop carrier. Connor saw Diaz shaking his head as if he was having a conversation with himself. He knew Flint would be speaking with the NEIIS in the other troop carrier, but he didn't have time to review that conversation. Connor needed time to process the things Raylore had spoken to them about. But for now, he just needed to focus on their immediate goals.

The cockpit had a live video feed on the holoscreen, along

with the standard HUD for the troop carrier's flight screen. Connor saw the remnants of a few long spires that ended in jagged edges, but they were long enough to poke through the thick overgrowth that covered most of the NEIIS buildings. The broad leaves of eggplant-colored flora made it difficult to see the ground. Winter still had its hold on this region of the continent, and the dormant plants they flew over speckled the view in a fawn-colored ground cover. The frigid wind gusts unleashed a barrage, causing the troop carrier's inertia compensators to spike their power draw. A blanket of gray clouds covered the area, and Connor wondered what this place was like when the NEIIS had lived here.

The rise and fall of the landscape throughout the interior of the city occurred too often for it to be natural. There must have been impact craters from a NEIIS war, but who had they fought? The Krake? Or each other? How many NEIIS had died during all their wars? Was the entire continent one big battlefield that had been swept away by an artificial ice age? Years ago, when Connor had first come out of stasis aboard the Ark and after they'd discovered that the comms buoys that led back to Earth were failing in artificial succession, the Vemus had been coming. Tobias Quinn had put forth the idea of packing them all back onto the Ark and leaving New Earth, but Connor had argued against it. It hadn't been Tobias's call to make, nor had it been Connor's. It was the decision of every colonist—over three hundred thousand of them at the time.

The population of the colony had grown since then. With all the work they'd put into building a new home for the last humans in the universe, Connor now wondered if he'd been wrong to argue against leaving all those years ago. Should they have found a new home instead of staying on New Earth? They'd sent out probes to other star systems that they suspected could support life, but they were still years from getting any response from them. If the Krake proved to be too powerful an enemy, should he put forth the idea of leaving New Earth forever?

Connor knew he was getting ahead of himself, but his thoughts had begun to run of their own accord. The NEIIS had fought the Krake for entire generations in a vicious cycle. He felt his jaw tighten, and he squelched the growing unrest inside. He needed to focus. They needed to learn all they could about the Krake, which included their motivations. If they could understand what the Krake wanted, they might figure out how to defeat them.

A sub-window appeared on the holoscreen, which showed Darius Cohen and Raylore in the auxiliary work area.

"Raylore says the place we're looking for is inside the city," Darius said, and Raylore spoke again. Darius read the translation and nodded. "Away from the spires."

"General Gates," Lieutenant Amos said, "we're tracking multiple groups of ryklars in the city. They're large packs. I think this would be classified as a den."

Connor heard Diaz mutter a curse and used his implants to show a map of the area. There were red indicators on the map where the ryklars had been detected. Several smaller groups broke away from the others and tried to follow them as the troop carriers flew over the city.

Connor looked at Darius Cohen's face on the sub-window. "There's significant ryklar activity. Ask him if he knows if there's a signal luring them here. We're not detecting any, but I want to be sure."

Connor watched as Darius spoke to Raylore for a few moments. "I'm sorry, General, but he doesn't know."

Connor nodded. The ryklars might have been lured there by a NEIIS signal, but when it had gone offline, they'd stayed out of habit. They'd observed similar behavior elsewhere.

"What do you want to do?" Diaz asked.

"We can use our own deterrent signals, but we can't make them all leave a city this big."

Connor was quiet for a few moments while he considered their options. They could use mobile ryklar deterrent signals, which would create pockets of safe areas, but he hadn't come there to institute ryklar population control. "Once we get over the designated area, begin broadcasting the ryklar deterrent signal. Maximum broadcast strength."

Lieutenant Amos informed the pilots on the other troop carrier ships, and they closed in on the waypoint. The ryklar deterrent signal was broadcast at ultrahigh frequency so nothing could be heard with the naked ear. As they reached the designated landing area, the broadcast began. Recon drones were launched, and they could see the ryklars scrambling to flee the area.

Spec Ops soldiers went off the troop carriers first to secure the area. Once the green light was given by Carl Flint, Connor and the rest of them went outside. The Hellcats were kept on standby should they need air support. The landing area was on top of a large dome-shaped building. The structure was relatively intact and certainly could handle the weight of the three troop carriers and the Hellcats.

They were all armed, with the exception of the NEIIS. Raylore told them the research center was inside this building. Connor ordered thermite charges to be set to make a hole for access. There was a flash of light and the smell of acrid smoke as the thermite burned through layers of overgrowth to the bronze metallic alloy the NEIIS had used in their building materials. A squad of CDF soldiers dropped into the hole first, then the rest of them followed. Connor left a squad of soldiers behind to secure the troop carriers.

They dropped into a wide-open area. The ground was covered in dirt, and some of the nearby walls glistened with streaks of ice. Small rodents scurried away at their approach.

Connor looked at Raylore. "Where do we go from here?"

Raylore didn't answer right away. He walked over to the nearest wall and began pulling away the moss, revealing the three intertwining triangles that were the symbol for the NEIIS military. Raylore pointed to the side where a ramp led downward. Connor motioned for several soldiers to take point and they followed.

"Doesn't look like any type of military installation I've ever seen," Diaz said.

"I would expect most of the buildings in the city to be connected to the NEIIS military in some way, so it's not that much of a surprise," Connor said.

"Right. Those come later," Diaz said dryly.

Connor glanced behind and saw Dash speaking with one of the other NEIIS. He used his implants to access the recon drones they'd sent ahead. They hadn't detected any energy signatures. The place was dead, at least at this level.

The ramp curved around, leading them deeper into the building, and it didn't take them long before they realized they were moving underground. The invading plants gave way to the NEIIS structure the farther they descended. For the next twenty minutes, they slowly made their way downward until they reached the bottom, where a thick metallic door was partially open.

"You'll find a cranking mechanism on the side to get that door open," Connor said to the soldiers on point.

Using that information, the soldiers opened the door, but the only light came from what they brought with them—combat suits and the edges of weapons. Diaz had been right. The place was completely without power, and there was little chance of discovering functioning stasis pods.

After getting through the door, they found themselves in a vast open area. Their lights had difficulty penetrating the darkness, but the CDF soldiers had implants with night vision. Across the way, rising out of the gloom, was an arch. Connor ordered flares to be shot to the far side of the room so the NEIIS could see it better. As red flares ignited in the distance, the surface of the arch reflected the light in glistening pools. On an elevated platform to the right of the arch was what looked to be a command center.

"Let's make a sweep of the area. Mark the location of anything that could be useful. Captain Flint, send a group of engineers over to the arch. We need to understand how it's different from ours," Connor said.

He looked at Raylore, but the NEIIS only peered at the arch. His still form remained motionless, mimicked by most of the other NEIIS.

"Just give them a few moments. This is a lot for them to take in," Darius said quietly.

Connor nodded and gave them some space. For the next few minutes, he coordinated with Flint and Diaz.

"Excuse me, Connor," Dash said. "There are some rooms off to the side that have consoles. I'd like to take Jory and a few of the other NEIIS with me to check them out. I brought a portable power generator suitable for bringing the console online to extract the data. Also, I want to see how the NEIIS use their own system."

"That's a good idea," Connor agreed and looked at Diaz. "Why don't you take a few soldiers and go with them."

"Yes, sir. Roger that. Make sure Dash doesn't screw anything up. Got it," Diaz said.

Dash smiled. "Weren't you the one who—"

"Come on, kid. I haven't got all day," Diaz said, starting to walk toward the rooms.

Dash quickly followed him, and Diaz shouted for a group of soldiers nearby to come with them.

"I think Raylore and the others are ready to talk now," Darius said, so Connor and Flint walked to where Darius and the NEIIS waited.

"Do you know if this arch was ever operational?" Connor asked.

"This place is one of three research efforts I'm aware of relating to the Krake arches, but there were many rumors started to prevent the Krake from finding this place. I would need to access the system consoles to determine whether it was ever used," Raylore said.

Connor started up the ramp that led to the NEIIS command center, where a soldier had connected a portable power generator to the main console. Connor had seen this type of console before and knew it used a local data storage supply. The portable power generator had the emergency shut-off enabled to prevent any latent NEIIS protocols from accidentally getting initiated.

The NEIIS console came online, and Connor gestured for Raylore to use it.

"I've already retrieved the data from the core, General," Corporal Tran said.

"Thank you. Carry on, Corporal," Connor said.

Raylore approached the console and began accessing the interface. Being quite familiar with the NEIIS interface, Connor watched as the NEIIS brought up different command windows. They'd put an enormous effort into understanding the NEIIS computer systems, but even so, Connor had a recon drone recording the entire session so it could be reviewed later.

"This archway was used one time before it was shut down permanently," Raylore said.

Connor read the translated record on the NEIIS console.

"Why would they only use it one time?" Darius asked.

"I'm not sure, but the log indicates that the emergency shutdown protocols were used for the entire facility," Raylore said.

Connor rubbed his chin for a moment and frowned. "There was a battle here—at least above us. I wonder if someone used the arch to escape. Can you access the navigation interface to see what the destination was?"

"I will try," Raylore said.

Connor was watching the NEIIS navigate the interface when the command comlink channel on his implant suddenly became active with multiple alerts.

"We're under attack," Flint said, bringing his rifle up.

Then Connor heard weapons fire.

16

CONNOR LOOKED BACK at Darius and the NEIIS. "Stay down."

The elevated platform gave them a high vantage point. Connor heard soldiers firing their weapons on the far side of the chamber, and he squatted down to peer to the other side, looking for what they were shooting at.

Flint was on the comlink channel, trying to get a status. Then Connor heard ryklar screeches over the weapons fire.

"Order them to fall back to the arch," Connor said.

Flint relayed his orders.

"Time to move," Connor said to Darius. "We stick together. Stay close."

They scrambled off the platform and raced toward the arch. The ryklar deterrents were still active, and Connor didn't know why they weren't working. The deterrent signals from the troop carriers would never penetrate this deep beneath the ground, which was why they'd brought their own.

As more CDF soldiers rushed to join them, Connor opened a comlink to Dash. "We've got ryklars in the area."

"I heard them. I've barricaded the door. We're in a room by the west wall not far from the arch."

"Good. Stay there," Connor said.

Connor noted the sounds of the ryklars becoming louder as he ran toward the arch and the CDF soldiers already gathered there. He looked at the far wall, only to see their staggering forms racing past him. Several ryklars stopped and looked at the arch. The beards of their tentacled faces were blood red, as if they were under the control of a NEIIS ryklar signal. Oddly, the sides of their heads were bald, and their ears seemed to be missing. Gray skin covered the area, but there was pink scar tissue where their ears should have been. The ryklars started racing toward them.

"We've got incoming!"

Connor brought up his weapon and began shooting at them. The other CDF soldiers followed suit, and the ryklars went down, their bodies sinking into unmoving heaps. Connor saw that several ryklars had stayed back by the wall as if they were trying to remain hidden, so he used his implants to access the configuration of his rifle and changed it to long-range mode. He aimed at the group of ryklars trying to stay hidden and fired one round. The ryklar on the end collapsed, startling the others near it. The ryklars grabbed their fallen comrade and dragged it out of sight. Something was off about the way they moved, but Connor didn't have time to think about it right then.

A bright flash of green light streaked over them.

"They're breaking off and retreating. Should we pursue them?" Flint asked.

Connor watched carefully as the ryklars began to withdraw. He caught a glimpse of one of their faces, and the bearded tentacles had faded in color to a dull pink. "Pursue them, but don't engage unless they attack. I want to know where they came from."

"Yes, General," Flint replied.

Connor looked toward where Darius and the NEIIS were hunkered down.

"Is it over?" Darius asked.

"They're retreating."

Darius nodded and blew out a breath. "What was that light? I thought this place didn't have power."

"We're not sure."

The NEIIS nearby looked wide-eyed and upset.

"Why didn't the deterrent work?" Darius asked.

"I think these ryklars were deaf," Connor replied. "They looked different than the ryklars above. There was a thick mass of tissue that covered where their ears should've been."

"I saw the same thing, General," Flint said.

Connor nodded. "Where's the engineering team?"

Flint gestured toward an area behind Connor, and they walked over to the engineers. Connor recognized one of them.

"Norma, can you get this thing to work for me?"

Norma Ellison smiled. "This one is dead, General Gates. Whatever the NEIIS used for powering it has long been corroded. But we have detailed scans of the internal components, some of which were missing from the ones we have on base."

"We can take pieces of this one back with us if needed. Will that save time?"

Norma nodded. "It might. I had just found an access panel with an undamaged data storage device when the ryklars attacked. We can take that with us and extract what we need."

"We're running short on time. Get what you need so we can get out of here," Connor said, walking back toward Darius and the NEIIS. He looked at Raylore and gestured toward his ear as he spoke. "Have you encountered ryklars that were immune to your control signals before?"

"This is beyond my knowledge," Raylore replied through the mobile translator.

Connor looked at the other NEIIS, and they kept glancing toward the far side of the chamber. Flint asked to speak to him away from the others.

"General, they found something that I think you should see. It might disturb *them* though," Flint said with a tilt of his head toward the NEIIS.

Connor nodded, and they went to the far side of the chamber. There were dead ryklars along the way. All of them appeared to have a mass of skin tissue where their ears should have been.

"They couldn't have been born this way," Flint said. "Someone did this to them."

"Let's have someone collect samples and see what R&D can make of it back home," Connor said.

They walked to where a group of CDF soldiers were gathered near a fallen figure. Connor looked down and saw what looked like a ryklar on its side. He circled around to the front of it and saw that part of its skin had come apart, revealing something brown inside. Connor pulled the skin away, exposing a NEIIS face.

His eyes widened. "What the hell!" The NEIIS was wearing the skin of a ryklar to conceal its identity. "Is this the only one?" he asked.

"It's the only one we found, General," the soldier next to him answered.

"I want this one wrapped up. We're taking it with us. Do not show it to anyone else. Is that understood?" Connor said.

The men set about covering the body and hauling it off to the troop carriers.

"We need to check the other bodies. See if there are any more of them," Connor said.

"There haven't been any other reports. I'll put a few soldiers on it," Flint replied.

Connor looked around the vast chamber. There were no power sources, so the likelihood of there being stasis pods in the area was remote. How had the NEIIS known they were there? Were they keeping watch? The NEIIS could have been from a different part of the city, but the team hadn't detected anything when they'd arrived. Why had the NEIIS attacked them?

Connor heard Flint asking for the status of the team pursuing the ryklars. He looked at Connor and shook his head. "They lost them."

"How did they even get in here?"

"The soldiers reported that part of the wall opened," Flint said and looked over at a nearby soldier. "Miller, tell General Gates what happened here."

"We walked right past the area and all was quiet. There must have been a hidden doorway because the ryklars were behind us when they attacked," Sergeant Miller said.

Connor looked at the wall. It was smooth, and there weren't any seams. Then he looked around the vast chamber and shook his head.

"General," Flint said, "I recommend that we leave this place as soon as possible."

Flint was right; it wasn't safe, and Connor knew it despite how much he wanted to stay. He wanted to figure out how the NEIIS were there and get everything they needed from the arch.

"All right, we'll start withdrawing," Connor said.

He and Flint headed back to the arch. The engineers were still getting what they needed. Darius and the NEIIS were with them, and Raylore was answering questions.

Connor looked at Flint. "I want four recon drones to stay here and record any activity for the next week. We'll send another recon team to retrieve them."

"Understood," Flint said, then quietly added, "This just gets weirder and weirder."

The man had a knack for understatements.

Connor gave a slight nod of his head toward Raylore and the

other NEIIS. "How do you think they'll react once they learn they're not the only NEIIS out of stasis?"

"If it were me, I'd be happy to learn there were other humans around, but with the NEIIS I'm not so sure. When are you going to tell them?"

"Not until we're away from here."

They went back to the arch and helped the engineers get what they needed. Within a half hour, they were returning to the troop carriers. Dash walked up next to Connor.

"Before the attack, I managed to get some info off the NEIIS console in that room we were holed up in. With Jory's help I found records indicating they were aware of the issues that might arise from going into stasis," Dash said.

"I can't say I'm surprised."

Dash shrugged. "But I found a reference to something they were developing to cure it at another site. I'd like permission to pursue it."

Connor looked at Dash, considering.

"Jory has the disease, and his cells will continue to degrade until he dies. He just came out of stasis a week ago. There's no way for us to know if the NEIIS inside the pod will suffer from this disease until after it's too late," Dash said.

"How long would it take?" Connor asked.

"It's pretty far away. We haven't explored that area too much, but it's closer to our side of the continent, within five thousand kilometers of Sanctuary. This is important and could improve relations with the NEIIS."

Connor gestured for Dash to walk with him away from the others. "I appreciate the effort, but this seems kinda personal."

Dash inhaled and swallowed. "I was the one who picked Jory's stasis pod to be revived. I feel responsible for what's happening to him. I know it doesn't make sense, but there it is."

"It makes sense to me, but it's not your fault."

"I know. It's just..."

"If we hadn't brought them out of stasis, it's unlikely that Jory or any of the others would have lived until the NEIIS revival protocols brought them out. Assuming they worked to begin with, that is."

Dash nodded.

"I'll authorize the mission. You'll take a CDF escort with you."

"Thank you, Connor. I'd like to bring Jory with me. He can help with accessing the NEIIS systems."

"All right. What I'm about to tell you is confidential, but you need to know," Connor said and proceeded to tell him about the NEIIS body they'd found.

Dash's eyes widened in shock. "Maybe a vault with stasis pods that we missed?"

"Your guess is as good as mine at this point, but I don't want this known just yet. I told you because I can trust you. And you needed to know since you're going to be out here."

Dash nodded. "I understand."

"I hope you do. The NEIIS inside attacked us. They weren't interested in communicating with us, and they were trying to hide the fact that they were there. At this point, I'm not sure we can trust any of them."

Dash pressed his lips together for a moment. "They're not all the same. If there are more like Jory or some of the others, then... They're not all the same. That's all I'm trying to say."

This whole situation was complicated. Connor knew it, and Dash knew it as well.

17

SWEAT GLISTENED on Sean's brow, and the muscles in his shoulders and arms burned with effort. Several beads of sweat splashed onto the exercise mat in front of his face, and he squeezed his eyes shut to keep the sweat from burning. He heard several hearty chuckles from the men around him.

"Ah ha! Fingertips only. If those palms touch the mat, you lose," Benton warned.

"It's all right, Colonel. It's been a while since you've trained with us," Boseman said.

Sean looked up from the plank pose he'd been holding for over ten minutes to see Boseman's tense face staring back at him from about a foot away. The veins were popped out of his forehead and down his neck to his muscled shoulders.

Sean blew out a breath, and several droplets of sweat flew toward the Spec Ops captain.

Boseman grinned and began to speak quietly. "First, it starts off as a dull ache in the shoulders. Then it runs down your arms until the ache begins in your lower back. Makes you start to lean to one side, so you tighten those abs, and that's when your forearms start to cramp. Then your muscles start to shake, and you start thinking maybe it's about time to stop now. Or you might slip. All that sweat running down your arms—"

"Stop trying to sweet talk me, Captain," Sean said. He cleared his mind. He just needed to hold on a little bit longer.

Benton and several other Spec Ops soldiers laughed and began shouting.

"What's the matter, Colonel? Am I distracting you?" Boseman asked.

Sean looked up and saw the hungry gleam in Boseman's eyes. He was strong and could probably hold this plank a lot longer than Sean could. Sean smirked. "No, it's just that your breath is horrible. I'm surprised no one has said anything. Good looks but bad breath make for a poor combination."

Boseman blinked in surprise and let out a hearty laugh.

"All right, that's time, gentlemen," Benton said.

Sean sank to the floor and rolled onto his back, breathing heavily. The crowd of soldiers walked away now that the contest was over. It had been a while since Sean had held a damn spider plank pose for fifteen minutes.

"When you said you wanted to blow off some steam, I didn't think you meant this," Boseman said, hardly sounding winded at all.

Sean rolled over and pushed himself into a standing position. The muscles in his chest twitched. He wasn't used to working out like that anymore.

"I missed you," Sean said, grabbing his bottle of water and chugging it down.

"Right," Boseman answered. He toweled some of the sweat off his face.

"Do I need an excuse to come down here?"

Boseman shrugged his thickly muscled shoulders. "It's your

ship. But if I had to guess, I'd say you were looking for an escape of some kind—if you don't mind me saying."

"And if I did mind?"

"Then that's just too damn bad, sir."

Sean snorted and shook his head. "Just tacked on that 'sir' for effect?"

"I could lie to you and say how much the boys love having their commanding officer down here to prove to us all that he's still got what it takes—"

Sean cut Boseman off by throwing his towel at the man's face and then performed a well-executed takedown. Boseman was on his back.

"I still have what it takes," Sean said.

Boseman quickly recovered and a grappling match ensued. Both sides had gotten a few good takedowns in, but Boseman managed to get Sean's arm pinned behind his back while Benton and a few other soldiers jeered from the side. Sean dropped to his knee and drove his elbow back. His sweat-slicked arm slipped from Boseman's grasp.

Sean spun around, and Boseman held up his hands. "I give. That's enough."

They walked over to the side of the room and sat down on one of the benches.

"You know, someone was looking for you—a pretty little thing by the name of Sophia. Long, brown, curly hair. Can't remember her last name," Boseman said.

Sean grimaced. "Reynolds. That's her last name."

Boseman arched an eyebrow toward him. "Is that a thing now?"

"No, not for months, and it was never really a thing. More like the right time, right place. Or the right time, wrong place, depending on how you look at it," Sean said.

"Don't tell me you're still hung up on that scientist," Boseman said, his deep voice making the accusation sound all the more severe.

"You're going to have to be more specific than that. We have a lot of scientists on the ship," Sean said, but he knew who Boseman was talking about.

Boseman leaned forward and rested his elbows on his knees. "So that's why you came down here. A certain Dr. Evans has finally returned to the ship. What's going on between you two?"

"Nothing is going on between us," Sean replied.

Sergeant Benton glanced over at them. "Are you talking about the SO named Evans? She's something else. Is she back on the ship? She's so tall, and she's got that long black hair," he said, making a "hmm-hmm" sound like he'd just eaten a tasty meal.

"Sergeant, when you gonna learn how to keep that mouth shut? Go on, get outta here," Boseman said.

Benton made a hasty retreat.

"That guy never learns," Sean said.

"He's just like the rest of them, but let's not get sidetracked," Boseman said.

"Don't make me pull rank here."

Boseman shook his head. "That's a low blow, even for you."

Sean sighed. "As I said before, nothing is going on."

Boseman compressed his lips for a moment. "What are you, in high school? What's the problem here? I've never seen you waver like this."

Sean sighed in exasperation. "We work well together. Honestly, she's an asset on that bridge."

"Don't give me that crap about 'we work well together and I don't want to jeopardize that.' You know that's bullshit. Is she interested?"

Sean stood up. "I need to hit the showers."

"Better make it a cold one," Boseman said with a grin.

"Fine, you want to gossip. There've been a few moments where this thing between us could... Honestly, I can't get a good bead on her. Sometimes she acts like she doesn't like me, and at other times, we just click," Sean said, snapping his fingers.

Boseman nodded. "Sounds like you're not giving her what she wants." He looked at Sean for a moment, considering. "Usually, when a woman's got a man twisted up like you are right now, it means you either got to fish or cut bait. So what's it gonna be?"

"I just want to let you know that I really enjoyed this pep talk. It means a lot to me that you care so much."

Sean started to walk away.

"Fine, don't tell me. But just remember that they don't wait around forever."

Sean waved and went to take a shower. Sometimes Oriana made him feel... She just brought out the foolish side of him. It was almost reactionary at times, like when she'd mentioned not coming back to the ship. And now he was being an idiot within the confines of his own mind. They were hours from embarking upon an unprecedented journey, and he needed to focus on the task at hand. He'd come down there to blow off some steam, and he'd really needed it. Boseman had been his friend for years. The man knew him well and had a nice, simple way of putting things. Simple, however, didn't mean it was easy. Sean just wanted to be near Oriana. He liked having her around, and he didn't know what to make of that, but he wasn't some sort of lovesick teenager. He was a soldier first and foremost. He'd seen other people struggle with balancing loved ones while doing this job, and he didn't envy them. He'd witnessed Nathan and Savannah bearing that weight, as well as Connor and Lenora. They weren't the only ones, and he didn't want to be like them. He liked the simplicity of his life. There wasn't room for anything beyond a short fling. That was how it had always been, and it was enough.

18

AFTER A NICE LONG shower and a hot meal, Sean felt completely refreshed. His military-grade implants were similar to the prototype NA Alliance implants Connor had, but without the high risk of rejection by the host. Sean required very little sleep, and generally speaking, a few hours a day would leave him well rested. But even though this was technically true, the human brain required certain outlets if it was going to function at peak performance. The brain did not operate as an island unto itself but was a harmonious connection to the body. Muscles needed to move, and Sean had gone far too long without physically exerting himself. He'd been overdue for a good workout and was glad he'd gone down to the Spec Ops platoon training area. The ship had multiple areas where the crew could find some sort of recreation, but there were also areas that were only accessible by people of a certain rank.

Sean headed for the elevator to the bridge and waited for the doors to open.

Oriana was inside. "Good morning."

"Today's the day. Any last-minute concerns you'd like to tell me about?"

The elevator began its ascent.

"None that haven't already been stated. The decision has been made, and I'm not going to question it."

Sean looked at Oriana for a moment, thinking she'd sounded like she had more to say. "If you've got something to say, you should just say it."

The elevator stopped and the doors began to open.

"I could say the same thing about you," Oriana said and walked off the elevator.

Sean shook his head. Sometimes when they spoke, it felt like they were having two different conversations at the same time.

He strode onto the bridge and headed for the command chair.

"Colonel Quinn," Specialist Sansky said, "I have Phoenix Station actual for you."

Sean sat down. "I'll take it here."

Savannah's face appeared on Sean's holoscreen. "On behalf of Phoenix Station, we wish you luck on your journey, Colonel Quinn."

"Thank you, Colonel Cross."

Sean knew Savannah didn't like the current plan and had proposed sending several reconnaissance drones to the space gate with a scheduled return. Sean had opposed the argument. They needed to take the offensive, and like it or not, a recon drone didn't have the sophistication to carry out everything they needed to learn about the Krake.

"The Colonial Defense Committee sent their warmest regards. I'll forward the actual message to you. I also wanted you to know that Dr. Grant has assured me the backup space gates will be up and running in a few weeks."

"Understood," Sean replied. "Thank him for me, and make sure he does it right."

He saw Oriana glance over at him from her workstation.

"Will do," Savannah replied, and the comlink closed.

Sean rubbed the bottom of his chin for a moment. "Ops, what's the status of the space gate?"

"Power taps have been engaged. We're spooling up reactors three and four, Colonel," Lieutenant Hoffman said.

"Comms, I want a broadcast channel to the entire battle group," Sean said.

"Yes, Colonel. Broadcast channel is open."

Sean waited a few moments before speaking. He'd once asked Connor how he knew what to say at moments like these, and Connor had replied that he usually didn't. "CDF Battle Group Trident, we are about to embark upon a journey beyond anything ever done before. We are the tip of the spear, but our main mission is to learn all we can about the Krake. Our secondary mission is to determine the location of the colonists who are MIA. I'm not one for making long speeches, so I expect you all to do your jobs with the absolute excellence that has come to be the hallmark of the Colonial Defense Force. Colonel Quinn out."

The broadcast channel closed.

"All right, Ops, let's get the ships ready to go through the gate."

The space gate status went to green, and Sean still found it disconcerting that there was no indication they were looking through a gateway into another universe. They had to rely on their instrumentation for that.

The *Vigilant* was positioned off to the side like a stalwart protector guarding the way forward. The destroyers would go through first, and the space gate was open wide enough to accommodate two of them at a time. Once they'd all gone through, there was no communication back into their universe other than a visual confirmation. Upon the successful transition of the first destroyer group, Sean sent the rest of them. The *Douglass* went through next and was followed by the carrier *Yorktown*.

"All ships have transitioned, Colonel," Lieutenant Hoffman said.

"Now it's our turn," Sean said. "Take us through, Lieutenant Edwards."

The *Vigilant's* maneuvering thrusters put them on a direct path with the space gate.

"Power taps are stable and tethers to the gate machines are all green," Lieutenant Hoffman said.

The main holoscreen showed the open space gate, and Sean could see the ships of the battle group ahead of them. He looked at Oriana. This was the first time they'd put her theory to the test. Either they'd be stranded in another universe until Phoenix Station built another space gate, or everything would be fine and they'd have the space gate with them.

"Increase the power draw to the gate," Sean said.

The front of the ship was already through the gateway and the sensors on the ship indicated that they were more than halfway through.

"Begin rolling of the gate machines," Sean said. "Tactical, confirm that the alignment is sustained."

He shared a look with Oriana. If Murphy was somewhere lurking in the shadows, waiting for the perfect opportunity to show up, this would be it. If the alignment wasn't maintained, the gateway would cease to exist. The *Vigilant* could find itself missing the aft section of the ship if it didn't clear the event horizon first.

"Alignment is in the green," Lieutenant Russo said.

Sean watched the data streams on the main holoscreen. Communications with the rest of the battle group had gone dark after they'd transitioned.

"We're through the space gate," Lieutenant Russo said.

They waited a few pregnant moments. "Gate machines are through and accounted for."

Sean heard the relief in the lieutenant's voice. He looked at

Oriana and smiled. It had worked. They were on the other side and had brought the space gate with them.

"Begin the power-down procedure and secure the gate machines," Sean said.

Specially designed tethers would attach the massive gate machines to the *Vigilant's* hull.

"Colonel Quinn, I have Major Brody from the *Douglass* for you on comms," Specialist Sansky said.

Sean opened the comlink on his personal holoscreen.

"Colonel Quinn, are you okay?"

"We're fine. Ship status report green."

Brody blew out a breath. "There was a gamma-ray burst when the gate machines came through. It was pretty powerful, according to our sensors."

Sean looked over at Lieutenant Russo. "Tactical, are you detecting anything on our scanners?"

"Negative, Colonel."

"We don't have anything on our sensors," Sean said.

Brody nodded. "Neither do we anymore. It was just when the space gate came through. It was strange, and it might have drawn attention to us."

"Understood. Stand by," Sean said. "Tactical, start passive scan suite. Helm, let's get some distance from this position. We might've inadvertently let the Krake know of our arrival. Comms, send the *Talbot* and *Vargas* on their scouting run."

His orders were confirmed. They would move away from their current position and start passive scans of the system. Two destroyers would start their scouting runs and reunite with the main group in thirty-six hours.

"Colonel Quinn," Gabriel's voice said over the speakers. "I've compared the current high-res optics feed with our last voyage into the alternate universe. I'm afraid there are anomalies."

"What kind of anomalies?"

"My findings are preliminary, but it looks like the planetary alignments are not where we expected them to be," Gabriel said.

Sean looked at Oriana. "Can you have your team confirm?"

"Of course. I'll have them working on it right away," Oriana said.

Sean had Gabriel put the report on the main holoscreen so they could study it together. The anomalies weren't glaringly obvious at first glance. Gabriel had assured him that an accurate assessment would require more data, but he thought it was prudent that Sean should know. Sean agreed. If they weren't in the universe they expected to be in, they needed to figure out where they were.

19

SEAN GLANCED at the time in the upper right corner of his internal heads-up display. They'd been in this mystery universe for over twenty-four hours and were making painstakingly slow progress toward understanding where they were. Gabriel's preliminary analysis was proving to be correct. They weren't in the universe they'd intended to go to, and Sean had become increasingly irritated by the fact that they didn't know where the hell they were.

He hastened down the corridor heading toward the bridge. CDF personnel stepped aside, making a hole so that he could pass through first. Near the bridge was a conference room where he could meet with the senior officers to discuss tactical situations and ship or fleet issues. He sometimes did this on the bridge, but he found that it was worth changing the meeting place for those issues from time to time. The bridge was a place to conduct the affairs of the ship and the battle group, not to strategize for long periods of time about their next move.

The door to the conference room hissed open and Sean walked in. Major Shelton and Captain Halsey stood up.

"Please be seated," Sean said.

Oriana was there, as well as two members of her science team. The wallscreen was displaying a similar conference room on the *Douglass*. Major Brody and his senior officers and scientific advisors were in attendance.

Sean glanced at Halsey. "Have there been any updates with the subspace communication capabilities?"

"Negative, Colonel Quinn. Five minutes is the limit before we have a total loss of the signal. We're experimenting with sending data through in a highly compressed format. The tests conducted so far have been positive."

Sean exhaled through his nose. "That's encouraging. Keep at it."

"Will do, Colonel."

"All right, it's time to talk about the elephant in the room," Sean said, directing his gaze at Oriana. "The reports from our passive scan analysis indicate that this is not the star system we've been to before. Planets are not in the expected positions, and we need to figure out why."

"We've gone through the calculations used to target the universe we've been to before," Oriana said. "It all checks out."

"You can't sit there and tell me that everything worked when we're not where we should be! This is unacceptable," Sean said.

He saw her cheeks redden in anger.

"I was giving you the status of our analysis of the situation, Colonel. The first step in root cause analysis is to determine whether there was some kind of fault in our equipment."

"The hardware reports I've read indicate that they're functioning normally. And since the fault isn't with the operation of the space gate, there has to be something wrong with the targeting parameters we used. There's a serious flaw in our methodology," Sean said.

Oriana glared at him for a moment and did not reply.

"Do you have any recommendations?" Sean asked.

"I made a recommendation before we came here, remember? You didn't listen to me then, so why would you listen to me now?"

Oriana had argued against sending the battle group through the space gate so soon.

"We're not here to discuss decisions that have already been made. We need to deal with the current situation," Sean said.

"Excuse me, Colonel Quinn," Brody said.

"Go ahead, Major Brody."

"It's been twenty-four hours since we arrived. Why don't we use our space gate to contact home? We open the gate and send a comms drone through it, then bring it back. If there's a standard CDF check-in with Phoenix Station, then at least we'll know we can still get home."

Sean nodded. "I think that's something we should seriously consider, but we do have the risk of the gamma burst. We don't know if there are Krake ships in this star system."

"The gamma burst only occurred when we brought the space gate through. It's something new, so perhaps there's little risk of alerting the Krake by simply using the gate for a normal check-in interval. Assuming, of course, that there are even Krake ships here to detect us using it," Brody said.

"Dr. Evans," Sean said, "what do you think of Major Brody's suggestion?"

"My team needs more time to analyze the data we have and compare it with what we had before, noting the differences between the two star systems. Doing this will help us understand why our targeting was off the mark," Oriana said and paused for a moment. "Regarding the suggestion to use the space gate to contact home, that might create more problems than it solves."

"Such as?"

"I wouldn't recommend re-feeding our target data and going through the gate again until we've done more analysis of the star system. The only thing using the space gate again will do for us is to create more complexity. It will make our jobs harder to figure out what went wrong. At least for the moment."

"I agree we need to be cautious," Major Shelton said. "We don't know if the Krake have any dormant systems here that could be tripped off if we make too much noise."

"Agreed," Sean said. "We don't want to give ourselves away. That's why we'll move the battle group toward planet Sagan. That should shield our presence while we use the space gate. Doing this will give everyone what they want. We'll get to see if we can contact our home universe and understand just how flawed our targeting capabilities for the space gates actually are."

Oriana nearly scowled at him. She didn't like being put on the spot like this, but he needed answers. Sean dismissed everyone, and Major Shelton asked for a few minutes of his time before they headed to the bridge. Sean glanced at Oriana as she stormed out of the conference room.

"What's on your mind, Major?" Sean asked.

"Permission to speak freely, Colonel Quinn."

"Granted."

"I understand the need to push people to get them to perform, but I think you're being too hard on our science team. They have a complex task, but people aren't going to perform for you if you throw them out the airlock."

"Have you worked with the scientists before?"

"The *Talbot* didn't have much in the way of accommodating scientists," Shelton said, referring to the destroyer command she'd left to become the XO of the *Vigilant*.

"I have some experience with scientists. Sometimes they get lost in the analysis-type tasks and make very little progress forward. They need to be pushed."

"Like I said before, I understand that, but it almost feels like you're making Dr. Evans personally responsible for something that is beyond her control. It's not fair to her, and as your XO, it's my duty to bring this to your attention. I won't belabor the point though. I've made my opinion known, and that's all there is to say on my part."

Major Shelton left and headed to the secondary bridge. Sean didn't think he was making this personal with Oriana, but he liked that Major Shelton had chosen to bring this to his attention. She had done it in a professional manner and had merely stated her opinion. She didn't want or need anything but his acknowledgment that he'd heard her. She was being proactive, and he very much approved of that.

Sean headed to the bridge and ordered the battle group to move to another set of coordinates, which took them a few hours to reach. Planet Sagan, or at least the fourth planet from the star in this system, was similar in composition to the fourth planet near New Earth. The planet would serve as a shield, blocking their view of the interior planets and anyone who might be monitoring for suspicious activity in the star system. They detached the space gate from the *Vigilant's* hull.

"Power taps connected to the space gate," Lieutenant Hoffman said from the operations workstation.

"Home universe targeting coordinates have been uploaded to the space gate interface," Oriana confirmed.

"Execute," Sean said.

Since there were no ships going through the space gate, it was at its smallest configuration, which was five thousand meters across. The power requirements were twenty percent of what they'd used in order to get there.

"Gateway is open, Colonel," Lieutenant Russo said.

"Ops, send the drone through," Sean said.

"Yes, Colonel, sending communications drone," Hoffman replied.

The drone left the *Vigilant* and flew towards the space gate.

The transition through the gateway was uneventful, and a countdown timer appeared on the main holoscreen. The bridge crew continued to perform their duties while waiting for the drone to return. Communication through the space gate was one way, so they wouldn't receive any response from the drone for any updates they sent it.

"Comms drone has returned," Lieutenant Russo said. "Shutting down the space gate."

"Understood. Let's bring back the power taps and secure the space gate," Sean said. "Ops, put the comms drone data on the main holoscreen."

A series of sub-windows appeared on the main holoscreen, presenting each of the communications drone's data feeds. They were all flatlined. No communications had been established with Phoenix Station.

"Run a diagnostic on the drones," Sean said.

"It's green, Colonel," Hoffman said. "Here's a live feed from the drone right now."

Another subset of windows appeared. Communication signals from the battle group instantly came to life. Sean glanced back at the other screens. They were all blank, including the optical data feed.

"So we didn't see anything and we didn't hear anything. Tactical, what's your analysis?" Sean asked.

Each workstation on the bridge had specialized protocols that were unique to the function the bridge officer on duty was called to perform.

"Colonel, the drone was configured expecting to detect a signal nearby. There wasn't one. The data shows that it was in a vacuum, and there were brief detections of distant stars. The area that the drone was in was dark, as if it was well outside of any star system or there was an obstruction blocking the optical sensor. Perhaps if we sent another drone, we could get a more detailed analysis," Lieutenant Russo said.

Sean felt his stomach sink a few inches toward the floor. They couldn't get home. He looked at Oriana, and she seemed to sense his gaze. She turned toward him, her face turning ashen as she came to the same realization.

"Colonel," Specialist Sansky said, "we just received the data burst from our scout force, including a high res image of New— the third planet from the star." He'd been about to say "New Earth" but corrected himself.

Sean felt his shoulders tighten. "On screen," he said, his voice sounding rough.

The data feeds on the main holoscreen faded and an image of a planet materialized into stunning clarity. The lower and upper hemispheres were covered in white, and only a wide band at the equatorial line seemed to have escaped the severe ice age choking the planet.

Sean's mouth slackened and his brows pulled together in consternation. He'd seen icy planets before. The moons that orbited around the gas giant Gigantor had several of them, but the planet on the main holoscreen was supposed to be New Earth—a planet well within the goldilocks zone. It should have been teeming with life, but instead, they'd found a planet on the cusp of a frozen grave.

Sean swallowed hard and his mind raced. They couldn't get home and they were in the wrong universe. He had to focus. "Priority message Alpha. Battle Group Trident to the rendezvous point. We'll meet with the scout force. Wait. I want the rendezvous point moved closer to the planet."

"Yes, Colonel," Specialist Sansky said. "I will inform the battle group."

Sean gazed at the frozen planet for a few moments and then shared a look with Oriana, mirroring the stark realization of their current situation. They were lost, but they weren't helpless. Sean walked over to Oriana and leaned over so only she could hear. "If you were looking for an 'I told you so moment,' I'd say the universe has delivered."

Oriana pressed her full lips together for a moment and gave a slight shake of her head. "I'm not looking for any moment. I just want to figure out how this happened. What went wrong."

"Me too."

The last of her anger vanished from her gaze—gone in an instant. If they were going to figure out where they were, they had to go to that planet. Sean returned to the command chair, brought up his personal holoscreen, and began issuing orders to the battle group. They couldn't achieve anything by staying where they were.

20

CONNOR HAD SPENT much of his adult life on one military base or another. They had a rhythm to them that usually coincided with the purpose for which the base had been designed. Camp Alpha was no different, at least in theory. It was a military base, but at the same time, it was also a place of research. The subtle differences at Camp Alpha stemmed from the fact that the NEIIS were there.

After leaving the NEIIS city, Connor and the others were still coming to grips with the fact that they'd discovered yet another faction of NEIIS that had been successfully hiding their presence from everyone. They had no idea how long the NEIIS had been hiding underground, and Connor had decided not to share this information with Raylore or the others of his kind. They'd been just as surprised by the ryklar attack as the colonists were. Currently, the information that their attackers hadn't been merely ryklars was known only to a few CDF personnel, and Connor intended to keep it that way for a little while longer.

It'd been ten hours since their return to Camp Alpha. He'd checked in with Lenora and then resisted the urge to contact her again. He hadn't told her about the recent development, but he would. It wasn't that he didn't trust her; he just didn't want her to have to deny knowledge of something until he was ready to share it with the Office of NEIIS Investigations. He had every intention of bringing the ONI into this, but first, he wanted his people in the CDF to run their own analysis. They'd share their findings with the ONI in short order.

Connor had borrowed Nathan's office at Camp Alpha since Nathan was at Sierra, and he reviewed his messages again. Flint had checked in to say that they'd taken the arch components back to the CDF base near New Haven. Connor had sent the NEIIS body to the CDF base by Delphi, which housed extensive biological research facilities.

Connor glanced at his messages once again and noticed that Dash hadn't checked in. He wasn't overdue, and Connor had sent a squad of CDF soldiers with him, so he would be well protected. Plus, he knew Dash had instituted a training regimen of his own that included hand-to-hand combat and a wider breadth of knowledge of civilian weapons. Connor couldn't fault the young man for wanting to be prepared, but he'd hoped there wouldn't be a situation where Dash had to use that training.

An alert appeared on his personal holoscreen, indicating that his next meeting was due to start in a few minutes, so Connor stood up and left the office. He went to the conference room and saw Diaz speaking with Major Brooks. He thought Diaz looked a bit tired. Darius Cohen and Kurt Johnson were also in the room. Brooks and Diaz stood up and saluted when Connor entered, then sat back down. Connor greeted Nathan, who, along with his staff, was on a video feed displayed on the central holoscreen.

"Good morning. We have a couple of guests with us today— Darius Cohen and Kurt Johnson," Connor said, gesturing toward the two men.

"Thank you for letting us listen in," Johnson said.

"Welcome, gentlemen," Nathan said. "Before we discuss the

events that occurred at the NEIIS city, we have some new developments of our own. Is that all right with you, Connor?"

"Of course."

"Thank you. As of two hours ago, the Trident Battle Group has missed its check-in."

Connor frowned in thought for a few moments. "I always thought the check-in intervals were too condensed given that we were having Sean explore a star system that might have a Krake presence."

Nathan nodded. "It *is* aggressive, but the red flags don't start going up unless they miss a series of check-ins. It's been over forty-eight hours since we've had any updates. Just to bring the others up to speed, we haven't heard from Colonel Quinn since they went through the space gate."

Connor didn't like it. He could tell that Nathan didn't either and said so. "When are the backup space gates due to be operational?"

"Soon. Within the next twenty-four to thirty-six hours was my last update from Phoenix Station. But after they're completed, they'll need to be tested."

"I don't see that we have a choice but to wait. If we send a comms drone out there broadcasting, it could hamper whatever Sean's trying to do."

"Excuse me, General Gates," Johnson said. "What exactly is Colonel Quinn doing?"

"He's on a reconnaissance mission in the star system where we detected the CDF signal. The battle group has a good amount of offensive capabilities that should enable Colonel Quinn to carry out his mission and possibly engage the Krake, if there's a need," Connor said and looked at Nathan. "How long before the third and fourth space gates are constructed?"

"It'll be at least another week. The plan was to deploy those gates at different, predetermined areas in our star system that the battle group is aware of with the intent to gain insight and provide Sean with alternative opportunities to check in, but I still don't like that we haven't heard anything from them."

"Neither do I, but let's think about this. I don't want to send another scout force through just yet, and I certainly don't want to pull ships from our home fleet, especially if Sean is in the middle of something like running some kind of covert operation. What we could do is send an observer through and let it do its thing. Then we could open the space gate again and bring the observer back."

Nathan considered this for a few moments, and Johnson looked like he wanted to say something.

"What is it?" Connor asked.

"The observers are the unmanned surveyor platform. Wouldn't it make sense to send another ship through and then bring them right back? Surely they could give us more information than the surveyor platform."

"Not necessarily," Nathan said. "The surveyor platform gives us a way to learn more about the star system without risking the potential loss of another ship." Nathan looked at Connor. "I think that's the way forward. I'll let Savannah know at Phoenix Station."

"All right, it's time to move on to our next order of business," Connor said and sipped some water. "We have a couple of new developments of our own. First, aside from the arch components collected by our engineers, I sent a squad with Dash DeWitt on another mission based on the data they extracted from a console at the city. The NEIIS were aware of the risk of cellular degeneration from going into stasis. However, there was some evidence uncovered that they might have had a cure for it."

"I've informed Raylore of this since Jory went with Mr. DeWitt. It's difficult to judge NEIIS reactions, but I feel it's safe to say that they were pleased by this news," Darius said.

"Can we expect more cooperation from them?" Johnson asked.

"It's a step in the right direction. These things take time."

Johnson nodded and entered some notes on his tablet computer.

"There's more that happened at the city that I've kept confidential until now," Connor said. He saw Johnson narrow his gaze slightly but otherwise remain impassive. "The ryklars were driven to attack us, and we discovered that there were NEIIS behind the attack. They were wearing ryklar skins to conceal their identities."

Darius Cohen's eyes went wide, and Johnson pressed his lips together for a moment before speaking.

"Did you retrieve any of the bodies?"

"They're being examined at our base in Delphi. I concealed this because I didn't want the NEIIS to know about it at the time. I will convey our findings to the ONI and invite them to come do their own analysis," Connor said and looked at the others in the room. "But first, we need to consider the implications of this discovery. The NEIIS in that city were trying extremely hard to keep their presence concealed. There was no power at the research center at all. And when we went poking around, they attacked us. Does anyone want to hazard a guess as to why they did that?"

Darius motioned that he wanted to speak. "We know the NEIIS are territorial, but I think you're implying that this is different, and I think you're right."

The diplomat sometimes surprised Connor with his realistic view of the situation. He wasn't overly optimistic, and he wasn't negative either. He seemed to maintain a good balance between pragmatism and idealism.

"They represent a new variable to be considered," Connor said. "We left reconnaissance drones to observe the area, and we'll send a retrieval team to get them in the next seventy-two hours. There's heavy ryklar activity in that city, but at some point we need to consider making contact with the NEIIS there.

Darius, I'd like to know your thoughts on how to approach this."

Darius considered for a few moments. "I'd say we wait. They're obviously suspicious of outsiders, so I think waiting is our best option, at least initially."

Connor nodded. "I agree, but what do you think about sharing this discovery with Raylore and the other NEIIS here?"

"They'll be shocked, is what I expect. After that..." Darius paused for a moment in thought. "They're going to want something in return. The subject of their life here at Camp Alpha has become a growing issue. They want their independence, and I realize that this is a major security concern for the colony."

"You're damn right it is," Johnson said. "Any decisions regarding the status of the NEIIS brought out of stasis requires oversight from the Colonial Defense Committee."

"This is just a conversation," Connor said. "No one is deciding anything, and no one is going to act without following the standard protocols we've agreed upon regarding the NEIIS."

Johnson frowned as if he hadn't expected Connor's response. Connor smiled inwardly and looked at Darius. "I think we should reinforce why we're restricting them to the camp. We're trying to help them reestablish themselves, and we'd like to share this world with them. At the same time, is there really any harm in discussing possible settlement sites with the NEIIS?" He'd been talking to Darius, but after a moment he looked at the others as well. "It might make them more cooperative if they have an end goal in sight."

"This might work in the short term," Darius replied. "But are we seriously considering this? The more we interact with the NEIIS, the more they understand certain nuances in our dealings. I'd rather not string them along."

"Well, as Johnson has pointed out, this is a decision for the Colonial Defense Committee. I think we should be upfront with some of our expectations from the NEIIS, and I realize this may put stress on our communications with them. I think if we approach this as if we're helping them purely out of the goodness of our hearts, it will be met with suspicion from them. Our expectation is that we'd like to form an alliance with them to help fight the Krake. We need the NEIIS to understand that we're not leaving this planet. We're here for the duration, and it would be better for everyone if we worked together," Connor said.

Johnson shook his head. "You'd be willing to set them free?"

"Yes."

"What about you, General Hayes? Same question."

"I agree with Connor. We took these precautions for Camp Alpha as a temporary initiative. It's necessary now, but at some point it becomes inappropriate. I don't think we're there yet, but as Connor stated, it doesn't hurt to begin having those conversations now."

Johnson looked at Darius Cohen expectantly.

"I agree, and I expect it might make them more cooperative. And at the same time, it also might make them realize that they do actually need our help."

Johnson nodded. "One of the concerns of the Defense Committee is the potential threat the NEIIS represent to the colony. What if they decide they don't want us here?"

Connor shrugged. "There will always be a significant risk regarding the NEIIS."

Johnson considered this for a moment. "What if they refuse to cooperate?"

Connor had his own opinion on this, but he glanced at Darius.

"When dealing with two independent entities, there is the possibility that the two parties involved cannot come to an agreement," Darius said.

"Yes, I understand that, but what would we do then?" Johnson asked, quickly following up with, "I mean, what would be the appropriate response?"

This time Darius looked at Connor before replying. "I expect that we would stop helping them."

"The NEIIS like to posture a lot," Connor said. "I think when push comes to shove, they'll arrive at the understanding that they need our help. We shouldn't underestimate that. We want their input because it will help us be better prepared to deal with the Krake, but at this point, I think they need us more than we need them."

Darius nodded. "That is an accurate summation of our dealings with the NEIIS."

Johnson nodded and seemed to be lost in thought for a few moments.

"This is a lot to take in," Connor said. "I think we all need some time to consider it. Johnson, I expect you to discuss this with your team and Governor Wolf. Then we can consider our next step."

Connor thought he saw a small smile from Nathan, but he ignored it.

"Yes, indeed," Johnson said. "You've given me much to think about."

The meeting ended and everyone left the conference room. Connor trailed behind and then slipped back into the room, telling Major Brooks that he was not to be disturbed for the next few minutes. She signaled to a nearby soldier to stand outside the conference room door so Connor wouldn't be disturbed.

The holoscreen flickered on to reveal Nathan alone as well.

"I figured you wanted to have a private chat," Nathan said.

"You know me so well."

Nathan grinned. "I know you wanted to be more cooperative with people like Johnson, but from all outward appearances I'd say you guys are becoming fast friends."

Connor tilted his head in a slight nod and smiled. "I'm sure you've heard the saying about keeping your enemies close."

Nathan shook his head and smiled. "You're all kinds of devious."

"I know Johnson is involved in quite a number of things. I figure if he believes I'm letting him in, he might give something away. So about the recon team..."

"Yes, I think they need some additional instructions for when they retrieve the reconnaissance drones."

"That they do. They need to do a thorough scouting of the area but try to be as discreet as possible. We need to locate where the NEIIS are living."

Nathan nodded, considering. "It's a tall order, but I agree it's something we need to do now. I'll make the arrangements."

Connor smiled. "And you didn't even make me ask for it."

"I know you've got something else up your sleeve."

"I do. I need to get to New Haven. The engineers should have had enough time to get the arch ready."

"Are you planning to be on the away team?"

"Not this time. Flint is going to lead the team that goes through."

If Nathan was surprised that Connor wouldn't be going through the arch, he hid it well. Connor *wanted* to be on the away mission, and he could have gone, but he recognized that they had other able-bodied people who could also take on those high-risk missions.

His call with Nathan ended and Connor left the conference room. He would check in with Darius before he left for New Haven. He suspected that Johnson would request to come with him, and the best way to keep an eye on Johnson was to keep him close.

Diaz was waiting for him outside the conference room. "Ready to go when you are."

Connor looked at him for a moment. "Are you feeling all right?"

Diaz nodded. "I'm fine. I keep remembering the NEIIS with the ryklar skin over him. It's messed up. I don't see how Darius can even think of coming up with a diplomatic way to deal with someone like that. Do you?"

Connor shrugged. "I don't know. We might not be able to deal with all of them, but we still have to try. I don't think... Let me rephrase that. I think they attacked us because they were protecting something, which means that the intent behind the attack was different than just being territorial."

"Yeah, but what were they protecting?"

Connor sighed. "That's the real question, isn't it?"

21

IN THE DAYS THAT FOLLOWED, Connor stayed at the CDF base near New Haven to oversee the operations to update their prototype arch. Looking up at it, he admired the shimmering metal based on technology they were just beginning to understand.

He was distracted by Norma Ellison yelling at one of her subordinates. The CDF engineer was determined that they get the archway working properly. On more than one occasion, Connor found himself wondering how Noah would've tackled the mystery that the arch had become. Would they have been further along if he hadn't gotten hurt?

Diaz crossed his arms and jutted his chin out toward the arch. "That thing still gives me the creeps." He eyed Connor for a moment. "What's on your mind?"

"Noah," Connor said. "I wonder what he would've done with the arch."

Diaz nodded with the trace of a frown on his face. "I've seen that kid do amazing things. Figure things out that I couldn't even begin to take a stab at."

"He's one of the good ones."

"Has there been any change in his condition?"

Connor shook his head.

"Still no word from Sean either."

"Sean can handle himself. He put together a good team to take with him. We trained him well."

Diaz tilted his head to the side and gave a small nod. "I know we did. I still worry about him, though. I don't normally get attached to the soldiers I've trained, but he was one of the first."

"The first or the last, it doesn't matter. We just connect with some of them and not others, and we see what they're made of as they learn what they can do. I truly believe Sean is going to outlive both of us."

Diaz chuckled. "Uh, maybe you, but I plan to live to a ripe old age."

Connor heard his name being called from over by the work being done near the arch. He turned around and saw Kurt Johnson walking toward him.

"I think I'll go check on Flint," Diaz said and walked away. He could hardly contain his dislike for the advisor.

Johnson walked over to Connor and stopped. Putting his hands on his hips, he blew out a long breath. "It's really quite remarkable, don't you think?"

Connor was getting a little tired of being around Johnson so much. Whenever they talked, Johnson always tried to soften Connor up with some idle chitchat instead of just getting to the point.

"What can I do for you?"

"As impressive as the arch is, and the space gate for that matter, are you worried that we're working with flawed technology?"

Connor gathered his thoughts for a moment. "Taking risks is part of the job. If we don't, especially where the arch and the space gate are concerned, we'll be blinded to what the Krake are capable of. I don't want to get caught with my pants down when they do come here."

Johnson arched an eyebrow. "Do you ever consider that the Krake might never come here?"

"Not for a single iota of a second. Neither should you."

Johnson was quiet for a few moments as he watched the work crews finish up near the arch. The soldiers who'd be going through were gathered nearby. "How do you even sleep at night? If you always think we're about to be under attack... doesn't it wear you out?"

Connor shook his head and exhaled. "Ignoring the problem isn't an option. I'd rather be prepared and take comfort in the fact that we're doing everything we can. So yeah, I sleep just fine for the little bit of sleep I need."

Johnson's eyebrows raised as he registered what had just been said. "That's right! I'd heard that about you. You only need a few hours of sleep. Maybe I should get those implants so I can be as productive."

"It does have a few side effects, but you'll have to excuse me, I need to take care of a few things," Connor said and began walking away.

"I wanted to ask you about Lars Mallory."

Connor stopped and turned around. Johnson walked toward him.

"I got the impression from our meetings with Darius Cohen that you were frustrated with the NEIIS lack of cooperation."

"I would've preferred to have gotten more information from them, but under the circumstances, I can't fault the NEIIS for being suspicious of us. What's this got to do with Lars?"

"As brutal as his approach was, he did get results. The intel we got from their covert base that Noah Barker found was quite informative. I was wondering whether you..." Johnson began and eyed Connor for a moment, "...approved of the rogue group's actions, at least on some level."

Flashes of annoyance ignited in Connor's mind. Did Johnson really think that, or was he just trying to get Connor to give something away?

"I realize this kind of thinking isn't popular among public circles, but sometimes in order to get the results, we need to take action that's generally frowned upon."

Connor regarded Johnson for a few moments. "It was that kind of thinking that led to a lot of problems with the NA Alliance. It was how groups like the Syndicate turned good people like Lars into someone cruel. They played upon our fears and desires to be safe. I watched Lars grow up. He was a good kid, and he didn't become like this on his own. Someone put him on this path. 'Manipulated' might be a better word."

Johnson leaned away. "I don't believe for a second that you think Lars Mallory is not responsible for his own actions."

"No, I know Lars is responsible for his actions, but the situation is rarely that simple. Lars is working for somebody. That much is obvious."

Johnson's face remained impassive. "Is there something you'd like to ask me?"

"Maybe there's something you'd like to share," Connor countered.

Johnson smiled and chuckled softly. "Please, General Gates, you've seen me in the field. I don't have the stomach for this sort of thing."

"Self-deprecation can only get you so far."

"I was merely raising the question with you. I don't like it either, but it is a valid approach to our current problem. If the NEIIS aren't cooperative on their own, we might have to consider being more forceful in order to get what we need. Given your life before the colony, I would have assumed that this was something you knew more about."

Connor took a few seconds before responding. "Just because we *could* do something like that doesn't mean we *should* do it. We might get more from the NEIIS if we're cooperative with them. I happen to think Darius Cohen has good instincts for dealing with the NEIIS."

"He's a good diplomat, but I'm talking about the darker side of diplomacy."

Connor's gaze hardened. "I know exactly what you're talking about. You only *think* you do. But I need to come out and ask you. Are you involved with what Lars Mallory has been doing?"

Johnson met his gaze. "No, I'm not, but I'm not afraid to take a more objective view of what's been done."

"In that case, I don't think the approach Lars took is something we should consider adopting."

Johnson nodded. "I appreciate your time, General Gates."

Connor resisted the urge to tell him what he could do with his appreciation. "I'm curious. Have you spoken with Meredith Cain about this?"

Johnson appeared unperturbed by Connor's question. "We speak often, but Meredith's opinion is more aligned with yours. I didn't bring the question up to you to raise your suspicions about anyone in particular. I just thought that if the danger the Krake represent is as grave as you feel it is, perhaps we need to consider a different approach."

Connor didn't believe him. "Is this something you'd recommend to Governor Wolf?"

"Only if I had to. I have to say that being out here watching the CDF puts things into a different perspective. I have a better understanding of where you're coming from."

"Observing a few meetings is one thing, but they're the ones who are defending everyone else," Connor said, gesturing toward the group of soldiers near the arch. "Just something to keep in mind when you consider these alternative approaches to dealing with the NEIIS. A short-term gain will definitely have unanticipated results. Soldiers are not robots. We train them to follow orders. And after they get done being soldiers, they need to be able to go back to being people again."

Johnson nodded. "I've always admired your work with the Recovery Institute at Sanctuary. I know you've helped a lot of people there, but I've taken up enough of your time."

Connor watched the short, pudgy man walk away. He'd never trust Johnson, and he didn't think anything was going to change that. Either Johnson was some kind of all-star manipulative bastard who thought he could get away with asking Connor those questions, or he was telling the truth and he had nothing to do with what Lars had been part of. He made a mental note to contact Damon Mills and follow up on the investigation Field Ops and Security was doing. He knew Damon would've investigated all the frontline suspects involved in this rogue group, but maybe there was something he'd missed.

After checking in with Flint and the rest of the away team, Connor and Diaz went back to the command center.

Dr. Volker greeted them. "The components you found at the NEIIS city have helped, as well as studying the arch there. The testing we've done shows a more stable gateway, but we're not able to detect the signal anymore. However, the probes we send through are able to detect an unfiltered version."

"Just so I'm sure I understand you correctly—the way we had the arch set up before allowed for a signal to come through, but now it doesn't. Any idea why?" Connor asked.

"Only theories, General Gates. Nothing we can prove now. But at least this won't be a one-way trip for them. They can come back through," Volker said.

There was a time when Volker would've started going through all the theories they were considering, but he'd learned to give Connor just the facts. "All right, get your team ready to open the arch."

Connor opened a comlink to Flint. They had fifty soldiers in combat suits and other equipment ready to go through.

"Are you sure you don't want to come along for the ride, General?" Flint asked.

"I'm tempted, but you'll need to tell me how the party goes. Go in and try to find the source of the signal. If you can find Rollins or Oliver Taylor, then do so. But I want regular check-ins. The archway will be open every three hours unless we hear otherwise from you."

"Understood, General. We'll get him back."

"Good luck."

Connor closed the comlink and looked at Volker. "Activate the arch."

The holoscreens nearby showed the live video feed from the arch, and Connor heard the engineers going through the startup sequence to power it up. A flash of light blazed in the middle of the archway and spread to the edges. A view of a fog-covered lake could be seen.

"Gateway is stable," Volker said.

"Understood. Comms, give them the green light," Connor said.

He watched the soldiers walk toward the arch and through it.

They were traveling light because this mission should take less than forty-eight hours, and a countdown timer appeared on the main holoscreen. A few minutes later, a small comms drone came back through the arch. It contained a basic status report from Captain Flint, indicating that they had successfully made it through.

"Now the waiting begins," Connor said, then glanced at Diaz. "Don't act like you didn't want to go with them."

"Just say the word and I'm there," Diaz said.

Connor sighed. "Not this time."

Diaz nodded slowly. "Yeah, not this time."

Connor watched the arch for a few minutes and then ordered the gateway to be closed.

22

RUMORS HAD SPREAD about their issues with the space gate, mainly the fact that they couldn't return to their home universe. Sean had made the announcement that they were doing everything they could to solve the problem with targeting. He encouraged everyone in the battle group to focus on their jobs, but if they had ideas to help them address the issues with targeting, they should share them with their commanding officer. To prevent his senior staff from becoming inundated with suggestions, Sean had Gabriel, the *Vigilant's* AI, make a preliminary analysis of the queries. Oriana and several other scientists, as well as his own XO, Major Shelton, had provided Gabriel with a framework from which to evaluate suggestions from the crew. This framework enabled Gabriel to provide immediate feedback. Fortunately, this filtered out most of the recommendations that would have taken up precious time on behalf of Sean's senior staff and had the added bonus of getting people to concentrate on their work.

One of the advantages of having a battle group was that Sean wasn't limited to one particular warship doing all the heavy lifting. The risk was spread as much as possible among the other ships.

Destroyers made excellent scouts, as well as providing backup for the heavy cruisers. But their only break so far was the lack of Krake ships in the star system.

Sean decided to divide the battle group and recon the planet that passed for New Earth. Other than having a similar orbit, there were distinct differences in the star system, particularly with New Earth. The planet had multiple moons and a small asteroid field near the main lunar body. Preliminary analysis indicated that the asteroid field used to be a small moon that had somehow been broken apart. And aside from the fact that in this universe, New Earth was in the middle of a severe ice age, the inner planets were in a much closer orbit to the star. As interesting as this was, it didn't give them insight into why the targeting data they'd used with the space gate interface had brought them to this universe instead of their intended target.

Sean glanced at the empty science officer's workstation on the bridge. Either Oriana or a member of her staff had occupied the auxiliary workstation so much that it had become their permanent workstation. But in order to focus on solving the problem with the space gate, Oriana and her staff had been working tirelessly on the issue off the bridge.

"Colonel Quinn," Lieutenant Scott said from the tactical workstation. "Captain Welch from the *Albany* and Captain Martinez from the *Dutchman* are in position."

"Understood," Sean said. He'd dispatched the two destroyers far enough away that if they were detected by any latent Krake forces, the battle group would be able to blindside their enemy should the need arise.

The main holoscreen displayed the tactical status of the *Vigilant*. A few moments later, their scanner array detected the active scans of the two destroyers. There was nothing for them to do but wait as the two destroyers wouldn't be sending the results of the active scan for a few minutes. Sean was keen to minimize the risk to the battle group, which called for a brief communications blackout.

"No Krake ships detected," Lieutenant Scott said.

"Very well, keep us at Condition Two," Sean said. "Lieutenant Edwards, take us to the planet. Tactical, I want our own scans of the planet and the immediate area."

His orders were confirmed. They'd regroup near the planet.

"Colonel Quinn," Specialist Sansky said, "I have Captain Welch on the comlink for you."

"Send it to my personal holoscreen," Sean replied.

Captain Lori Welch of the destroyer *Albany* appeared on his screen. "Colonel, our preliminary scans indicate that there are structures on the lunar surface. We've confirmed this with our high-res optics. However, there is nothing in orbit, which strikes me as odd. Sending to you now for review."

"Receiving," Sean replied. He brought up the scan data and peered at it. "Stand by, Captain Welch."

Sean looked at the data, and the scans did indicate some type of structure on the closest moon to the planet. "Good work. Proceed to the moon for further analysis."

"Yes, Colonel."

Sean opened a comlink to Major Brody on the *Douglass*.

"This is *Douglass* actual," Brody said.

"A change in plans. I want you to take your task force and begin surveying the planet surface for any signs of civilization."

"Understood, Colonel. Did something else happen?"

"Captain Welch detected what might be a lunar base. We're going to investigate," Sean said.

"Understood, Colonel. I'll let you know if we find anything. Happy hunting."

The comlink closed and Sean opened another one to Oriana. "Dr. Evans, can I interest you in a field exercise?"

Oriana frowned. "I don't understand."

"We found something on one of the moons near the planet that requires further investigation. I'd like you to join the away team."

Oriana was field certified, so it wasn't a question of whether she could function in an EVA.

"I don't think I'd have anything to offer on the field exercise, Colonel."

"Are you any closer to figuring out what's wrong with the targeting protocols we're using?"

"We're still updating our variables, but we don't have a plausible reason for the failure yet."

Sean nodded. "That's what I thought. I think you need new data. Assuming there *is* a lunar base, it would have been put there by the Krake, and there might be something there that we can use to figure out what we're doing wrong. I think it would be better if you came along in person rather than advising as you watch a video feed."

Oriana considered this for a moment. "You said 'we.' Are you on the away team?"

"I will be. We'll keep you safe. I really need you with me on this; otherwise, I wouldn't have asked."

Oriana looked at him for a moment and then nodded. "All right, I'll go, but I'd like to bring a few more of my people."

"Bring as many as you'd like. We depart in thirty."

23

THREE COMBAT SHUTTLES left the *Vigilant* on a trajectory toward the primary moon of the ice planet. Sean couldn't think of the planet as New Earth, even if it was in another universe. He'd ordered limited communications between the task forces for the duration of their missions. Comms would only be risked if there were enemy ships detected and the rest of the battle group needed to be warned.

They'd assumed that the installation on the moon was of Krake origin, which Sean felt was a safe assumption. Gabriel's preliminary analysis of the high-res images in comparison with the destroyer class vessels they'd faced six months ago indicated that they were of similar design.

Sean looked at the combat shuttle's main holoscreen and saw a large dome-shaped structure that bulged out of the ground like a wide protrusion.

"Is that all there is?" Boseman asked.

"There's probably more underground," Sean replied.

Starlight glinted from the top of the bronze metallic alloy of the dome, reminding Sean of the NEIIS architecture on New

Earth, but it would have to be significantly more refined if it were to protect the occupants from solar radiation. There was a multitude of craters near it, and parts of the dome were covered in lunar dirt. The shuttle flew around the structure, and they landed near an area most likely to have an entrance.

"No energy signatures detected, Colonel," Boseman said.

Captain Chad Boseman was Sean's friend, and they'd served together in the Spec Ops forces of the CDF. They checked their equipment. Sean wore a CDF combat suit while Oriana and the others wore regular EVA suits.

Sean looked at Oriana. "Are you ready for this?"

"A walk in the park."

Sean smiled. "Good. Once we're inside, if you see something you'd like to take a closer look at, let me know and I'll make sure it happens. I don't want you or other members of your team to go investigate anything on your own until I've had my people check out the area first."

"Right, safety first," Oriana said, glancing at her companions. "We got it," she said and looked back at Sean.

They vented the atmosphere in the combat shuttle and the loading ramp lowered to the lunar surface. Captain Boseman and his team exited the shuttle first, and Sean and the others followed. He noticed a few of the scientists stumble as they stepped onto the lunar surface. The lower gravity could be tricky if it had been awhile since they'd had spacewalk training.

The dome was near the LZ, and they soon found a partially covered door. Sean ordered the Spec Ops team engineer to use thermite charges to make a hole. Thermite could burn anywhere from within the vacuum of space to deep underwater. There was a flash of light and then the engineer banged the weakened section, knocking it away from them. There was a three-meter drop to the floor inside.

"How old do you think this place is?" Oriana asked Sean once they were all inside.

"It's hard to tell. There're some big craters nearby, and their impact could've just covered this place."

They walked down a featureless corridor of smooth walls, coming to a room that had several dead consoles that looked as if they hadn't been used in a while. There was no atmosphere inside the base, so it was difficult to determine the last time anyone had been there. The consoles were built into the wall, but there were no screens that Sean could see, so he assumed they'd used holoscreens.

Sean looked at Boseman. "Send a team ahead to look for a way to restore the power."

Boseman complied, and they continued to explore the area.

"What makes you think the power will still work?" Oriana asked.

"It doesn't look like whoever was here left in a hurry. It almost seems as if this place was decommissioned and they just left."

They were still exploring the area when one of Boseman's advance teams contacted them saying that they'd found what they thought was a command center. The base had a basic grid-style layout, so it was easy to navigate. Sean estimated that the structure was only two hundred meters in diameter, so it didn't take them long to find the command center. There were four primary work areas that had large pedestal-type tables, waist high. One of the CDF soldiers was on his hands and knees looking inside an open panel.

One of the other teams found a power station that was connected to a generator, and Sean gave the go-ahead to turn it on. They then hooked up their own portable power supply to jumpstart the generator. It seemed that the NEIIS based most of their technology on the Krake; otherwise, what they'd attempted would never have worked. Several holoscreens flickered to life, outlined in a pale green.

Sean skimmed the symbols on the screen. "Now that looks familiar. Let's try using the NEIIS translator on this and see if we can read any of it."

One of the advantages of neural implants was that the internal heads-up display could put an overlay on just about anything that came within the person's field of vision. This included the Krake holoscreen in front of them. Sean began navigating the interface and Oriana stood at his side.

"This just looks like log-type data."

They opened a few of the logs and Sean looked at Oriana. "What do you think?"

She frowned as she read some of the entries. "They seem to be in chronological order. We should find a way to take this data with us and have Gabriel help with the translation and analysis."

"That's a good idea, but we don't know where the data is stored. It must be around here somewhere," Sean said, looking around. "Boseman, get Allgood and Harris here. Have them try to trace where this console is connected. We may have to take it with us."

"I'm on it, Colonel."

Sean glanced back at the holoscreen, and Oriana was reading what appeared to be a summary. "This is one of the final entries," she said. "If the translation is correct, it looks like a list of things that might be experiments. But they all have this classification that translates to 'nonviable.' It might be an error in translation, but if it's not..."

Sean read the report. "Look at how they put the heading on these entries. I think the headings are the key to this. Let's see if we can get some help."

He opened a comlink back to the *Vigilant*. "Gabriel, I'm going to open a connection to my suit computer so you can observe what I'm seeing."

"Standing by, Colonel Quinn."

The data connection registered with his combat suit and Sean navigated through several log entries. He just needed a sample to give Gabriel a high-level overview of what they were seeing.

Lieutenant Harris came over to Sean. "Colonel, there's a connection to the data storage accessible through the panel below."

"I brought my tablet. Could we patch it to that data connection and perhaps speed this up?" Oriana said.

Harris nodded and took the tablet from Oriana. A few moments later, a much smaller representation of the holoscreen output showed on Oriana's tablet, and Sean connected to the tablet using his implants. He then handed the connection over to Gabriel.

"Accessing," the *Vigilant's* AI said, and there was a flash of multiple log entries briefly appearing on the holoscreen. "Dr. Evans is correct. These log entries appear to be observational logs of a scientific nature."

Sean read the information on the screen. "They were observing the planet. That was the purpose of this place being set up like a monitoring station." His eyes widened and he looked at Oriana. "They were manipulating the beings on the planet and trying to predict the outcome."

"Why would they do that?" Oriana asked.

Sean frowned for a moment. "Gabriel, are all these logs linked by some kind of prediction or hypothesis?"

"That is correct, Colonel. All of these log entries have what we would call a resolution code indicating whether, or to what degree of accuracy, their prediction was proved."

Oriana looked at Sean, her face pale. "Nonviable," she said. "Whatever they did here, they determined this place was nonviable. The planet is in the middle of an ice age. They just up and left after their experiment was over."

Sean pressed his lips together thinly. "It looks that way, but we'll have to take some time to do a thorough analysis of this data."

Even from within the EVA suit, Sean could see her tense up.

"Gabriel," Oriana said, "is there anything in the system on the space gates?"

"Negative, there is no space gate interface on this system."

"It was worth a shot," Sean said. "Gabriel, since you have access to the data, can you download it to an isolated system on the *Vigilant*?"

"Affirmative, Colonel."

"Excellent. Begin the download. Get what you can."

Another comlink from the *Vigilant* pinged Sean's combat suit. It was from Major Shelton.

"Colonel, we have multiple ship detections from the nearby asteroid field. I hope you found what you're looking for. I must advise you to evacuate immediately," she said.

"Understood, Major. Have they detected us?"

"Negative, Colonel. At least not yet. We don't have a visual yet, and I've restricted our scans to passive."

"Good. We'll wrap this up and get back to the *Vigilant* ASAP."

The comlink closed.

Sean let Boseman and the Spec Ops team know that they needed to leave. They realized they'd have to leave Oriana's tablet connected to the Krake console because they needed the physical connection in order to access the system so the data dump could be completed.

"Gabriel, once the data dump is completed, or if we're about to go out of range of the signal, I want you to initiate a remote wipe of that tablet. I want nothing for the Krake to find other than a useless piece of hardware."

"Remote wipe command confirmed, Colonel."

They headed back to the combat shuttle, and Sean resisted the urge to contact the *Vigilant* for a status update. Major Shelton would inform him if she had new pertinent information that required his immediate attention. The only thing they knew at this point was that there were ships in the area, but they didn't know what kind of ships they were. More importantly, they didn't know whether those ships had detected them.

24

THE RECONNAISSANCE DRONE came through the gateway, and Connor watched as its signal was reacquired at the command center.

"No updates from Captain Flint, General," Specialist Morgan said.

Connor gritted his teeth and shook his head. "Send a drone back through. I want it to fly up to fifteen-hundred meters and give us the lay of the land."

"Yes, General. Sending updated mission parameters now."

Connor watched the video feed on the main holoscreen as the drone sped through the gateway and another countdown appeared. "Very well, alert me of any new developments."

He stepped out of the command center and Diaz followed. Flint had checked in like clockwork for the first twenty hours he'd been deployed and then had asked for another day to further scout the area. They hadn't heard from him since. Connor looked at Diaz. "I hate this."

"So do I. What do you wanna do about it?"

Connor knew precisely what he wanted to do. He took a deep

breath. "I don't know if it's the fact that we haven't heard from Sean, and now Flint, and this is just making me have a knee-jerk reaction, but I can't sit by while we lose more people."

"So we send another team through and figure out what happened."

"It's not that simple. If I send another team that's equipped the same way Flint's platoon was, it might not be enough."

"Then we send a bigger team— Hold on, you don't need me to tell you this. What's going on?"

Connor closed his eyes and gathered his thoughts for a moment, then looked at Diaz. "I'm making an effort not to be the first one through on these missions. I sent Flint and then Sean, both perfectly capable soldiers. Now they're both missing and I... I need to go."

"Well, I can't stop you. You outrank me."

A soldier stepped out of the command center and saw Connor. "Excuse me, General Gates. You have a comlink from Darius Cohen. He said it was important."

Connor walked back into the command center and sat at the workstation he'd used before. A video comlink appeared on his personal holoscreen, showing Darius.

"Thanks for taking my comlink, General Gates."

"Have you learned anything we can use?"

"Raylore and some of the other NEIIS spoke about... It's more another request that we bring their protectors out of stasis."

"I know. We talked about this. Did you tell him we were reviewing his request?"

"Yes, and he understands that, but he thinks they'll have more information about how to deal with the Krake—the information he suspects you want."

Connor frowned and gave Darius a meaningful look. He supposed every intelligent creature out there would work their own angle to get what they wanted. "It seems a little convenient, don't you think, Darius?"

"It's give and take. Compromise and we bear the risk, but we might gain something, too. Raylore and the other NEIIS here didn't actually fight the Krake. They were aware of the struggle, and it was certainly part of their lives, but it's different for people like you. If you could speak to the NEIIS equivalent of someone like yourself, wouldn't that be valuable to you?"

Connor glanced at the countdown timer for the reconnaissance drone. It was almost time for it to return. "Run the request past Nathan. And I understand that this call is a courtesy, and I appreciate it. We might not have a choice but to give Raylore what he wants. However, we need some assurances. Like how do we know that whatever agreement Raylore makes with us will be accepted by anyone else we bring out of stasis? Can he even give us that?"

"It's a fair point, but we can bring them out in small numbers. Like I said before, it's give and take. If Raylore and the other NEIIS are only taking and not giving us anything, then we can just stop," Darius said.

"I can agree with that kind of approach. Run it past Nathan, and you two should brief Governor Wolf and the rest of the Defense Committee on it."

Darius frowned for a moment. "I would've thought you'd want to be involved in those meetings."

"I would," Connor said, watching the timer expire, "but I don't think I'm gonna be available. I have to go, Darius. I'll follow up with you when I have a moment."

Connor severed the comlink and stood up. The reconnaissance drone came back through the gateway and they powered down the arch. The main holoscreen showed a recorded video feed from the reconnaissance drone. The Krake forward-operating base was several kilometers away, and Flint's last update had indicated that the base was abandoned. They were moving toward the signal from Rollins, which was farther away, and that was the last they'd heard from them.

"Lieutenant Cook, what else have you got from the reconnaissance drone?"

Cook was doing a quick analysis from his workstation and then he put it up on the main holoscreen. "A CDF emergency beacon, along with a list of combat suit self-destruction sequences initiated."

Connor's eyes widened as he read the names of ten soldiers whose combat suits had been destroyed. Typically, a self-destruct sequence was initiated in the event that a soldier died. This prevented an enemy force from learning about the suits.

Connor's mouth formed a grim line. "Is there anything else?"

"Negative, General. That's all there was," Lieutenant Cook replied.

Connor turned and saw Major Henderson standing nearby. "Alert the reserve force. I want them assembled and ready to go in five hours."

"Right away, General," Major Henderson replied.

"Specialist Morgan," Connor said, "I need you to contact the CDF bases at New Haven and Delphi. I'm transferring new orders for select combat battalions at those bases to assemble here ASAP."

"Understood, General. I have the new orders and I am transferring them now."

Kurt Johnson, who'd been speaking with Dr. Volker, walked over to Connor. "What are you going to do? Are you sending another team?"

"I'm going to lead another team," Connor said and looked at Diaz. "You know who else to contact. Get on it."

Diaz turned and left the command center.

"You're going to lead them? But I thought the reserve team was led by Captain Ryan Olson. Is that not right?"

"I'm changing our response protocols. Come along if you want to find out more," Connor said.

He didn't wait for Johnson to reply. He knew the reserve force there could be ready within the hour, but he had something else in mind, which was why they needed more time. He remembered something Raylore had said to him when he'd met with the NEIIS, that the Krake were master manipulators who liked to create scenarios and predict the outcomes. Connor was going to change the status quo.

"Let's see if the Krake can predict what I'm about to do."

25

IN THE PAST FOUR HOURS, Connor had assembled a significant ground force of nearly two hundred soldiers. Two lines of combat-suit heavies lined up near the arch, head and shoulders above the regulars. Behind them was a complement of armored rovers mounted with M-180 gauss cannons. The remaining ground forces were outfitted in the combat version of Noah's multipurpose protection suit. Connor had considered bringing Hellcats with them through the arch gateway but decided against it. They brought combat drones instead, which would be enough to provide air support for what they had to do.

He watched the CDF soldiers assemble through a live video feed on a nearby holoscreen in General Hayes' office.

There was a soft knock at the door and Diaz stuck his head in. "Ten minutes."

"I'll be right there," Connor replied.

He opened the video comlink to Sanctuary, and Lenora answered. She was in her lab, which wasn't showing the usual buzz of activity. She looked at him with her brilliant blue eyes, her long auburn hair pushed behind her ears, and smiled at him warmly.

Connor felt a tinge of guilt spread across his face as he returned her smile.

"What happened?" she asked.

He told her.

"How long will you be gone?"

"At least twelve hours, and possibly a day at the most. We're going to move pretty fast. The NEIIS at Camp Alpha have told us some things about the Krake, but it's not enough. There's something else you need to know."

Lenora met his gaze and nodded. "All right, what is it?"

"We found NEIIS out of their stasis pods. Actually, we're not sure if they ever went into stasis. They tried to disguise themselves as ryklars and attacked us when we investigated another arch."

Lenora frowned as she collected her thoughts. "They even attacked their own kind?"

"I don't think they knew we had NEIIS with us."

"I see," she said. "At some point, we're going to have to refer to them by their own name—the Ovarrow."

"I know. Old habits." Connor paused for a moment and pressed his lips together. "I know I said I was going to try to limit my field missions, but this is something I have to do."

"I know that, Connor. You are who you are. Lauren and I will be here when you get back."

Lenora's understanding meant the world to him. "You know, I do miss our field assignments. Camping out under the stars, just the two of us."

"Careful. Keep this up and I might have to abscond you to some secret, out-of-the-way place."

Connor smiled, but he could hear a little bit of tension in her voice. Just because she understood didn't mean she wouldn't worry about him.

"Be careful," she said.

"I will. I was wondering if you could do something for me."

Lenora tilted her head to the side with a nod as she waited for Connor to continue.

"We took the NEIIS bodies to Delphi, but I was hoping you could start looking at the NEIIS data repositories for any mention of a group that didn't go into stasis or what faction was in the location of the city we went to. Contact Darius Cohen if you want him to ask the NEIIS there."

"I'd already written it down. I was going to do it anyway as soon as you mentioned it. I assume you have another team going out there to try and find them?"

"I do. I've invited the ONI to be involved, so they'll be reaching out to you as well."

"What about Dash? Shouldn't he have returned by now? Has he checked in?"

Connor pulled up the mission check-in logs and saw that Dash had indeed been in regular contact. "He's still investigating the medical cache to help deal with the cellular degenerative disease that's affecting the NEIIS. I have a squad of soldiers with them, so he should be well protected."

Lenora looked as if she wanted to say something else but stopped. She didn't like that he was going away again. She looked away from the camera for a moment and then swung her gaze back toward him. "You'd better come back," she said and closed the comlink.

Connor drew in a deep breath and sighed. Should he have expected anything different from his conversation with Lenora? They supported each other, but he was probably asking too much from her. Yet this was something he had to do.

He walked out of the office where Diaz was waiting for him with a somber expression.

"Lenora?" Diaz asked.

"Is it that obvious?"

Diaz shrugged.

"How does Victoria react when you tell her you're going away?" Connor asked. Diaz looked away for a moment and Connor narrowed his gaze. "You do tell her before you go, right?"

Diaz grimaced. "Most of the time. Sometimes it's just best not to worry them."

Connor frowned and shook his head. "Diaz, come on, you need to tell her."

They started walking down the long hallway that led outside. "I do tell her. I don't keep anything from my wife."

"So you've already told her then."

Diaz tilted his head and shrugged again. "Sometimes a prerecorded video message is just better than talking to her right before we have to leave."

Connor's mouth hung halfway between disbelief and exasperation. "You're afraid to tell her, aren't you?"

Diaz shook his head vigorously. "I'm not afraid to tell her."

"You just prefer to record the message and send it after we've already left."

"Well, it's not like it happens that often." Connor was about to reply but Diaz continued. "Look how well it went when you told Lenora you're going away again. Not just going away, but we're going to an alternate universe where there are things that are going to try to kill us. Tell me, how did that conversation go?"

The door opened and they went outside. He found himself agreeing with his friend a little bit, even if he didn't entirely agree with his method of handling the issue. It hadn't gone well, but those conversations never went well.

"It's your wife, and you have to live with her."

"Don't give me that, Connor. It's just better when I get back home and Victoria has calmed down."

Connor regarded Diaz for a moment. His friend had five

wonderful children. Diaz had often joked that when Connor became a father again, it would change him, but he hadn't counted on how it would change his perspective regarding his fellow soldiers, particularly the ones who were parents.

"You know, you don't *have* to come on this mission. I'm not ordering you to. It might be a good idea if you stayed. Who else is going to come rescue me if I get into trouble?"

Diaz simply stared at him. "I know right now you're speaking as my friend and not as my commanding officer, so I'm going to assume we're off the record here. I'm your friend. We've been through a lot, and I'm not going to let you go through that thing," he said, gesturing toward the arch, "without watching your back. So let's get it over with already."

They walked in silence for a few moments.

"I didn't say we were off the record."

Diaz made as if he was going to punch him, and Connor grinned as they walked to the last rover in the line of soldiers in front of the arch. It was a bit bigger than the others, being the mobile command center. Connor stepped inside and the soldiers saluted him.

"Welcome, General Gates," Major Wilson said. He was tall and lean, with brown skin.

"Thank you, Major Wilson. Are we ready to go?"

"Just say the word, General Gates."

There was a brief flash of light and the gateway opened. Then, the soldiers began going through. First, the combat-suit heavies entered, followed by infantrymen, then the rover mobile units, and lastly the command center. Connor tried to sense when they actually passed through the arch but couldn't. One moment they were home, and the next, the landscape showing on the holoscreen had changed. They were through.

26

THE CDF COMBAT shuttles flew into the main hangar bay of the *Vigilant* and Sean was the first one out. He ran to the equipment storage area and exited his combat suit, leaving it in the capable hands of the PFC on duty. Condition One had already been set, and the crew of the *Vigilant* was at their battle stations as Sean raced to the bridge.

"Sitrep," Sean said to Major Shelton as he approached the command area.

Major Shelton stood up and moved to the auxiliary workstation next to the command chair. "Two unknown ships detected on passive scans. I have tactical attempting to trace their trajectories so we can figure out where they came from."

"Do we have a visual of the ship?"

"Negative, Colonel."

"Tactical, I want a firing solution on those two ships. Helm, put us on an intercept course. XO, I want the *Albany* and the *Dutchman* to help us box them in."

Sean's orders were confirmed. There were only two ships,

which meant that this might just be a scouting force, but why would they come back there?

"Colonel, the *Albany* and the *Dutchman* are on an intercept course with the unknown ships," Major Shelton said.

"Very well," Sean said.

He looked at the PRADIS output on the main holoscreen, recalling the last time he'd faced Krake warships. They'd almost destroyed his ship.

"Tactical, I want two subsequent firing solutions with the objective of disabling the ships. Primary firing solution is clean sweep," Sean said.

"Confirm, Alpha and Bravo firing solutions, Colonel," Lieutenant Russo said.

"Colonel, should we try to raise them on comms?" Major Shelton asked.

CDF rules of engagement usually prohibited firing upon an unknown vessel unless being fired upon first. That ROE carried too much risk, but if he fired his weapons first and those ships attempted to communicate with his battle group, *he* would be the aggressor.

"We'll attempt comms first but not until we're in attack position," Sean said.

He brought up the status of the *Douglass* on his personal holoscreen. They were conducting a planetary survey, looking for any signs of civilization. Their current location was on the other side of the planet out of direct comms range.

"Comms, I need a communication drone ready to deploy to Bravo task force. Comms package Condition One, including relevant scan data on the two ships detected," Sean said.

A few moments later, "Comms drone ready at your command, Colonel," Specialist Sansky replied.

"Colonel Quinn," Major Shelton said, gesturing for Sean's

attention. "We could try the subspace transmitter. I realize we've only gotten it to work in five-minute intervals, but we could still transmit the scan data and your orders while conserving our drones."

Sean looked at Major Shelton and smiled. "Thank you, Major Shelton. Comms, keep the drone at the ready. Let's try subspace communication first. I want Major Brody to confirm he has received his orders."

They waited a few moments for Sansky to access the subspace communication interface. Major Shelton went over to the comms workstation to help. A few seconds later Sean saw Sansky nodding his thanks to Major Shelton, and then she returned to the auxiliary workstation.

"Subspace communication link is established and data package sent, Colonel," Specialist Sansky said and paused for a few moments. "Confirmed, message was received." He almost sounded as if he couldn't quite believe it.

Sean looked at Major Shelton, and she shrugged her shoulders slightly. He gave himself a mental kick. He shouldn't have overlooked the advantage of subspace communication. He frowned as a thought came to his mind. "Specialist Sansky, is it possible to scan subspace for open comms chatter?"

"I can try, Colonel."

"Please do so, and let me know if you detect anything."

"Yes, Colonel."

Sean looked at Major Shelton. "We have issues keeping links open, but there haven't been any problems scanning subspace frequencies."

"I reviewed the previous engagement you had with the Krake, and there's no mention of subspace communication. I guess we wouldn't have known if they had that capability at the time," Shelton said.

Sean nodded. "We have it now, so we might as well use it.

Good job suggesting that. Feel free to make all the intelligent suggestions you want."

"Thank you, Colonel," Shelton said and turned her attention to her personal holoscreen.

Sean waited a few more minutes for the battle group to be closer to the unknown ships. "Ops, begin active scans."

Within seconds, active scan data appeared on the main holoscreen.

"The unknown ships don't match the Krake warship signature. The mass of the ship is similar to one of our freighters, Colonel," Lieutenant Russo said.

Sean looked at the plot, taking in the position of the ships. "They're in an asteroid field. These could be scavengers or mining ships. There has to be a space gate nearby."

"Colonel Quinn," Specialist Sansky said from the comms workstation, "I received a comms package via subspace from the *Douglass*. No active civilization detected. Planetary scans indicate that the current ice age has been in place for hundreds of years, possibly more. These are best-guess estimates based on the rapid ice age instituted by the NEIIS on New Earth."

Sean glanced at the empty seat of the science officer workstation. He would've liked to have had Oriana there, or someone from her team, but their first priority was to work out the targeting capabilities of the space gate.

"Understood," Sean replied. "Tactical, I want the secondary firing solution ready to disable those ships. Target their main engines. Comms, try hailing the ships."

"Firing solution ready, Colonel."

"Attempting to hail unknown vessels on all known frequencies, and there has been no reply. Subspace is quiet as well, Colonel."

Sean acknowledged them and waited. They were closing in on the two ships. If they had any kind of passive scanner, they should have detected the battle group by now.

"Course change for both ships. Increased velocity. They're trying to run, Colonel," Lieutenant Russo said.

"Fire," Sean said.

"Yes, Colonel, firing a salvo of Hornet B missiles."

Four groups of new points appeared on the plot, showing the Hornet Bs racing toward their target. The freighters were moving faster than Sean thought they were capable, but the Hornets closed in on them.

"Confirm hit on both targets. Their main engine pods are disabled," Lieutenant Russo said.

Sean glanced at Specialist Sansky.

"Still no reply to our communication attempts, Colonel."

"Ops, scan along their trajectory. There has to be a space gate."

"Scanning. Space gate energy signature detected," Lieutenant Hoffman said.

A new point appeared on the plot that showed the probable location of a space gate ten thousand kilometers from the fleeing ships. There was no way those ships were going to make it with maneuvering thrusters alone.

"Colonel, I'm detecting a broadcast signal from the two ships."

They're calling for help. "Tactical, can you identify their comms array?"

"Negative, Colonel. We'd be firing blind."

"Comms, broadcast the following on the same frequency. 'Attention, unknown ships. Cease broadcast immediately, or we will destroy you.' End message," Sean said. "Tactical, Alpha firing solution ready?"

"Yes, Colonel," Lieutenant Russo replied.

"No reply, Colonel," Specialist Sansky said.

Sean gritted his teeth. He had no choice. "Destroy them."

"Yes, Colonel, execute Alpha firing solution," Lieutenant Russo said.

"Ops, those ships are communicating with the space gate. Can we access those comms?" Sean asked. At the same time, he used his implants to send a text message to Oriana requesting that she come to the bridge immediately.

"Colonel, I can attempt to access the space gate, but we do not have any access to those ships," Lieutenant Hoffman said.

"Negative, Lieutenant Hoffman. Unless we can hijack that signal, accessing the space gate isn't going to help us," Sean said and looked at the main hall display. "Comms, raise the *Albany*. They're closer. Tell Captain Welch to configure their comms array to intercept the signal from those two ships."

Sean's orders were confirmed, and a few minutes later Oriana came onto the bridge. She headed immediately for the science officer's workstation.

"I'm trying to capture a Krake comms session with the space gate we detected. I'm hoping you'll be able to look at it and determine why our targeting protocols keep failing," Sean said.

Oriana considered this for a moment and then nodded. "It can help, but it will only confirm the targeted universe that those ships want to communicate with. It will take time for me to analyze the difference between their protocols and ours. But I can cross reference that data with what we currently have. There could be something there," she said and paused for a moment. "I'm telling you this because I want to set expectations. I don't think I'll be able to come up with a quick solution to the targeting problem."

Sean squelched a flash of annoyance. It wasn't her fault, and she was right to manage his expectations. "Understood," he said and looked at Major Shelton. "Thoughts?"

"Colonel, I think we should move the battle group away from this area. Head to the outer system."

Sean grimaced. "Retreat?"

Major Shelton nodded. "Yes, Colonel. We have the advantage now, but we don't know who's on the other side of that space gate and what their capabilities are. They represent an unknown, and right now I'm willing to bet that their broadcast for help only indicates that they've been attacked by unknown ships. There's no way those scavenger ships can accurately identify us."

Sean frowned in thought. The primary objective was to recon the enemy and engage them only if necessary.

"Colonel," Lieutenant Russo said, "escape pods have jettisoned from the scavenger ships. Should we target them?"

"Negative, tactical. Have the *Albany* capture those escape pods," Sean replied.

A few moments later the two scavenger ships were destroyed.

"The *Albany* is on an intercept course, Colonel. Combat shuttles have been deployed to capture the escape pods."

"Very well," Sean replied.

He went through his options in his mind. They could destroy the space gate and temporarily prevent the Krake from accessing the system for a time. If he did that, they'd also know that Sean and the battle group knew the value of the space gate. It was a small thing, but he didn't want to tip his hand. He didn't know what the Krake response would be. Would they send a small scout force to investigate, or something more powerful? Whatever passed for Krake central command already knew the CDF existed, but they didn't know the CDF could traverse between universes.

"Comms, send CDF encrypted broadcast Alpha priority to the battle group. Rendezvous at Charlie coordinates."

They were withdrawing, at least for the moment. The space gate had deactivated when the ships were destroyed. Its location was well within the asteroid field.

Sean looked at Major Shelton. "Major, I want holding cells prepared for our prisoners. Decontamination protocols must be observed."

"Yes, Colonel," Major Shelton replied, then left the bridge.

"Excuse me, Colonel," Oriana said.

"What is it, Dr. Evans?"

"I just want to make you aware that we have the targeting data those ships used to call for help. I thought that since we're supposed to be looking for the Krake, perhaps we should account for that in our next move."

Sean exhaled through his nose and smiled. "Careful, I might put you in charge."

Oriana regarded him for a moment, impassively. "If I'm no longer needed on the bridge, I'd like to return to my team to work on the data we retrieved from the Krake installation on the moon and also any and all space gate-related data from this encounter. I'll have an update for you in a few hours."

She was still mad at him.

"Dismissed," Sean said.

"Colonel Quinn," Specialist Sansky said, "confirmed all ships in Battle Group Trident best speed to rendezvous coordinates."

Sean thanked him. They needed to regroup and evaluate the new information they had on hand. Hopefully, coming to this universe wouldn't be a total loss for them. The more he thought about it, the more he believed they'd been lucky they *had* come there. Things could have been much worse for them if they'd gone to a universe where the Krake had no presence at all, like what they'd detected when they tried to return to their home universe. Sean had made too many assumptions before. He realized it now with the benefit of hindsight, but they'd had to act, and he couldn't change what had been done.

Their primary objective now was to recon the Krake, but he also wanted to return to the universe they'd been to before where Connor had detected the distress beacon from Rollins. But any hope of a rescue mission from Sean's battle group was off the table for the moment. He didn't like the thought of leaving people behind, and he hoped he wasn't about to find himself in another situation where he'd be unable to help. Given what they were doing, there was the real possibility that they might be faced with leaving people behind. Their mission was one of high risk, and every commanding officer in the battle group understood that, but Sean hoped he could bring all his people back home alive.

He glanced at the main holoscreen, which showed Battle Group Trident. There was, of course, a chain of command, but out in the field, Sean had no one but himself. He had good people to support him, but ultimately the decisions for the group were up to him. He brought up tactical engagement scenarios on his personal holoscreen and began reviewing them, opening a comlink to the *Dutchman* and the *Ajax*. Captains Martinez and Vargas appeared on his personal holoscreen.

"Gentlemen, I have a job for you. I'm going to need both of you to stay in the asteroid field for a while," Sean said and began telling the two destroyer captains what he needed from them.

27

ONE OF THE most influencing factors Connor had considered
when designating the site for the new CDF base near New Haven
was its proximity to the arch they'd found at the lake bottom. In
the alternate universe, that area was the location for the Krake's
forward-operating base on the planet that corresponded with New
Earth. The CDF base was located five kilometers from the lake in
order to ensure it was away from any path that ran along the
shoreline in the alternate universe. They'd built their own arch
there, which would allow them to sneak into the alternate
universe without alerting the Krake to their presence. However,
given the substantial fighting force Connor had brought with him,
this also extinguished the possibility that the Krake would
continue to overlook their vulnerability when all was said and
done. A simple flyover by a Krake ship would detect that a
substantial fighting force had recently come to the area.

They beat a path to the Krake forward-operating base easily,
traversing the slimy, withering brush. Much of the base was in
ruins, and the massive arch was almost completely submerged in
the lake water. When Connor had been there six months ago, he'd

ordered the combat shuttle pilot to take out the arch support foundations, which had toppled it. The Krake hadn't rebuilt it.

"Why would they abandon this place?" Diaz asked.

"Your guess is as good as mine," Connor replied.

"Maybe they finished whatever they were doing here and decided to leave," Major Wilson said.

"After they'd been attacked?" Diaz asked doubtfully.

Wilson glanced around. "Who'd want to defend this place?"

"Point taken."

"Let's hold up here for a little while and investigate the area. There was a substantial underground facility," Connor said.

He sent multiple teams to canvas the area and then left the command center, accompanied by Diaz and Wilson, to have a look around. Scorch marks scarred many of the buildings that hadn't been destroyed during the attack, and it appeared that the Krake had made no effort to rebuild at all. As the CDF teams explored the military base, they found extensive damage to the underground facilities. Tunnels and entrances had either collapsed or were impassable.

"Are you looking for it?" Diaz asked.

"It has to be around here somewhere. I remember that we came out..." Connor paused for a moment, looking around while he got his bearings, "...just over there, so there has to be a way inside nearby."

DIAZ NODDED, then glanced at the metallic rooftops of the nearby buildings. "I keep expecting Krake soldiers to come out of nowhere and attack us."

Connor knew the feeling. He and Diaz had been trapped on a rooftop, waiting for extraction.

They continued onward and found the entrance to the base underground, which looked fairly intact despite some damage nearby. The door was sealed and wouldn't open. Connor called in a demolition team.

"What do you expect to find down there?" Major Wilson asked.

Sergeant Harkness set an explosive charge and then shouted a warning. There was a small flash and a section of the door fell away, leaving a gaping hole.

"There was some kind of control center inside that was patched into the arch. The Krake were recording different gateways, noting the times they'd been accessed, as well as an image of what could be seen beyond it," Connor said.

They went through the opening and down a long corridor. Scorch marks marred the walls, reminding him of when he and Diaz had fled through this area with the Krake hot on their heels. There was no power in the facility, so they were reliant on their enhanced vision capabilities, as well as combat suit systems. Soon, they found the control center, but the wall of holoscreens Connor remembered was gone. He walked toward one of the rounded workstations. It was as high as his chest and appeared undamaged. Connor gestured to Sergeant Harkness. "There should be a data core underneath there."

Sergeant Harkness squatted down and forced open the access panel.

"Why would they use local data storage instead of a secure data repository?" Major Wilson asked.

"They probably do, but they'll hold some data here at the consoles as well," Connor said and squatted down to look inside the access panel. "You can do a data dump from these points right here," he said, gesturing inside the panel.

Major Wilson arched an eyebrow toward him.

"Years of extracting NEIIS data cores is paying off. We think they emulated the Krake systems they'd come in contact with," Connor replied.

Diaz walked over to the door and looked down the corridor. "There's a lot of blockage down that way. We're not getting through there."

"What was down there?" Wilson asked.

"Holding cells. They had a lot of prisoners here," Connor said.

He wondered what had happened to all of them. He glanced at Diaz and could tell he was thinking the same thing. They left Sergeant Harkness to continue his work and headed back outside.

As they arrived back at the command center, the other teams began reporting in. A video feed from Lieutenant Greaves showed some kind of small living area.

"As you can see," Greaves said, "it looks like somebody was recently living here. They barricaded themselves in, cobbling most of this stuff together. They might've done it after this place was abandoned."

Connor listened as the various teams reported in with their findings. They'd found some Krake equipment, and Sergeant Harkness eventually reported that he'd finished his data dump of the available Krake systems.

Connor looked at Major Wilson. "Those are high priority. Let's send a small team back to our waypoint with the equipment and the data dump. I want them sent back through the gateway. If they hurry, they should make the next check-in. After that, have them secure the area."

They maneuvered their way to the north side of the Krake military base. They still hadn't received any broadcast from Flint or the Spec Ops team.

"General Gates," Specialist Myers said, "I'm detecting the CDF distress beacon with John Rollins' identification."

"What's the location?"

"About ten kilometers north of the base, General."

Major Wilson frowned. "If Rollins was hiding from the Krake soldiers, why would he stay so close to this area?"

"I don't even know how he could've survived on his own here," Diaz said.

"Maybe he wasn't alone, but as for why he stayed so close to the area, my guess would be that he thought this was the best place to get back home," Connor replied.

"The other missing colonist, Oliver Taylor, was a research scientist. His record indicates that he didn't have any survival skills," Wilson said.

They sent a scout force half a klick north of the Krake military base where they found evidence of recent travel, including tracks from CDF combat suits. Flint must've come this way.

Connor looked at the reconnaissance drone video feeds they'd deployed. There were areas of thick fog but not everywhere. Some areas had high levels of sulfur dioxide, which made Connor thankful they weren't forced to breathe the air there. The recon drones indicated that there were areas where the SO_2 levels were minimal. Survival was possible, but no one would enjoy being on this planet for very long.

"It's time for us to move out. Let's head for that beacon," Connor said.

"General," Major Wilson said, "should we send out a broadcast to Captain Flint and his team?"

They hadn't received any communication signals since they'd arrived. If Flint was watching the Krake military base, even from a distance, he would've sent word.

"Not yet."

"I know we're monitoring for comlink signals, but why wouldn't we broadcast? Do you think there are Krake forces nearby?"

"Possibly, and we don't know if they can detect our broadcasts. If Captain Flint is alive and monitoring the area, he'll see us coming," Connor replied.

They hadn't detected any Krake presence there, but if there

were Krake ships orbiting the planet, monitoring their position, there wasn't much they could do if they decided to bombard the area. They had no choice but to head to the beacon.

"Tell the soldiers to stay focused. We don't know what's waiting for us where that beacon is," Connor said.

"Understood, sir," Wilson said.

They could cover ten kilometers in a relatively short amount of time, but they would proceed cautiously. There was no telling what waited for them, and since they hadn't heard from the Spec Ops team, Connor felt it was safe to assume they were heading into danger.

28

CONNOR ACCESSED one of the reconnaissance drones that had scouted ahead of their large fighting force. These drones were capable of multi-spectrum analyses of the area, which included anything from sampling atmospheric composition to video feeds, along with acoustics that could be filtered to the tiniest decibel. Aside from plant life struggling to survive, there was little detected. Undulating sulfur dioxide levels continued to be detected, as well as increased seismic activity. They accessed the microphone feed from the reconnaissance drone, and there was a near-constant hissing noise coming from the ground. There were several vents in the ground from which water vapor with significant amounts of sulfur dioxide billowed into the atmosphere. The pressure beneath the ground gave rise to an almost squeal-like sound as the gas escaped.

Diaz, who'd been listening in, shook his head. "That's all we need. This whole area is a big damn volcanic caldera. This isn't creepy at all. Between that noise and the fog that rolls in and out at will, I can't wait to get out of here."

Connor couldn't disagree with him. The atmosphere was

almost toxic in some areas, which made him glad that all the soldiers were in combat suits with their own supply of oxygen.

They'd received a report that the materials collected from the Krake military base had been successfully taken through the gateway. The team was hunkering down and securing the area.

They entered the beginnings of a foothill region, and the walls of the caldera were more than fifty kilometers away. Beyond that were the actual mountains.

"What do you think the odds are of a volcano going off right about now?" Diaz asked.

"If we're lucky, not for a long time," Connor replied. "Either way, we're not going to be here long enough to find out."

An alarm chimed from one of the reconnaissance drones and Connor brought the video feed to prominence on his holoscreen. The mists had cleared just enough to reveal the top of a wall.

"Is this another base?" Diaz asked.

More of the mists disappeared to reveal dark wooden huts grouped together behind the wall. The damp wood sagged as if it were about to collapse.

"This isn't a base," Connor replied, peering at the video feed. "It looks more like a refugee camp."

The mists continued to clear away, and the camp looked to be a collection of scavenged materials, some of which Connor recognized from the military base.

He looked at Diaz. "There are too many huts for just one person. I think the Krake released their prisoners, and they built this place."

Diaz's frown sank into a scowl. "When those bastards left, they just cut the prisoners loose? That's not just a death sentence; that's torture."

"If that's what happened," Wilson said, "where'd all the prisoners go?"

Connor continued to look at the video feed. "That's what we need to find out."

The soldiers scouted the area, and the mobile command center pushed through the makeshift wall. The other armored rovers went to the outer perimeter to provide backup to the soldiers who were checking the area.

"The beacon is located atop one of those structures, General," Specialist Myers said.

An area in the central region of the camp became highlighted on the holoscreen, and Connor and the others left the mobile command center to have a look at it. As he walked up to the hut with the small antenna and dish sticking out on top, Connor noticed that several of the huts seemed to have collapsed recently.

A soldier climbed to the top to examine it. After a few moments, he looked down at Connor and the others. "It's a basic set up. Whoever did this knew our broadcast frequencies, and it seems to rotate broadcasting to conserve power," Sergeant Galloway said.

"How is it powered?" Connor asked.

The soldier reached in and disconnected something. The broadcast stopped. "This doesn't look like one of ours. Probably from that base," Galloway said. He looked at it for a few moments and then put it back.

Connor was about to reply when the noise level from the volcanic vents seemed to subside all at once, and a sudden stillness gripped the area. Then he heard shouting from the far side of the camp, followed by weapons fire.

He heard Major Wilson trying to get a status from the soldiers.

"Tell them to fall back and form a perimeter," Connor said.

He brought his weapon up and tried to peer through the fog beyond the makeshift wall. Diaz had his weapon up and was scanning the area. A comlink opened from Specialist Myers at the command center.

"General Gates, we've received a comlink from Captain Flint—"

Whatever else Myers was about to say was cut off, and a red glow came from the surrounding area. The lights gleamed brighter and Connor heard snarling in the distance, followed by the scream of a soldier. The screaming didn't stop, and the soldiers on the perimeter began to fire their weapons. M-180 gauss cannons fired from the armored rovers.

Connor sent a broadcast signal to activate the combat drones. They launched from the command center and rose up into the air. "Come on, we need to see what we're up against," he said and ran back toward the mobile command center.

The soldiers continued to fire their weapons in spurts, but they didn't know if they were hitting anything. Suddenly, dark shapes burst from the fog to attack them, and the red lights coming from the creatures' bodies pulsed through the thick fog blowing in.

Connor climbed inside the command center and walked up to the wall of holoscreens. There were video feeds from the combat drones, as well as the reconnaissance drones. They caught a view of one of the creatures, and Connor froze the image. Thick armored plating went down its back and onto a long tail. It ran on four legs but had an extra set of shoulder joints and large arms. The creature had scarlet glowing points along its spine and neck from some sort of bioluminescence, and it had thick, powerful jaws.

Another video feed showed the creatures closing in on the camp all at once. The soldiers fired their weapons, and it looked like several of the creatures went down, but Connor couldn't be sure. He looked at the communications specialist. "Get me Captain Flint, now." The comlink came online. "What's your status, Captain?"

"General Gates, you have to get out of there. There are hundreds of them coming. They ambushed us, and I lost half my men fighting them. We have Rollins, but he's in bad shape. I'm not sure if he's gonna make it."

"Where are you?"

"We're in the foothills. There's no way we can make it to your position. We've been monitoring the camp, but we've had some problems of our own and didn't see you arrive."

Connor brought up a map of the area based on reconnaissance drone surveys. A glowing waypoint indicated Flint's relative position. "If we're able to keep these things occupied, do you think you could make it back to the Krake military base? Or even the gateway location?"

"Yes, General. We'll have to circle around to avoid those creatures. It's rough terrain, so it's going to take a little while."

"Get started, and get a move on it," Connor said. He looked at Specialist Myers. "Task one of the combat drones to fly air support for them."

"Yes, General," Specialist Myers said.

The CDF soldiers formed a perimeter within the camp, and Connor ordered them back the way they'd come. The creatures attacking them ranged in size from two meters to almost as much as six meters in length. Given the extreme length of their bodies, the red bioluminescence was prominent along their spines and never seemed to fade. If anything, it grew with the intensity of their attacks.

The CDF combat heavies unleashed a barrage of attacks that cut a swath through the approaching fighting force. The soldiers made a steady withdrawal, and the creatures continued to probe their defenses, looking for a way through.

The command center tipped to the side as something large slammed into it, and the M-180 gauss cannon on top could be heard firing. More of the creatures slammed into the vehicle from the other side.

"What the hell are they doing?" Diaz said.

"They're changing their tactics and attacking the rovers," Connor said and ordered the soldiers to form up around the armored rovers. They needed to move faster. He watched as soldiers on screen got snatched by the creatures' powerful jaws and thrown behind as they attacked with reckless abandon. Connor narrowed his gaze. He'd only witnessed an attack like that once before on New Earth—ryklars under the influence of a NEIIS command-and-control signal. These beasts were being controlled somehow.

"Specialist Myers, can you scan for any control frequencies?"

"I don't detect anything, General."

Something massive slammed into the command center. Connor braced himself as the command center toppled to its side and the gauss cannon on the roof went quiet. Several more creatures slammed into the bottom and the vehicle slowly spun around until it came to a stop.

Connor helped those around him onto their feet. "Grab your weapons. We have to get out of here."

There was heavy fighting outside, but after a few moments, Major Wilson gave him a nod. "We've got a window."

Connor grabbed his rifle and they left the vehicle. The mobile command center was missing a few wheels, and there was significant damage to the bottom. He looked at Diaz. "Can you set this thing to explode in a few minutes?"

Diaz smiled. "Not a problem," he said and went to the front of the vehicle. Several soldiers covered his flank while he worked.

"They're regrouping for another attack," Major Wilson said.

A few moments later, Diaz came back and CDF soldiers pressed in around them, forming a protective shield. Connor saw some of the beasts sprinting with deadly grace as they galloped over the slippery terrain. They coordinated their attacks, with some creatures feinting while others actually attacked. The other rovers were left largely alone.

They quickly moved away from the area, and a bright flash reflected off the fog as the mobile command unit exploded. The self-destruct had been tied into the fuel cells, and Connor heard the loud thumps of the creatures' bodies as they landed nearby. Diaz let out a hearty laugh as Connor glanced at him. Without warning, a dark shape sprang up behind Diaz and snatched him back into the fog. Diaz cried out, and in only a few moments, he sounded farther away.

Connor charged toward him and heard Wilson shouting orders for soldiers to follow. He didn't think about the creatures trying to lure him out; he just reacted. He caught sight of a red glow to the side, and Connor fired his weapon into the beast's muzzle. The force of this blow caused it to spin around and tumble to the ground.

Diaz cried out again, and it sounded like he was being dragged. Connor screamed for his friend. Several combat drones flew overhead, firing at creatures that were closing in all around him. Two soldiers caught up to him, and they continued forward. Connor saw Diaz ahead.

"Let go of me, you son of a bitch!" Diaz screamed.

The creature was holding Diaz by his leg, shaking him violently. Connor aimed and fired his weapon, catching the creature's hindquarters. It let go of Diaz's leg and backed away into the fog as the soldiers laid down covering fire. Diaz was bleeding badly, but he'd propped himself up onto an elbow and had his rifle aimed where the creature had been swallowed by the fog.

Connor and the soldiers quickly reached him, but then a wall of red bioluminescence seemed to glow all at once in a heady promise of certain death. The creatures towered over them.

Thinking quickly, Connor accessed his combat suit controls and activated the exterior lights using the same red spectrum of the bioluminescence. He cranked up the power until the light was so bright that it blinded the creatures, and they backed away.

Connor ordered the soldiers to use their combat suit lights also. The beasts flinched and growled but did not attack.

"Grab him," Connor said, gesturing to Diaz.

Connor pulsed his combat suit lights like he'd seen the creatures do, which resulted in more of them arriving. A rover pulled up behind them, and the M-180 gauss cannon unleashed its fury, scattering the beasts. He grabbed hold of Diaz, helping the soldiers carry him to the rover where they passed Diaz off to a soldier inside. Connor then climbed to the top of the rover and began shooting at the creatures as the vehicle backed away. He kept aiming and shooting all the while, trying not to think about how much blood he'd seen on his friend.

He heard combat drones flying overhead, raining hellfire missiles onto the ground. They were able to drive the creatures back, giving the rover time to escape.

Connor opened the comlink to Major Wilson. "Have anyone in a suit turn on their lights using the same spectrum as the creatures'. It'll confuse them. I think it's some kind of intimidation tactic before they attack."

"Understood, General," Major Wilson said.

The rover reached the others, and they continued their trek toward the Krake military base. The area around the CDF soldiers glowed with a red light of its own, and it stalled the attack from the creatures. Connor didn't know how long this would work, but he knew it only had to work for a short while longer.

29

SEVERAL SOLDIERS CLIMBED atop the rover and took up positions near Connor.

One of the soldiers turned toward him, and his eyes widened. "General Gates, sir," he said, and some of the others looked at Connor in surprise.

"Stay focused," Connor said.

The name of the soldier nearest him appeared on Connor's internal heads-up display. "Small world, Sergeant Galloway."

The other soldiers readied their weapons and pointed them toward where the creatures were gathering in the mists. Connor heard the thumping cadence of the combat suit heavies walking near the rover. The growling and hissing seemed to increase, but they could only see shadows through the thick fog.

Connor switched to infrared and saw hundreds of creatures barely fifty meters from them.

"They're going to regroup and attack again, I know it," a soldier said.

Connor looked over at the soldier. The name Private Woods appeared on his HUD. "Hold your fire. Wait for them to commit."

"Yes, sir – Uh, sorry, General Gates," Woods said.

Connor looked through the scope on his rifle. They'd stalled them with the lights, but that wasn't going to last. If the creatures pressed forward, they might be able to hold them off for a little while, but it was going to cost lives.

"Excuse me, General Gates, I have an idea," Sergeant Galloway said.

Connor didn't look away from the creatures. "What is it, Sergeant?"

"These things reacted to the beacon at the camp when we turned it off. I wonder if turning it back on would make them back off a bit."

Connor frowned and considered for a moment. "That might be a little too convenient, don't you think?"

"I'll take convenient if it works, General."

"All right, give it a try. See if you can remote-access it."

Sergeant Galloway lowered his weapon and brought up his suit computer on his forearm. After a few moments, he shook his head. "I can't access it at all from here," he said and glanced in the direction of the camp multiple kilometers away.

"Did you remove the power supply?"

"No, it's still attached. I just turned off the beacon."

Connor watched as Galloway looked toward the camp, a thoughtful frown on his face.

Connor shook his head. "No one is going back there."

"What if I have one of the comms drones mimic the distress beacon and have it activate at the camp?"

"Good idea. Give it a try," Connor said.

They waited as Sergeant Galloway took control of the nearest reconnaissance drone and sent it back to the camp. Connor watched as it streaked across the sky. Once it reached the camp, Galloway activated the distress beacon, and they continued to wait. Nothing happened. The creatures didn't react at all. Instead, they began to press closer toward them.

Galloway muttered a curse. "It's not working."

He was right; the beacon had no effect, but Connor had another idea. He seized control of the reconnaissance drone, and Sergeant Galloway glanced at him. Connor had a great deal of experience squeezing every ounce of capability out of a recon drone. A video feed from the drone appeared on Connor's internal heads-up display. As it hovered near the makeshift antenna, he could see inside the access panel. Connor engaged the drone's mechanical arms, which emerged from beneath the camera feed. He eased the drone toward the access panel and used the arm to reach inside and activate the beacon.

"The beacon is active," Sergeant Galloway said. "I didn't know recon drones could do that."

Connor looked at the creatures, and their advance seemed to have stalled again. An idea came to his mind, and Connor decided to have the drone power the beacon off and then back on. Each time he did it, the creatures seemed divided as to what they wanted to do.

Connor smiled. "Kill the lights," he said and sent a quick comlink broadcast. Within a few moments, the red lights around the soldiers went out. Connor power-cycled the beacon again, and this time the creatures began running away back toward the camp.

"Let's pick up the pace," Connor said and looked to Galloway. "Keep an eye on them."

They quickly retraced their steps while keeping a watchful eye on their flank. Aerial combat drones monitored the creatures, which were still moving back toward the camp. They reached the Krake military base and Connor sent a comlink to the soldiers guarding the gateway. The check-in was about to occur, and he ordered them to inform the CDF base to keep the gateway active so they could get home. He used his implants to access the rover's systems and saw that Flint was almost to the waypoint near the gateway.

"General, the beacon is now offline. I think the power cell is depleted," Galloway said.

"Understood," Connor replied.

They made it to the gateway, and the soldiers began going through. Connor climbed down from the rover and opened one of the storage hatches, recalling two combat drones to his location. He began unloading a heavy container, and Sergeant Galloway gave him a hand.

"What's this, sir?"

"It's a little gift for the Krake when they come back here—if they come back here," Connor said.

They finished attaching the new payload to the combat drones, and Connor sent them speeding away. Once they reached their destinations, they would go into low-power mode and wait.

The soldiers quickly went through the gateway. Wilson told him that Diaz was severely wounded and had been among the first group to go through. Connor watched the sky, looking for some sign of a Krake ship, but nothing came.

"Time to go, General," Major Wilson said.

Connor went through the gateway and returned home.

30

HOME.

Connor tried to feel some sort of sensation as he stepped through the gateway, but there wasn't any. He couldn't feel a thing, and it seemed to trip his brain up because he had once again anticipated feeling some sort of resistance at crossing between universes.

The uninjured soldiers lined up over to the left and went through decontamination procedures. To the right, wounded soldiers were waiting to be checked by teams of medics. The more serious cases were carried on stretchers to a tent where the doctors were.

Connor walked over to Major Wilson. "Do you know how many casualties there were?"

"At least thirty-six, General," Wilson replied.

They'd taken over two hundred soldiers with them, and given what they'd faced, the loss of thirty-six wasn't bad on a report; but the day Connor was comfortable with the loss of any soldier would be the day he turned in his stars for good.

"Understood, Major. Double-check that number, will you?"

"Will do, sir," Wilson said and walked away.

A medic checked Connor over. He didn't have any injuries, so he was waved onward. Connor quickly went through decontamination protocols and removed his combat suit, noticing the lingering smell of sulfur dioxide in the air due to its high concentration. The circulation system would be working in overdrive to get the smell out.

Nathan Hayes met Connor as he came out of the decontamination tent.

"I see they finally let you leave Sierra," Connor said.

"I left as soon as I received word that you were leading the fighting force yourself. Looks like things got pretty rough there."

Connor exhaled and nodded. "I'll tell you all about it, but first, where's Flint?"

"Flint and his team are quarantined. The doctors are checking them out, as well as Rollins. I should warn you though—he looks really bad."

Rollins had somehow survived for over six months on that hellish world. How was he supposed to look?

Nathan led Connor to the quarantine area where Flint and his team were being examined.

Flint saw Connor and Nathan walk in and smiled. "Thanks for coming to get us, sir."

"I'm glad we got there in time. What happened?" Connor asked.

The doctor finished his examination and handed Flint a bottle of water with electrolytes, instructing him to drink it.

"We went through and made our way to the military base. It was abandoned, but we looked around anyway. The distress beacon cut out so we decided to hold up at the base for a little while. Then we found the camp that was housing the beacon, and that's when we found Rollins. He's not well. I think he may have lost his mind because he fled the camp when we showed up. We followed him, and that's when the ambush occurred. Those creatures..." Flint paused for a moment and drank from the bottle. "We followed Rollins to a cave. The creatures didn't pursue us very far, but their surprise attack— Several of us were down before we knew it. We reached a cave and were able to keep them from getting inside, but we had to restrain Rollins to keep him from running away. The man was starving—withered away to nothing but skin and bones. I've never seen anything like it."

Flint drank more of his water and then continued. "I sent a small team to try and make it back to the waypoint, but they were ambushed and overwhelmed. We were going to take another go at it if you hadn't shown up."

Connor nodded. "Get some rest and we'll meet up later."

Connor and Nathan moved on to a solitary area where Rollins lay in a bed behind a glass wall. He was unconscious. They looked through the glass and collectively sucked in a breath. Connor had never seen anyone that emaciated before. There were IVs hooked up to his thin arms, and he could see Rollins' bony shoulders through his clothing. His gaunt face looked brittle and stiff. There was a nurse cleaning him up.

A doctor left the room and walked over to Connor. "Hello, I'm Dr. Grady."

"How's he doing?" Connor asked.

"Severe starvation and dehydration coupled with extreme exposure. I don't know how he's still alive, to be completely honest with you."

Connor looked through the window again, remembering when Rollins first came to the Recovery Institute when he'd been the new mayor of Sanctuary. Rollins had a mean streak to him that stretched the patience of anyone he came into contact with, and his demeanor hadn't been improved by what he'd experienced during the Vemus War. Connor had tried to help him, and Rollins was getting better. He would probably never be considered one of the nice guys, but he was worth saving.

Connor looked back at Dr. Grady. "Is he gonna live?"

"We should be able to keep him alive by giving him nutrients and rehydrating him, but it's too soon to determine how severe his condition is. If he does live, we won't know how much damage was done to his brain until he stabilizes. We have medical nanites in his system that are repairing his organs. He's in for a rough time if he survives." Dr. Grady paused and frowned. "I understand you want information from him, but I feel I need to warn you that this might be a tall order. I've spoken with Captain Flint, and he described Rollins' behavior. I'm not sure how much of the man you knew is inside that room."

Connor shared a glance with Nathan and swallowed hard. "Understood. Please do what you can and keep us apprised of his condition."

Over the next few hours, Connor and Nathan met with each of the soldiers who'd gone to the alternate universe with Flint. In some cases, the debriefings were short, and longer in others. Connor received an update that Diaz was in stable condition but was still unconscious. He suppressed a shudder when he heard the news, thankful he didn't have to tell Victoria and Diaz's five children that their father was dead.

Nathan glanced at him. "Are you all right?"

Connor shook his head. "No, not really. But I'm glad Diaz is going to recover."

"Me, too," Nathan replied.

They went to the command center. All gateway activity had been locked down since their return, and the area by the arch was now clear of any soldiers. Connor had a reconnaissance drone on standby, hovering twenty meters away, along with automated, high-powered turrets aimed at the gateway.

Nathan looked at him. "What do you hope to find?"

Connor watched the drone video feed on the main holoscreen. "You'll see."

The arch was activated, and a stable gateway was established. The reconnaissance drone went through and a timer appeared on the main holoscreen. After a few minutes, the drone returned, tendrils of smoke rising from its ceramic-alloy panels.

They accessed the recorded data on the main holoscreen, and Connor watched as a decimated landscape appeared that stretched as far as the drone could see through its optics. The atmospheric sensor showed temperatures were well above normal, and there were high levels of radiation. The area where the Krake military base had been was simply destroyed, and there were remnants of Krake ships nearby that had crashed into the ground. Connor looked at the feed with grim satisfaction.

Nathan eyed him for a moment. "You left the trap."

Connor smiled wolfishly. "Yes, I did. I suspected the Krake were going to return. They had laid a trap for us, but mine was better. Looks like they lost at least four of their ships."

Nathan whistled in appreciation. "What do you think they were hoping to learn?"

"I'm not sure, exactly, but it felt good to hit them back for a change. The one thing the NEIIS seemed to agree on regarding the Krake was that they like to manipulate. This might've just been a test for them."

Connor ordered the arch to be powered down. "We should move it to another location."

"Agreed," Nathan said. "I already have people working on the data you recovered from their systems."

"It's a start," Connor said.

He sent a copy of the drone data feed to Flint. At least he would know that they'd finally hit the Krake back—a cold comfort for the Spec Ops soldiers who'd lost their lives.

"The Colonial Defense Committee is going to want a debriefing in the next few days."

"I expected as much. I'm going home to Sanctuary first. Then I'll meet you in Sierra," Connor said.

"Kurt Johnson was looking for you. He said he wanted to speak to you before he left," Nathan said.

Connor crossed his arms, thinking that if he demoted himself — He terminated that line of thought. "He knows how to find me."

They left the command center.

"Dana Wolf asked me to relay to you that she appreciates the effort you've been making to keep her office in the loop," Nathan said.

Connor arched an eyebrow and smirked. "Maybe she was just happy to be rid of Johnson for a few days."

Nathan waggled a brow in response.

31

BATTLE GROUP TRIDENT reached the rendezvous point in six hours. Sean had ordered Captain Martinez and Captain Vargas, COs of the *Dutchman* and *Ajax,* respectively, to check in every four hours using subspace comms only. This limited their communication capability, but it also minimized the risk of being detected by Krake forces. They were still limited to five-minute intervals, but at least they could send data packages across the link if needed. There hadn't been time to do significant load testing, so Sean didn't know what the upper limits of the subspace communication link actually were.

He was sitting in the command chair on the bridge when an alert appeared on his personal holoscreen, indicating that his senior officers had assembled in the conference room near the bridge. He closed his console and stood up.

"Lieutenant Russo, you have the con."

"Yes, Colonel, I have the con," she confirmed and took his place in the command chair.

Sean left the bridge and went to the conference room. As he walked in, he saw that Major Shelton and Lieutenant Scott were already there. Oriana was also there but without the other scientists that usually accompanied her to these meetings. The main holoscreen showed the commanding officers of the rest of the battle group, minus the *Dutchman* and the *Ajax*. Since the battle group was in close proximity, they were able to use tight-beam communication, which minimized the risk of any detection from Krake forces even though there were none in the system at the moment. It was a given that it was only a matter of time before the Krake arrived.

"All right, let's get started," Sean said as he sat down. "According to Captain Martinez of the *Dutchman*, the space gate is still quiet."

Leaving the two destroyers to monitor the area while using the asteroid field as camouflage presented a high degree of risk to those ships, but Sean knew the commanding officers were more than up to the task. They understood the risks and how important the objective was. They were to monitor the space gate and report when the Krake forces arrived. Sean needed eyes on that gate, and he'd left the two destroyers there so they'd have a fighting chance of sending word to the battle group if they were discovered.

"I know I'm not the only one who wonders what the Krake response will be to the distress call that went out," Sean said. He saw several of his officers bobbing their heads on the holoscreen. "Some of you may be wondering why I chose to move the battle group out near what would be Sagan's orbit back home. The answer is simple. At some point, Colonel Cross from Phoenix Station will send another probe, which will mean they've finished their space gate. We've missed our scheduled check-in, and I expect they'll be working double time to get it up and running. We'll monitor the space gate in the star system and be ready to send an update to the comms drone that will no doubt come from Phoenix Station."

"Excuse me, Colonel Quinn," Major Brody said. "Given the

issues we have with our targeting capabilities for the space gate, it raises the real possibility that we may never hear from Phoenix Station."

Sean glanced at Oriana. They'd discussed this at length before the meeting. "It is a possibility."

"How long do you intend for us to wait out here?" Brody asked.

"It could be another three to five days before we hear from Phoenix Station; however, we will not be idle. Dr. Evans and her team have been working on the issue, as well as the analysis of the data we extracted from the Krake research base on the moon."

Sean looked at Oriana. "I think this would be a good time for you to give an update, Dr. Evans."

"Thank you, Colonel Quinn," Oriana said. "Nothing in the data that we've recovered sheds any light on the targeting issues we're experiencing. We understand how to send a set of coordinates to the space gate based on the data we have on hand, but for some reason, we continue to have unanticipated results. It's an intricate set of calculations we're struggling to understand. Ultimately, it's alien technology. The heart of the issue is: why doesn't the same set of coordinates work anymore? I think the problem has to do with time. Six months have passed since the *Vigilant* went through the Krake space gate. We also know that the space gate the NEIIS created was somehow linked to the arch on the planet, which activated when the Krake opened a gateway from another universe. The NEIIS were attempting to reverse engineer the space gate. We took that knowledge and combined it with what we learned in the alternate universe. We got the space gate to work, and we also assumed the coordinates would still work." Oriana glanced at Sean for a moment, then continued. "We tried to tweak our calculations, but thus far we've been unable to test our changes to determine whether they'll work. Given the current situation, my recommendation to Colonel Quinn was to wait until after the current crisis has passed before trying the space gate again."

Sean nodded. "I expect that the Krake will send some sort of scouting force here at any time. I don't want to be testing our space gate when they get here." He gestured for Oriana to continue.

"Our analysis of the data from the moon base does indicate a research initiative. We think their goal was to be able to accurately predict every outcome, no matter how extreme. I still have Gabriel helping with the core analysis of that data. At first, the experiments we were able to translate appeared to be almost chaotic in nature. On the surface, it seems ruthlessly scientific. The range of experiments has no set pattern other than what we think was their main objective. We also know the data set that we retrieved is incomplete, as far as we can tell."

Sean watched as the other commanding officers took a few moments to consider what Oriana had said. The more they learned about the Krake, the more of a mystery they became. "The power to accurately predict any outcome is highly valuable. We know from our research into the NEIIS on New Earth that the Krake didn't appear to be interested in conquering them. There was strong evidence of significant manipulation over a long period of time."

Major Shelton cleared her throat. "I just want to be sure I'm understanding this correctly. From a scientific perspective, Dr. Evans, you think the Krake travel from universe to universe attempting to manipulate events to see if they can accurately predict the outcome? Like some bizarre form of fortune-telling?"

"I'll be honest with you, Major Shelton. I don't know what to think about what we've found so far. It seems too soon to make that determination. Even though the evidence we have does support that theory, I wouldn't present it as a fact just yet. We need more information," Oriana said.

Major Shelton looked at Sean. "What do you think, Colonel Quinn?"

"I think that if I could accurately predict an enemy's movements, I would never lose a battle."

Major Shelton considered this for a few moments and then nodded.

"Dr. Evans is correct," Sean continued. "We need to gather more data. We need to do more reconnaissance. That's our main objective, and it hasn't changed, even in light of our current challenges."

Major Brody indicated that he had another question, and Sean nodded for him to speak.

"How is this related to what happened with the escape pods?"

Sean looked at Captain Welch from the destroyer *Albany* on the holoscreen. "Captain, would you share what occurred as you attempted to retrieve the escape pods?"

"Yes, Colonel," Captain Welch said. "We sent out our combat shuttles to retrieve the pods. Once the Krake inside realized what was occurring, they began to initiate a self-destruct sequence."

"Why would they commit suicide?" Brody asked.

"We don't know," Sean said. "The only reason we were able to retrieve any of the escape pods was because the self-destruct mechanism failed in some. Those escape pods are now aboard the Vigilant, and we've moved the prisoners into holding cells where they've been restrained."

"What are you planning to do with them?"

"We're going to interrogate them."

"I figured as much, but do you think they'll be... that they'll give us reliable intel?"

"We're trying to keep them alive as long as possible, and I want to see what they know about the space gates. We *do* know that, based on the ship design, these Krake are not military. They're either scavengers or miners who came here on a routine run for resources. I was initially hoping that they'd be more forthcoming with information, but the fact that they chose to end their lives rather than be captured speaks volumes about who they actually are."

"One more question, if that's all right, Colonel," Brody said.

"Go ahead."

"Assuming we can communicate with the prisoners and they can help us with our targeting problem, what will we do then, Colonel?"

Sean didn't have to look at the other commanding officers to know that the very same question was on all their minds, given their current situation. Brody's question wasn't an audacious challenge to Sean's authority but was merely the voice of the crew, as it were.

"I understand that you're all concerned about our current situation and that the crews of your ships share those concerns. If we can work out our targeting issues, I plan to send an update to Phoenix Station for them to transmit to COMCENT. After that, I intend to continue with our mission, which is to learn what we can about the Krake," Sean said and paused for a moment. "Our mission hasn't changed. We cannot return with the little bit we know now. We need to find out exactly who the Krake are and what they're capable of. Only then can we figure out a way to defeat them. That is our mission, which came straight from the top. I will carry out my orders, and so will you."

"Understood, Colonel," Brody said in a tone that showed he meant it.

The windows surrounding Captain Welch on the holoscreen illuminated on the edges, indicating she wanted to speak.

"Go ahead, Captain Welch."

"We had difficulty communicating with the Krake. I was just wondering how you plan to work around that, Colonel."

"We can't even speak with the NEIIS back home, so I'm not

surprised you had difficulty when your soldiers retrieved the escape pods. I'm going to use the NEIIS translator on the holoscreen interface. We know that the computer system language the NEIIS used was a derivative of the Krake systems. I'm hoping the Krake will recognize those symbols and be able to use them to answer us. Since they're our prisoners, I'm not concerned with giving away the fact that we're quite different from the NEIIS. I'll also have Gabriel record the sessions so we can start putting a phonetic alphabet together to one day speak with them in the more traditional sense."

"Thank you, Colonel," Captain Welch replied.

Sean ended the meeting and told his senior officers to keep their respective crews up to date. They needed to focus on their jobs. That was what they'd trained for. He saw Oriana look at him and turned toward her. "What's on your mind?"

"When you question the Krake, do you want me to come with you?"

Sean almost thought she sounded a bit concerned but resisted the urge to tease her. They were under enough stress. "I wouldn't want to risk it. You can be the voice in my ear and observe from a place of safety."

"I understand, and I'll prepare a visualization of the calculations we're using for the space gate interface so you can show it to them. It shouldn't take that long. Are you going to question the Krake personally?" Oriana asked.

She was concerned, and Sean felt his lips curve upward just a little bit. "Yes, I am. I need to look them in the eyes to get a feel for who they are. Any insight I can get by meeting with them face-to-face is only going to help us in the long run."

"Understood, Colonel. If you'll excuse me, I'll get those ready."

"I would appreciate that," Sean said.

Oriana left the conference room, and he was alone with Major Shelton.

"Colonel, I hope you're going in there armed."

Sean smiled. "Of course. Me and a squad of Spec Ops soldiers. I'm not worried about what the Krake will do to me in there."

Major Shelton nodded. "I can see that, Colonel. It's just that, given what we've learned about them, they seem kind of rigid."

"What do you mean?"

"If they *are* obsessed with being able to accurately predict any outcome, perhaps the Krake in the escape pods determined that they were going to die anyway and simply chose to end their lives as soon as possible."

Sean thought about it for a moment and nodded. "That makes sense, and I agree it is troubling. We'll take every precaution to keep them alive, but it definitely does shed some light on who we're dealing with."

They left the conference room, with Major Shelton heading for the bridge and Sean went to the holding cells. He'd been anxious to go there as soon as the Krake were brought aboard, but he'd had to meet with his senior officers first. Now that that was out of the way, he could at last look his enemy in the eye.

32

THE HOLDING cells were in a storage area away from critical ship systems. When Sean had ordered the cells to be set up, he'd anticipated having more prisoners than the number that actually arrived.

Boseman met him outside the holding area with Sergeant Benton at his side.

"How many prisoners are there?" Sean asked.

"There are six left now," Boseman replied.

Sean blinked his eyes. "Fourteen of them took their own lives before we could stop them?"

"Affirmative, Colonel," Boseman said and gave a slight shake of his head. "We have them separated and restrained."

Sean frowned and looked at the aisle of empty holding cells. There were soldiers posted at each of the cells containing Krake prisoners.

"Gabriel, have you been monitoring their vital signs?" Sean asked.

"Since they were forced from their escape pods, Colonel."

"Is there anything I should be aware of?"

"While there are some similarities in physical appearance to that of an NEIIS, they would be classified as a separate evolutionary line as their genetic profile is a bit different. Using the Stolzmann biological classification system, they would be considered a separate species."

Sean exhaled through his nose. "Understood. Keep an eye on them and alert me of any critical developments. Otherwise, I just want you to observe our interaction with them. Is that clear, Gabriel?"

"Crystal clear, Colonel Quinn."

Sean looked at Boseman. "How did fourteen Krake prisoners die?"

"It was the craziest thing I've ever seen. Once they were in their cells, they just started dropping to the floor—dead. It was part of their suit computers. A shock to the heart. We were able to get to the others using our stunners, which prevented their suits from working. We removed their envirosuits and restrained them."

Sean walked up to the nearest holding cell that had a CDF soldier standing guard. There was an active holoscreen on the door that showed the interior of the cell. A Krake was sitting in a large chair. Thick metallic bands held its wrists to the arms of the chair, and similar bands were at the its feet and torso. The magnetic bindings were active, locking the prisoner in place. Unless the Krake could rend battle steel alloy, there was no way it was going to move. There was even a collar around its neck that held its head securely in place.

"Open the door," Sean said.

The soldier opened the door, and Sean stepped inside. Boseman and Benton followed.

The Krake's pale blue eyes had vertical irises and were set more forward on its face than on the NEIIS'. Its cobalt skin had dark gray streaks, making it almost shimmer in the light. Broad tentacles hung from both sides of its mouth.

The Krake's eyes flicked toward Sean, and it appeared as if the creature was glaring at him, but he couldn't be sure because it hadn't made any outward show of aggression. Regardless of what the Krake was thinking, Sean wasn't intimidated. If they were anything like the NEIIS, they respected a certain amount of posturing.

Sean stepped closer to the Krake. He then walked to the side and around the chair until he came to stand in front of it again. The Krake's eyes tracked him as far as they could.

Sean used his implants to disable the magnetic lock around the Krake's neck. The creature's head bobbed forward for a moment at the sudden freedom, and it drew in a deep breath. Sean powered on the holoscreen on the wall and gestured toward it. The NEIIS translator software was already preloaded into the interface.

"Why did you come here?" Sean asked.

A series of NEIIS symbols scrolled across the holoscreen. Sean made a swiping gesture and sent the holoscreen to hover near the Krake's face. The Krake seemed to consider the message for a few moments before the screen split in half. One side of the screen was blank, and a series of NEIIS symbols appeared on a holographic interface below it. Sean sent the release signal for one of the Krake's wrists.

Sean repeated his question and the NEIIS translation flashed for a moment, snatching the Krake's attention. Sean then gestured toward the holographic interface.

The Krake reached out, seemingly comfortable with a holographic interface, confirming that they were already familiar with this type of technology. It swiped through the different options for NEIIS words until it found one and selected it.

"Resource acquisition."

"Why did the other Krake prisoners kill themselves?"

Sean knew the NEIIS translation wouldn't be an exact match,

but it should convey the meaning enough for the Krake to understand. At least he hoped so.

The Krake didn't respond.

Sean stepped closer and repeated his question.

"We are already dead."

Sean frowned. "Gabriel, is this translation correct?"

"Affirmative, Colonel."

Sean pressed his lips together for a moment and then used his implants to bring up the video feeds of the other holding cells. The other Krake sat in chairs similar to the one in this holding cell and they were all clearly alive. Sean looked at the Krake. "Not dead."

Sean killed the video feeds and they disappeared.

The Krake did not respond.

"Who did you call for help?"

"We did not call for help. An alert was sent. That is all."

"Are there more of you coming?"

The Krake simply looked away.

Sean decided to change his tactics and brought up an image of the space gate along with the targeting calculation Oriana had given him to share. They'd gotten it from the Krake space gate. "We got this from one of the other prisoners. Do you know where it goes?"

The Krake turned its gaze toward him and sneered.

Sean pulled out his pistol and pointed it at the Krake prisoner. The Krake jabbed his long finger at a symbol on the interface and leaned his head forward. "Death."

Sean wasn't going to shoot him. He'd been foolish to pull out his weapon, and he holstered it.

"All calculations indicate that death is inevitable. You will learn nothing from any of us."

Sean sneered in disgust and reengaged the Krake's restraints.

Then he accessed the chair controls and the chair straightened so the Krake was forced to its feet.

"Death is the coward's way out. You might not want to speak with us, but some of the others do. Why don't you think about that for a while?"

Sean waited a few moments for the Krake to read the NEIIS symbols, then powered off the holoscreen and left the room.

As soon as the door was shut, Boseman blew out a harsh breath, shaking his head in dismay. "It's like they don't care about anything. They've already made up their minds about how this is going to turn out. Makes it hard to find their pain points."

"I didn't expect that they'd be so rigid. They had no weapons on the escape pods. This wasn't even a soldier."

"Why did you tell him the other ones were cooperating?"

Sean shrugged. "I'm trying to keep them off-balance. I thought he reacted to it the first time, so why not let him stew a little?"

"Colonel Quinn," Gabriel said. "I can confirm that the Krake's vital signs did elevate when you mentioned that the others had cooperated with you."

Sean looked at Boseman. "Maybe they're not as rigid as they seem to be."

"If you ask me, I'd say he didn't like using that interface."

"What do you mean?"

"It was more than just the inconvenience of having to enter his reply. Once you turned the translator on and he realized they were NEIIS symbols... I just had the impression he didn't approve."

Sean tried to remember the Krake's reaction to the translator, but it could have just been that the Krake didn't like being held prisoner. Who does? "I'll keep that in mind."

"Colonel Quinn," Gabriel said. "Your presence is requested on the bridge."

"I'll be right there," Sean said and looked at Boseman. "Can you take over with the others? Just ask them a few questions to see if their answers are any different than what we already have."

"Of course, Colonel, but I'm hardly qualified to interrogate anyone."

"Neither am I. I'm kinda making this up as I go along. I don't want them harmed, but I don't want them comfortable either."

"Understood, Colonel."

Sean left the holding cell area and headed for the bridge. It took him almost ten minutes to reach the bridge, where he headed for the command area.

Major Shelton saw him coming. "Colonel Quinn, we received word from the *Dutchman* that several Krake ships have arrived. Five ships in all—three destroyer class vessels and two larger vessels that we're designating as cruiser class. Communication from the *Dutchman* was through subspace, and they're waiting for orders."

"Were the *Dutchman* or the *Ajax* detected?"

"Negative, Colonel. They transmitted passive scan data and essentially an optical feed of the ships traversing through the space gate."

"Put it on the main holoscreen."

A moment later the scanner data with an image of the Krake warships appeared on the main holoscreen.

"Colonel," Specialist Sansky said, "I'm receiving another update from the *Dutchman*. The Krake attack force has divided into two groups. Two of their ships have changed course and are heading toward the planet, while the others are canvassing the asteroid belt. Captain Martinez believes they're looking for the salvage ship wreckage."

Sean's lips formed a thin line. He knew the *Dutchman* and the *Ajax* were using the asteroid field as cover, giving them some natural camouflage, but he wasn't sure how long it would last. He looked at Shelton. "What do you think, Major?"

"I don't know how much time the *Dutchman* and the *Ajax* have. If we were responding to a distress beacon, we'd be looking for wreckage. I believe they'll concentrate their search on the wreckage and try to piece together what happened."

"That's what I think as well. They'll put together that their ships were attacked and that we could still be in the area," Sean said and glanced at the main holoscreen for a moment. "We need to draw them out."

"You mean lay a trap?" Major Shelton asked.

"That's exactly what I mean. They split their forces. Let's test their response. We draw them out here and disable their ships. All I need is one of them left intact to determine how they use the space gate."

"What about our prisoners?"

"I don't think they're going to be much help."

Sean could tell that Major Shelton had other questions regarding the prisoners but was smart enough not to bring them up on the bridge.

"Do you think the Krake would be interested in getting their people back?" Major Shelton asked instead.

Sean shook his head. "No, I don't."

"Understood, Colonel."

"Tactical, set Condition Two throughout the ship."

The announcement was made throughout the ship and the battle group.

"How do you plan to lure them out here?" Major Shelton asked.

"We think they're looking for wreckage, so I'm thinking the escape pod transmitters would make a good lure. Don't you?"

Major Shelton nodded.

"Comms, send this update to the *Dutchman* and the *Ajax*. They are to hold their positions unless detected. We're formulating an attack plan. Details forthcoming. Continue to monitor the space gate and the Krake ships on passive."

"Yes, Colonel, the message has been sent," Specialist Sansky said.

The *Vigilant* was the flagship for the battle group, and as such, they had double occupancy for certain key workstations. They would need all of them to engage the Krake. Sean had superior numbers in terms of ships, but firepower would possibly be an issue. He had to use the element of surprise. It was the only way they could achieve their objective, which was to take one of those ships intact.

Sean looked at Major Shelton. "Let's get started."

33

"COLONEL QUINN," Specialist Sansky said, "the *Yorktown* has checked in. Space gate is on standby."

"Acknowledged," Sean replied.

Since he was taking the *Vigilant* into a hot zone, he'd decided that the best way to protect their only means of escaping this universe was to leave their space gate behind, along with the *Yorktown*. The converted freighter was their carrier vessel for the Talon-Vs he had deployed.

In order to lure the Krake into his trap, Sean had to move the battle group closer to the ice planet. The enemy's escape pods were put on a trajectory that took them away from the asteroid field and nearer the planet.

Sean's gaze swept across the bridge from his command chair. They were fully staffed, with reserves on standby. The crew of the *Vigilant* wore envirosuits with their helmets retracted into small storage containers below the necks. The envirosuits were light-duty spacesuits that were invaluable to any member of the crew who found themselves in a part of the ship experiencing a sudden loss of atmospheric pressure. They were equipped with micro-thrusters and mag-boots, and carried a twenty-four hour supply of oxygen. Given what they were about to do, it was a necessary precaution. It was one thing to suddenly have a battle thrust upon them, which was what they'd faced over six months ago; it was quite another thing to know they were going into conflict with a highly capable enemy force.

Sean felt a quiet increase in tension on the bridge—a build-up of anticipation depicted in the subtle fidgeting by some members of the crew that resulted in them checking and rechecking the data feeds on the main holoscreen. There was a single-minded determination to make sure everything that could be done was being done. He'd experienced the same thing when preparing for the Vemus invasion. Even though the circumstances were quite different, the familiar sense of anticipation was the same, manifesting as a tingling in the back of the mind, knowing they were about to do something extremely dangerous.

"Colonel," Lieutenant Russo said, "Captain Williams has confirmed that the package has been delivered. Combat shuttle squadron Shadowhawks are on their way back to the *Douglass*."

"Understood," Sean replied and watched the data on the main holoscreen refresh with the escape pods' locations.

Since they weren't using active scans, they were reliant upon less exact means of determining enemy ship positions. The Trident Battle Group had been deployed and was waiting to ambush the Krake. When they came to investigate their escape pods, he would spring the trap. Surprise and speed were their greatest weapons. Sean intended to strike a crippling blow to the Krake ships, which would severely limit any counterattack they could muster.

Oriana sat to his left at the science officer's workstation. This wasn't the first time she'd seen battle, but she looked a little pale. She caught sight of him looking at her and smoothed her features.

"I wish I could've figured out the targeting so we wouldn't need to do this," Oriana said.

"You will, and we're going to help you do it," Sean replied. Using the space gate to travel to another universe had proven to be more difficult than they'd initially thought, Sean included. It wasn't her fault, and Sean tried to tell her that.

He and the rest of the senior officers understood that they needed to engage the Krake, since this was an opportunity to gain credible intel on their enemy. And more than half the effort of fighting a battle was the preparation that occurred before the first shot was fired. They were playing a game of cat and mouse. The Krake seemed to be playing this game also but a bit on the reckless side, and that alone was insightful. They were responding to a distress beacon from scavenger ships, and by now they'd had enough time to analyze the remains of the ships Sean had destroyed. There was a clear and present danger, yet no ship in the entire battle group had detected any type of active scan from the Krake ships. Maybe they weren't being reckless, Sean thought, trying to limit his assumptions when devising his strategy to engage the enemy. They knew so little about the Krake, and it was important that he not let certain biases cloud his judgment.

The Krake ships were still on the fringes of the asteroid field near the ice planet's farthest moon, and the wreckage of the scavenger ships was nearby. The combat shuttles had returned to the *Douglass*. Sean had deployed the battle group in a formation that resembled an open maw, with the *Vigilant* on one side and the *Douglass* on the other. Their destroyers were dispersed between them, and they remained far enough away that the Krake wouldn't be able to detect them unless they began using active scans. If they did, Sean could close the trap relatively quickly. The missile tubes on all ships were loaded with HADES V missiles, and Talon-V Lancer and Stinger squadrons were deployed amid the ships with a mission to protect them from Krake attack drones. Talon-V Storm class squadrons would remain in reserve until an opportunity presented itself for them to storm an enemy ship. They didn't know what else the Krake had in their arsenal because nothing else had been used against them in their previous engagement. The attack drones were vulnerable to railgun armament at any stage of activation but resistant to point defense lasers when in combat mode.

"Lieutenant Russo," Sean said, "activate the Krake escape pod distress beacon."

"Yes, Colonel. Activating escape pod distress beacon now."

"Acknowledged," Sean said.

He heard Specialist Sansky record an update for the battle group. They couldn't do single broadcasts through subspace comlinks, but they could open multiple individual channels to each of the ships and send the same data through. The upper right corner of the main holoscreen showed Condition One readiness throughout the *Vigilant* and the entire battle group.

"Captain Vargas from the *Ajax* reports the Krake ships are on the move, Colonel," Specialist Sansky said.

Major Shelton looked at Sean. "They took the bait."

Sean nodded and resisted the urge to cross his arms in front of his chest. He wanted to stand up and disperse some of his excess energy, but he didn't. "Tactical, can you confirm Krake ship positions?"

"Tracking, Colonel," Lieutenant Russo said and initialized a passive scan sweep. "Confirm that the Krake ships are on an intercept course with the escape pods. Relative velocity is within known Krake ship capabilities."

Krake ships were fast. It was theorized that their ships were powered by a reactors that utilized the Casimir effect. The generation of vacuum energy had long been sought after as a method of power creation and had stymied scientists since it had first been theorized. Essentially, a Casimir reactor was more efficient and powerful than their own fusion reactors.

Over the next thirty minutes, Sean watched as the three Krake ships closed in on the escape pods. One of them, a destroyer class, sped ahead of the others. The front of the ship had an elongated oval shape that seemed to maintain consistent form toward the stern. The light brown hull had accents of dark brown, outlining sections at the front, and the overall design was sleek and symmetrical. Even the large, heavy-cruiser-class ship seemed to be a bigger version of the destroyer.

Sean didn't want to make any assumptions where Krake ship capabilities were concerned, especially with an unknown vessel like the heavy cruiser. Warships were constructed for a specific purpose, and just because the outward appearance of the two ship classes were the same didn't at all indicate that they possessed similar capabilities but on a grander scale.

Sean drew in a deep breath and exhaled.

"Tactical, execute firing solution Alpha."

Targeting priorities had been previously assigned to the battle group. There were specific ships with high-value target locations, such as the engines and known attack drone launch tubes. They'd encountered Krake destroyer class vessels before, but the cruiser class was something different. Firing solution Alpha would hit the cruiser hard.

With subspace communication capabilities, the Trident Battle Group was able to communicate in real time. Whether or not the Krake could detect subspace communication was unknown; however, they'd achieved a level of coordination previously unheard of in any human military throughout history.

HADES V missiles launched from the *Vigilant* and the *Douglass* at precisely the same time. The six destroyers wouldn't fire their salvo until the next wave.

"Active scan pulses detected, Colonel," Lieutenant Russo said.

"Ops, go active scan," Sean said.

The HADES Vs sped to their targets, and Sean's gut clenched as he urged them onward. The trap had been sprung.

CAPTAIN OLIVIER MARTINEZ of the CDF destroyer *Dutchman* shifted in his command chair. After years of training and running simulated battles, he found himself on the sidelines, and it sucked. He understood the importance of his mission, but he wanted to fight with the battle group against the Krake. They'd been in prime tactical position, virtually undetected by the enemy. Instead, the *Dutchman* was hidden near an asteroid for the purposes of monitoring the Krake space gate. At least they weren't completely in the dark about what was happening, thanks to the subspace communicator they had. He had to admit, when they'd first been deployed with its limited-use capabilities, he never would've thought he would come to rely upon it so much. The subspace communicator had been a bit of a joke at Phoenix Station. Five-minute intervals for comms wasn't a huge gain, and they sometimes lost the subspace comms link after a hundred and twenty seconds. Yet here he was, supremely appreciative that they had the device aboard their ship.

"Captain, I'm detecting a power spike from the Krake space gate," Lieutenant Sandeep Harish said from the tactical workstation.

Martinez looked up in alarm. "On screen."

The main holoscreen showed a video feed of the Krake space gate. The only visual signs that the gate was active were the glowing points near the edges. The visual beyond the space gate looked the same as it had before. A few moments later, a dark shadow loomed into view like a leviathan emerging from the gloomy depths.

Martinez' stomach sank and the breath caught in his throat as a succession of Krake warships began to emerge through the space gate. The crew on the bridge of the *Dutchman* went silent, watching as one Krake warship after another and sped off toward the battle.

"Tactical, I need an accurate count of how many enemy ships are coming through. Comms, alert Colonel Quinn that they have enemy ships heading their way," Olivier said.

His orders were confirmed, and the bridge crew snapped out of shock and went to work.

"Fifteen Krake destroyers came through the space gate. The gate is still active, but no more ships have come through, Captain," Lieutenant Harish said.

It had all happened so fast, and Olivier's thoughts raced. He briefly considered disabling the space gate but then discarded the idea. The Krake forces were already here, and the CDF battle group was in trouble. Olivier's mouth compressed to a grim line.

"Tactical, I need a firing solution on those ships. We need to draw them away from the battle group," Olivier said.

"Yes... yes, Captain."

Olivier heard the catch in his tactical officer's voice. Engaging the Krake forces to draw them off the battle group would expose them. With their own space gate so far away, there was very little chance that either the *Dutchman* or the *Ajax* would reach the rendezvous point.

Olivier stood up. "Stay focused. I know it looks grim, but we have a job to do."

The bridge crew went back to their tasks.

"Comms, open a comlink to *Ajax* actual. I need to speak to Captain Vargas."

THE HEAVY ARMORED plating at the tip of the HADES V missile was designed for penetrating deeply into the hulls of enemy ships. And even though the scans and reports confirmed that they'd taken the enemy completely by surprise, they'd still been able to launch their dreaded attack drones. This was why Sean had rotated missile salvo deployment among his destroyers. The combat suite AI coordinated the detonation of the HADES V missiles to both blind the Krake attack drones and then destroy them. The Krake heavy cruiser was a hulking wreck, broken apart, leaving the two Krake destroyers to engage the battle group.

The two Krake warships broke formation and went on an intercept course for the *Vigilant* and the *Douglass*. Even with limited engine capacity, the Krake destroyers were still closing in fast.

"Colonel, I have an Alpha priority message from the *Dutchman*. Fifteen Krake warships have come through the space gate and are heading in our direction," Specialist Sansky said, his voice rising at the end of this disclosure.

Sean frowned. "Say again, Specialist."

"Fifteen Krake warships have come through the space gate. The Krake cruiser and destroyer vessels that were surveying the planet are also on an intercept course, but they'll arrive after the others, Colonel."

Sean looked at the PRADIS output and saw new enemy marks appear on the plot. His brows pulled together, and his nostrils flared. Seventeen Krake warships were coming right for them.

He noted the location of the two closest Krake destroyers and did a quick calculation in his head. His lips curled in disgust. They wouldn't have time to board either destroyer, and there was no chance for them to collect any usable intel to operate the space gates. This mission was a bust.

Seventeen fully operational enemy ships were heading towards them, but their surprise attack had left the CDF battle group entirely unscathed. His mind raced as he tried to come up with a course of action that wouldn't end in their own destruction. How had the tables turned so quickly? He glanced at Major Shelton and could see that she'd arrived at a similar conclusion. They had no other choice.

Sean glared at the main holoscreen, focusing on the two Krake destroyers nearby. "Tactical, I want a firing solution to take out those two ships. Light them up." He walked back to the command chair and sat down. "Ops, send out orders for the battle group to retreat to the space gate. Comms, alert Major McKay on the *Yorktown* to bring up our space gate ASAP. We are coming in hot."

His orders were confirmed.

"Ops, inform Talon-V Stormer squadron commanders to board the nearest ship for transition through the gate. The rest are on escort duty."

Sean felt hollow inside. They hadn't even detected a space gate signal calling for reinforcements, and he was kicking himself for not having thought of it. Unless... He frowned in thought. Unless there hadn't been a call for reinforcements. This whole thing might have been part of the Krake strategy to get Sean to reveal himself. He shook his head slightly and opened a comlink to the *Douglass*.

"Major Brody, I want you to head to the space gate ahead of the group and take over the power tap from the *Yorktown*. The carrier doesn't stand a chance on this side of the gate."

"Understood, Colonel," Brody said. "May I ask where the *Vigilant* will be during the retreat?"

"We'll be buying you as much time as we can. I'm going to have the *Dutchman* and the *Ajax* attack the Krake forces from behind. It should stall their approach."

"Colonel, there's no way the *Vigilant* can take on that many ships for long. They'll simply divide their forces and come for us. We have to retreat to our gate together."

Sean clenched his teeth. He was about to do the one thing he'd hoped he would never have to do. He looked at Major Brody and nodded. "We won't be far behind. You have your orders, Major Brody."

Sean closed the comlink and recorded a message for Captain Martinez and Captain Vargas. He laid out their roles in their retreat and hated himself for it. The two CDF ships monitoring the Krake space gate had even less of a chance of surviving than the *Vigilant* had.

"Excuse me, Colonel," Oriana said.

Her voice pierced through his thoughts, and Sean grimaced. As he turned toward her, she almost flinched. He was about to order the almost certain death of two destroyer crews. "What is it?" he said harshly.

"The report from the *Dutchman* indicates that the Krake space gate is still active."

"Get to the point, Dr. Evans."

Oriana met his gaze. "The *Dutchman* and the *Ajax* can use the Krake space gate to escape. I don't know what they'll find on the other side, but it's better than remaining here. Wouldn't you agree, Colonel?"

Sean drew in a hasty breath. "The space gate is already open, and it's one way. How the hell would they—" Sean's eyes widened as he finally understood what Oriana was saying, and he smiled. "Thank you, Dr. Evans!"

He turned away from her and began recording a new set of orders for the two CDF destroyers. In the void, some chance was better than no chance at all.

"We could use the same coordinates with our own space gate and meet them on the other side," Oriana said.

Sean sent updated orders to the *Douglass*.

Retreating from a superior enemy force was almost as much of a challenge as committing to a battle in the first place, probably more so since they were now retreating through their own space gate. It wasn't as simple as ordering "all full ahead" and "run your ass off." They had to quite literally thread the needle.

The *Douglass* fired a salvo of HADES V missiles, which command and control was handing off to the *Vigilant*. Sean had placed the *Vigilant* in the center of the battle group, with three destroyers on either side of him as they made their withdrawal. The Krake attack force swooped towards them, led by hundreds of glowing attack drones.

"Gabriel, will the attack drones reach us before we go through the space gate?" Sean asked.

"Affirmative, Colonel. There is a ninety percent certainty that the attack drones will pierce our missile screen and reach the battle group."

He had to do something to decrease that margin. "Major Shelton, order the destroyer escort to increase velocity by thirty percent. Helm, steady as she goes."

The CDF heavy cruiser had more combat capabilities than its destroyer escort, and he needed to give the battle group time to transition through the space gate. The only problem was that the *Vigilant* was going to have to bear the brunt of the Krake attack while they did it. Even if he did make it to the space gate, he still needed time for the *Douglass* to make it through.

"Colonel, destroyer escorts have increased their velocity," Major Shelton said.

"Acknowledged, Major. Now I need you to go to the secondary bridge."

"At once, Colonel," Major Shelton said and ran off the bridge.

CDF heavy cruisers had two command bridges. The secondary bridge was in another location to provide backup in case the primary bridge was damaged. Sean was playing the odds as best he could.

"Colonel Quinn, the *Dutchman* and the *Ajax* have engaged Krake forces," Lieutenant Russo said.

The two destroyers would fire their salvos as quickly as possible, bringing to bear the full armament of which they were capable.

"Acknowledged," Sean replied.

Even if part of the Krake attack force broke away, there were still more than enough ships for them to engage the battle group. Sean glanced at the battle group status on his personal holoscreen. The *Yorktown* was grayed out on the display. It had transitioned through the space gate.

"Come on," Sean said quietly.

"Krake attack drones have penetrated through the missile defense screen. I also have confirmed detonations of HADES Vs on enemy ships, Colonel," Lieutenant Russo said.

As the Krake attack drones rushed toward them, the *Vigilant's* mag cannons functioned at a near constant rate of fire in tandem with point defense lasers. The point defense lasers had little effect on the Krake attack drones by themselves, but when they were hit by the mag cannons, it caused them to become vulnerable.

"Power draw reaching critical levels, Colonel," Lieutenant Burrows said.

"Acknowledged," Sean said.

There was nothing Sean could do. Gabriel would reroute power as best he could to bolster their defenses.

The Krake attack drones changed formation. Instead of a moving wall of glowing death heading toward them, they spiraled, forming several long columns lancing toward them. The effect was almost immediate. The attack drones were pushing past their defenses.

"Go to individual life support," Sean ordered.

Automatic helmets came on and the bridge crew were already in their EVA suits. Sean glanced at the battle group ship status and saw that the destroyer names were quickly graying out on the screen.

"Tactical, launch HORNET II missiles targeting the heads of those columns. We might be able to stall their attack and give us time to get within the *Douglass's* point defense range."

The mid-range missiles carried a lighter payload but were excellent for quick precision strikes.

"Missiles away, Colonel," Lieutenant Russo said.

The video feed on the main holoscreen flashed as the attack drone's advance was momentarily pushed back. Then they regrouped. Glowing columns of drones spiraled around, splitting into even smaller groups and pushing closer to the *Vigilant*. Klaxon alarms blared as they penetrated the hull. A visual of the space gate was on the main holoscreen. Somehow, they stayed on course. Sean knew the *Douglass* was unleashing its armament as best it could, but it was at half capacity because they were powering the space gate.

"Transition in five," Gabriel said and continued to count down.

The *Vigilant's* combat computers targeted the nearest attack drones and focused their fire. The *Douglass* would need every second if it was going to make it through the space gate.

The *Vigilant* passed through the gate, along with any Krake attack drones in the vicinity, and the automated ship defenses ceased firing so they wouldn't damage the gate.

"Colonel," Lieutenant Russo said, "I'm showing the attack drones have gone offline. They're dormant."

A video feed came to prominence on the main holoscreen, and Sean saw the attack drones lose power. It was like watching the end of a power cycle as the glowing drones suddenly became dim and lifeless.

"Show me the space gate," Sean said.

They couldn't actually see the gate, but they could see the area of space where the battle raged on. The *Douglass* was transitioning through the gate, stern side first. The glowing engine pods slightly diminished as maneuvering thrusters from the bow of the ship struggled to push it through quickly. When the *Douglass* was halfway through, Sean saw the gateway expand.

"Detecting a buildup of gamma radiation," Lieutenant Burrows said.

Sean had only seen a recording of when they'd transitioned through the space gate. There was an immense buildup of power, and he heard Oriana gasp.

"It's out of alignment. The space gate is out of alignment," Oriana said.

There was a bright flash of light that blinded them for a moment and the *Vigilant's* sensor array cycled to reset, which it did automatically in the presence of an intense energy burst.

"Damage report," Sean said.

"Sensors are still offline. They're cycling. We have hull breaches on decks five through eighteen. Automatic bulkhead doors have sealed off the damaged areas of the ship. Waiting on other critical systems," Lieutenant Burrows said.

They'd pushed the combat capabilities of the *Vigilant* to the limit and beyond. It was a miracle the ship was still in one piece.

"Comms, try to reach the *Douglass*," Sean said.

"I get no response, Colonel," Specialist Sansky replied.

"Tactical, can we get a visual of the *Douglass*?"

A few moments later an image appeared on the main holoscreen. The *Douglass* had rolled onto its side, adrift through space. Sean's eyes widened. More than a third of the ship was simply gone. They were venting atmosphere, and it looked to be barely holding together. The image updated as Gabriel highlighted the space gate machines nearby. There were whole groups of gate machines missing. They wouldn't be going anywhere for a while.

"Ops, begin rescue operations for the *Douglass* immediately. Comms, I want a status report from the other ships..."

34

DASH HAD LEARNED over the years that searching for anything related to the NEIIS was complicated, even when they had a map to their location. Over the hundreds of years the NEIIS had been in stasis, the landscape had changed, and whole cities had been destroyed in a war he didn't know much about.

They'd been searching for the medical cache for almost two days, and Dash knew Captain Jennings' patience was wearing a bit thin. Pretty soon she was going to insist they return to base. For the most part, Captain Jennings kept the soldiers under her command in line; however, Dash was beginning to catch muttered comments about the futility of the mission. The soldiers didn't much care for being around the NEIIS, a fact that Dash was sure Jory was aware of as well. He stayed near Jory, acting as a barrier between the CDF and the NEIIS.

Dash glanced at where Jory sat on a fallen tree. They'd camped in the forest the night before and would be leaving soon. Given the NEIIS physiology, they naturally walked with a bit of a stoop, but Dash wasn't sure that was the only cause. It could also be due to the disease. Cellular degeneration accelerated when the NEIIS came out of stasis.

Specialist Karen Wagner walked over to Dash. "I need to check his vitals."

Karen was one of the few soldiers who was more tolerant of the NEIIS. She seemed to genuinely care whether Jory lived or died, and that kind of compassion made her an excellent medic.

Dash stood up and wiped his hands on his pants. Jory looked over at him and Dash gestured toward Karen. They'd been through this before. She just needed to run a quick scan. Jory stood up and waited for Karen to approach.

The medic brought up a small scanner and held it a foot away from Jory's face. She lowered the scanner, pausing at Jory's chest, and then raised it back toward his head. She then scanned along the NEIIS's arms and turned it off. She looked at Dash. "It's happening faster now."

Dash nodded. "That's how it works. It starts off slowly, and as time goes on, it gets exponentially worse."

Karen looked at Jory. "Thank you."

The translated text appeared on the mobile holoscreen, and Jory sat down.

Karen looked back at Dash. "I just don't understand how this could happen. I heard you mention that it was some form of cellular degenerative disease."

"It has to do with the stasis technology the NEIIS used. We all experience cellular degeneration as we grow older. That's really what it is. They're growing older at an accelerated rate, compounded by the fact that they were in stasis."

"How long will he live?"

"Maybe a few months. In about six weeks he won't be able to walk anymore."

"Oh God, that's horrible."

It's even worse to see, Dash thought to himself.

He heard somebody else walking over and turned to see Stillman give him a friendly wave and then glance at Jory for a moment.

"All done, Specialist?" Stillman asked.

"Yes, Lieutenant. The NEIIS checks out."

"Good. Gather your things because we'll be leaving soon," Stillman said, and when Karen left, he looked at Dash. "If we don't find anything today, Captain Jennings has decided that we'll head back to New Haven to resupply."

"Maybe we'll get lucky then."

Lieutenant Stillman smiled and shrugged. "I now have to say I have more of an appreciation for what you're trying to do than I did before."

Dash arched an eyebrow. "Oh yeah, which part?"

"Searching for these NEIIS settlements. You're able to spot things I would've sworn weren't there."

"It's what I've been doing for the past few years. You just get an eye for it."

Stillman nodded. "Assuming we find something, how do you know whether the NEIIS will be able to identify exactly what we're looking for?" His face assumed a pained expression. "You know what I mean. Was he a doctor or something?"

Dash shook his head. "The translator isn't one hundred percent accurate, so when I've asked him what his job was, it says he was a repairer. That could mean he was something like a maintenance tech, but perhaps he worked with healers."

Stillman frowned. "If the translation isn't accurate, then..."

"I've seen the records that refer to the stasis pods the NEIIS used. They were aware of the issues and were... at least some of them were working on dealing with it."

"Okay, I think I understand. We'll be leaving in fifteen minutes. Did you share the coordinates yet?"

"Yeah, they have it. If it's any consolation, it's south of here, which is almost like being on our way home," Dash said and smiled.

"There's always someone who's going to complain. It's not personal, but if it gets out of line, let me know."

Stillman left him and Dash began gathering his things, communicating to Jory that they were leaving. The NEIIS looked tired. Perhaps it would be best if they just headed back to Camp Alpha. He had to admit that Jory was extremely brave to have come out there with them—either that or he just trusted Dash. It was probably the latter, and Dash hoped he wouldn't let the NEIIS down.

35

DASH SAT near the front of the Hellcat. He had his holoscreen open and was reading through the subject headers of his messages when one caught his eye. It was from Merissa.

Dinner?

Dash opened the message.

Dash, it was so good to see you. I understand you're busy. We all are. But I would love it if we could have dinner when you return to Sanctuary.

Merissa.

He heard a nearby soldier let out a hearty laugh. "Look at that. No, no, I'm serious. Look at Dash."

Dash looked up and saw Compton watching him with a broad grin. Compton used his elbow to snatch the attention of his friend and gave Dash an approving nod. "Only one thing can put a smile like that on a man's face," said Compton.

"What?" Dash asked, unable to banish the smile from his face.

"What?" Compton said, imitating him.

Karen, who was sitting across from them, looked up from her own personal holoscreen.

"What's her name?" Compton asked.

Dash took a breath and chuckled. "Merissa. She's a friend."

Compton repeated her name and smirked toward him. "Come on—a friend? Friends don't put that kind of smile on our faces. What's the deal? Spill it."

A few of the other soldiers urged Dash to speak up, and he noticed that Jory glanced in his direction as well. Even though the NEIIS couldn't understand what they were saying, they always watched.

"She wants to meet for dinner when I get back."

Compton smiled and nodded approvingly. Dash glanced at Karen, who rolled her eyes and grinned.

"We've got our very own Casanova," Compton said.

Dash frowned. "Who?"

"Oh man. You don't know who Casanova was? Let's just say he was a ladies' man. So what are you gonna do? Are you gonna see her?" Compton asked.

Dash glanced at the message on his holoscreen and then powered it off. "Probably, yeah. Do you want to come? I could see if she has a friend," he offered.

Compton held up his hand and shook his head. "No, thank you. I have no problems where that's concerned. I'm just glad to see you're not always working."

Lieutenant Stillman stepped out from the cockpit and looked at Dash. "We need your help."

Dash unbuckled the straps and went with Stillman.

They were above the foothills of the mountain range that could be found across the entire continent. It connected to other mountain ranges, but they were all part of the same system. Dash spotted a small NEIIS city. From their vantage point, they could see shallow depressions in the areas around the city. A long time ago there'd been a battle there. There were remnants of NEIIS buildings—rounded architecture with an extensive network of ramps. The area was surrounded by forest, and a large waterfall could be seen off to the side.

"These are the coordinates. I'm just not sure where we should put down," Captain Jennings said.

Dash studied the main holoscreen for a few moments.

"You think Jory would know?" Jennings asked.

"Probably not. I don't think they traveled that extensively before going into stasis. But he'll be able to help if we find any intact systems down there," Dash replied.

He looked away from the city and back at the waterfall again, following the water down to the end. "Can we zoom in on the bottom of that waterfall, please?"

The pilot did as Dash asked. A scan of the area showed a cave entrance nearby.

"Can you take us down there? I'd like to check that area out."

Jennings frowned. "You don't think the medical cache is in the city?"

Dash flattened his lips for a moment. "I wouldn't rule it out, but the bunkers were sometimes found away from cities—somewhere that had a chance of being overlooked."

Jennings nodded and then ordered the pilot to take them down there.

Dash returned to his seat and told Jory what they'd found. Soon after the Hellcat landed near the river bank, they were walking towards the cave opening.

His gamble paid off. As soon as they were through the entrance, they found a path that led to a NEIIS-made substructure. The NEIIS must have found the cave and made it bigger, hollowing it out years ago. There were several large storage containers throughout the chamber. Some of them were open, and their contents were exposed to the elements.

As they went deeper into the chamber, Jory stumbled but quickly regained his footing and pointed toward the path, which was his way of saying he wanted to keep going. There were several open crevices on the ceiling through which sunlight spilled, bathing the ground in pools of light. Dash was thankful for the enhanced implants that allowed him to see through the darkness between those pools of light, and he knew the CDF soldiers had no problem seeing in the dim light either. He removed the flashlight from his pack and handed it to Jory.

Jory swung the flashlight around and spotted a smaller storage container tucked behind one of the larger ones. They went over to it and saw that it was marked with a partial symbol Dash didn't recognize. Jory used the crank on the side to open the container. He reached inside but was unable to lift what was in there. Knowing that the NEIIS was getting weaker by the day, Dash gestured that he would do it. Inside was an oval-shaped metallic container a meter across, which was heavier than it looked. Dash pulled it out and set it on the ground, but when he moved to open it, Jory stopped him.

Dash brought up the mobile NEIIS translator and activated it.

"This could be it. It has the proper symbols," Jory said.

"I need to open it so we can see what's inside. I can't bring it with us unless we open it," Dash said.

The NEIIS tilted his head to the side, which was their equivalent of a nod.

Several loud moans came from deeper in the cave. Dash's eyes widened, and he looked back at Compton. The soldier had heard it, too, and gestured for Dash to be quiet.

"There's something else here," Compton said on the broadcast comlink.

Dash glanced around. The pathway curved away from them so he couldn't see what was on the other side. Several loud, breathy pants were coming from a large creature. Then something big dropped almost on top of Dash, knocking him into the cave wall.

His MPS activated and prevented him from being hurt by the jagged rocks, but he heard Jory cry out.

"What the hell is it?" Compton cried.

A colossal, lumbering shadow stood over the medical cache and stomped on it. The beast had thick brown fur and an elongated snout, and as it turned toward Dash, it snarled.

Berwolf! It was the size of a grizzly bear but as agile as a wolf.

Dash pulled out his sonic hand blaster and pointed it at the berwolf, then squeezed the trigger. A powerful wave of kinetic energy slammed into the creature, and it howled in pain, stumbling away from them. Dash regained his feet, went over to Jory, and shouted for the others, telling them what it was. He helped Jory to his feet and grabbed the medical cache. The berwolf was stumbling around, disoriented from the sonic blast, but Dash heard other berwolves in the area.

Compton yelled for Dash to follow him, so he urged Jory behind him and kept his weapon ready while dragging the medical cache with them. There were so many distinct growls occurring at the same time that Dash had no idea how many berwolves were in the cave. They kept running amid the storage crates as the CDF soldiers struggled to shoot them.

Dash heard Captain Jennings shouting orders, and a screeching, high-pitched alarm sounded throughout the cavern. Dash flinched, dropping the container and covering his ears. Jory did the same. The berwolves went quiet and seemed to disappear.

The screeching stopped.

"Don't move," a loud voice said from a speaker on a comms drone hovering above them. "If any of you try anything, I'll invite my berwolves back inside."

Dash saw Compton swing his weapon around, trying to find a target. A shot rang out and made a small crater in the rock wall just behind him.

"That was a warning. We have you surrounded."

The voice sounded artificially deep due to the use of a synthesizer to protect the identity of the speaker.

"I am Captain Vera Jennings of the Colonial Defense Force. To whom am I speaking?"

"I'm not your enemy, Captain Jennings. The real enemy is already among you."

It all clicked into place for Dash, and he waved to Captain Jennings. "It's Lars Mallory," he said and looked up at the comms drone. "Drop the act, Lars. I know it's you."

The comms drone swung around, and Dash knew the camera was pointed at him.

"Mr. DeWitt, how nice to see you again."

"Why don't you come on down here?" Dash said with a sneer.

Lars laughed. "I don't need to. We have the high ground and superior numbers, as Captain Jennings already knows. I wasn't kidding when I said I'm not your enemy, and I know CDF ROE prevents you from engaging with colonists."

"We will defend ourselves, Mr. Mallory," Captain Jennings said.

"I don't want to hurt any of you. I just want what's in the case," Lars said.

Dash stepped in front of the medical cache, and Jory moved to his side.

"Don't be stupid. The NEIIS are not your friends."

"I have a job to do, Mr. Mallory. If you and your men attack us, we will use deadly force," Captain Jennings said.

Dash used his implants to access the comms drone, then activated one of the programs Noah had shown him for secure systems. He couldn't take control of the comms drone, but he could list all the comlinks currently connected to it. Lars wasn't lying. He had over fifty men in this cavern with him. Somehow, he could command berwolves, too.

Dash's stomach turned over. They were in trouble, and he

desperately searched for something he could do. "So what's your plan? Are you just going to kill us?" Dash asked.

"You know we don't harm colonists," Lars said.

"Tell that to Noah."

Lars ignored him. "NEIIS, on the other hand…"

Several red dots appeared on Jory's chest, and Dash used his body to shield the NEIIS. The red dots were now on his chest.

"This is pointless. The NEIIS are not your friends. You don't know what I know. They will betray you all," Lars said.

"I've heard this all before. Where have you been for the last six months? And if you know so much, why don't you tell us all about it? We can go to Sierra right now," Dash said.

"What makes you think I'd be welcome in Sierra?"

Dash glanced at Jory and saw another crimson dot appear on the side of his head. He shoved the NEIIS back.

"Captain," Compton said over the team comlink, "he's not bluffing. I've got over fifty of them. They're above us."

"Stop this, Lars. We need the NEIIS to help us fight the Krake," Dash said.

"The NEIIS had their shot, and they failed."

"They didn't fail. They're still here. They need our help and we need theirs."

"On that, we'll have to disagr—"

"Do you know what we're doing here? Do you know what we're trying to find?" Dash asked, cutting Lars off.

"It doesn't really matter."

"That's where you're wrong, Lars. He's dying. You don't need to kill him because he'll be dead in a few months anyway. We're out here looking for medicinals that the NEIIS stored."

"Why should I care about that? All the more reason to stop you."

"Do you know what happens to them when they come out of stasis? Do you know about the rapid aging?"

"I do, but it's not fast enough."

"I read the records. They were using what's in that container to combat the disease. There are a lot of R&D folks who want to study it. This might actually help the colony."

"We don't need their help."

"Damn it, Lars. If you could just ease off the trigger finger for five minutes, you might understand what I'm trying to tell you. Your friend has been lying in a coma for the past six months, and it's all your damn fault. Yet the contents of this storage case might actually help him. If you destroy it, you'll have killed Noah... again." Dash paused for a moment. "Isn't it worth a shot at least? The chance to help Noah? I saw you. I saw the look on your face when he got hurt, and I know you didn't mean to hurt him," he said and breathed deeply. He picked up the container. "I'm gonna take this case and walk out of here. If you want to stop me, you're gonna have to kill me."

Dash swallowed hard and stepped away from the rock wall, gesturing for Jory to follow him. A few of the CDF soldiers glanced at him but most kept their attention above them. Dash walked out from cover. His legs shook, and he felt that at any moment he was about to die, despite Lars saying he didn't want to hurt any colonists.

He glanced up at the comms drone and kept moving. Compton stayed by his side, and the other CDF soldiers gathered around him.

The comms drone sped toward Dash, stopping just above his head. Dash froze.

"This is a onetime pass. Take it and go."

Dash heard the sneer in Lars's voice. He glared at the comms drone and backed away from it. He wished he could've met Lars face-to-face. How he hated that man!

Compton whispered to him to get moving, and they beat a hasty retreat out of the cave. Dash kept looking behind them and saw the comms drone hovering in the air, and he knew that Lars was watching them.

They climbed back into the Hellcat and left.

Captain Jennings came over to Dash. "How did you know it was him?"

"If I told you I was guessing, would you be angry?"

Jennings tilted her head to the side. "Remind me never to play poker with you. I'll need to put this all in my report. I'm sure General Gates will want to know about it." She seemed to regard him for a moment. "You did well."

"I wish we could've caught him."

Jennings nodded. "At least we got to walk away."

Dash sat there for a few minutes, lost in his own thoughts. He kept going over the conversation in his mind. He had no real idea that whatever they'd found would help Noah. He'd lied. There was no reason to believe that NEIIS medicine was in any way compatible with human physiology. The R&D folks would research it, but he didn't think there was a miracle cure for Noah. Yet Lars had allowed him to walk away with it, which meant there was some part of him that possibly regretted what had happened to Noah. Why else would Lars have spared them?

Dash sank back into his chair and sighed.

36

THE NEIIS HAD a proclivity for building some of their settlements underground, and this made Lars wonder if the species that had become the NEIIS had once lived underground. He and his people were currently returning to a place deep in a mountainous region where he'd found the remains of an NEIIS military bunker. It was a good place to hide, although he didn't think of it as hiding but rather as a secure location away from the colony. There had been a few other bases, and Lars liked to rotate the people under his command among them.

The two Hellcats were flying in formation, using enhanced stealth. All transponders and automatic registers had been removed from the ship's systems so they couldn't be traced by Field Ops or the Colonial Defense Force. As they approached their destination, the Hellcats flew through the bunker doors and landed in the LZ. He ordered that the berwolves be returned to their pens. This had been their first successful operation with the creatures, and he was pleased with the result, assured it was one project that would move forward when he reported it up the chain.

Evans climbed off the loading ramp from the other Hellcat and stormed over to him. "What was that?"

"I let them go."

"I had the shot. Why didn't you give me the green light?"

"It was one NEIIS. Dying, by the looks of it."

"Not soon enough. We need to take them out wherever we can."

Evans was a bit of a hothead, and Lars knew it. He'd calm down eventually.

"Why don't you go shower up," Lars said.

"I have to report this."

"I have nothing to hide."

Evans regarded him for a moment and then nodded. "Just tell me this wasn't because you feel guilty."

Lars watched as the berwolves were guided away from the Hellcats. "If we'd killed that NEIIS, the CDF soldiers would've returned fire. Do you want to be responsible for killing soldiers?"

"We could've disabled them without killing any of them."

Lars shook his head. "Wasn't worth the risk. Right now, the CDF won't engage with us because we're colonists. We may not conduct ourselves out in the open, but ultimately, we only have Field Operations and Security to contend with. However, if we push the CDF too far and we don't have the backing we need, we could be declared enemies. In other words, what you fail to grasp is that if the CDF wanted to find us, they could. If a soldier had been accidentally killed, it would've been our fault, and they'd unleash the hounds on us."

Evans started to protest, and Lars grabbed him and slammed him against the wall. "Listen to me, and let it penetrate into your brain. You were a soldier. Right now, they don't know what to do about us, but if we start killing soldiers, we become the enemy. We need more support. Do you understand me?" Lars said.

Evans sucked in a deep breath and sighed. Then he nodded, and Lars let him go.

"It's been a long mission, but the work we're doing is important. Pretty soon the right people will learn that we've been right all along. We just need to be patient."

"Yes, sir," Evans said and walked away.

Lars headed to his office. They'd happened to be within two hundred kilometers when they detected the CDF Hellcats, but he hadn't known Dash DeWitt would be with them. Dash still blamed him for what had happened to Noah.

Lars walked into his office and tossed his backpack onto the floor. He brought up his personal holoscreen and opened the secure comlink to Sierra.

"There's been a new development," Lars said and began the debriefing for his superiors.

"Let them continue to make friends with the locals. It only makes our position stronger when it blows up in their faces."

The voice was disguised in case even their secure channel was compromised. Lars wasn't sure which of his superiors he was reporting to.

"They have to be ready to listen to reason by now. Let me reach out to Connor. I can get him to listen to me," Lars said.

"Not yet. I have something else for you to do first."

Lars stifled the protest that had been forming in his mind and listened as the next phase of their plan was laid out for him.

37

CONNOR WALKED into the medical center at Sanctuary and headed for Diaz's room. He'd spent a few days with his family, and it had left him feeling recharged, but now there was something in the back of his mind, urging him to get to work. He made his way to Diaz's room and knocked on the door, glancing through the window at his friend. Diaz was sitting up in bed, but his eyes were closed. His arm was in a sling from where the creature had nearly torn it off, and Diaz's face also showed signs of recent healing. Connor felt someone tap him on the shoulder, and he turned to see Ashley standing behind him.

"I'm glad I caught you before you went in to see him."

"How's he doing?" Connor asked.

"His injuries are healing well, but he's still really shaken up."

Connor nodded. "It was pretty bad, Ashley. I'm not going to kid you. He almost died."

Ashley gave him a long look. "I know he's your friend, Connor, but this recommendation is coming from me as a doctor. Diaz needs to be moved off the active duty roster for a while."

Connor waited for her to continue.

"He loves you. You guys have been friends since you first got here. You watch each other's backs, and I understand that. He's not going to like it at all. He's not going to like not going with you wherever it is that you're going from here, but it's for the best," Ashley said, gesturing toward the window where Diaz sat dozing.

"You're right; he's really gonna hate it, but I think you're right. He's been different lately. Tired."

"Everyone has their limits, Connor. We can push past them for a little while, but I think Diaz has reached his, at least for now." She reached out and put her hand on his shoulder, giving it a gentle squeeze. Then she left him, and Connor went inside Diaz's room.

Diaz opened his eyes and looked at Connor. "It's about time you came to see me."

"I've been keeping an eye on you. I hear you'll be getting out soon."

Diaz nodded and raised his arm in its sling. "It'll be a few more weeks for this and the leg. That thing crushed them like they were paper."

"Maybe he just didn't like how you tasted and spit you out."

Diaz grinned softly. Then he shivered and looked up at Connor guiltily.

"Don't do that," Connor said. "Nothing wrong— It was... Hell, it would've shaken anybody up."

Diaz swallowed and looked away. "I know."

Connor was quiet for a moment, stalling for more time. He didn't want to say what he needed to say right then. "I think you need to take some time off. I mean, after you're all healed up. Maybe think about sticking around Sanctuary and taking a post training the troops again? Or we can come up with something else," he said while resisting the urge to look away from his friend.

Diaz looked at him for a long moment. He wasn't fooled, but

he wasn't protesting either. "Yeah, maybe that might be a good idea for a while until I'm back on my feet."

Connor nodded and blew out a breath of relief. "Good. Ashley just sent me a message. She needs to talk to me, so I'll let you get some rest. Send my love to Victoria."

It was a lie, and Diaz probably knew it.

"I heard you set a trap for them," Diaz said.

Connor nodded.

Diaz leaned back and rested his head on his pillow. "Good."

Connor left the room, a guilty pang twisting inside his chest. He didn't know what was worse—taking his friend off active duty so he didn't get killed or feeling like he couldn't do the same for himself. He moved a few steps away from Diaz's room and took a deep breath. He turned and glanced back at the door, and his throat became thick. "Damn it," he hissed and then walked away.

Connor found himself walking to the long-term care wing of the medical center. Noah's room was just ahead. He stopped outside the door and glanced through the window to see the room dimly lit and no one visiting. He opened the door and stepped inside.

Noah lay on the bed. There was a quiet hum from the machines that were keeping his friend alive. Connor glanced at the monitoring station. Noah's vital signs were stable.

He walked over to the bed. "Hey there," Connor said, looking down at his unconscious friend. "I figured I'd stop by and check on you."

He looked at Noah's eyelids, hoping to see some sign that his friend knew he was there, but nothing changed. Noah remained as unresponsive as always. "I could really use your help. These things we're facing—" Connor said and shook his head. He wanted to tell him to wake up. Noah's body was healed. Why wouldn't he wake up already? Connor needed his help.

The door opened and Ashley stepped inside. "I thought I might find you here."

"He still looks the same," Connor said without looking up.

Ashley stayed near the door. "We've been noticing increased brain activity at times. We think he's dreaming. The episodes are intermittent so they're hard to predict." Connor looked at her as she continued. "This is a good thing, Connor. It means he's still with us."

He pressed his lips together, refusing to get his hopes up. "How long can he stay like this?"

She walked to his side. "You're not going to like any answer I can give you," she said in a soothing tone. "We've been researching different treatments for a person in Noah's condition to see if we can help wake him from his coma. We'll keep trying."

Connor sighed and looked at her. "We should talk about Sean."

Ashley looked away from him. "I've been afraid for my son ever since he snuck off to join you in that Search and Rescue platoon. I knew then that he'd chosen a dangerous line of work."

"I wouldn't count him out. He's still out there, Ashley. We'll find him, or he'll make it back to us. Sean is smart and has all the right instincts." He paused for a moment. "I have absolute faith in him."

"I know you do," she said and regarded him for a moment. "I know you love him like he was one of your own, but I can't lose him. Do you understand? I can't lose my son."

Connor had rarely seen Ashley as emotional as she was right then. He remembered her grieving for Tobias when he'd died, and he didn't want to see her go through that again. The brilliant woman she was struggled with the fact that her child was in real danger.

"I understand, Ashley, and I'll do everything I can. You know that."

She nodded, but the worry in her gaze made her look oddly vulnerable. Together, they left the room.

CONNOR WALKED out of the medical center feeling as if he'd run the whole way from New Haven to Sanctuary. It was as if everything that had happened had just compressed into the last thirty minutes. Seeing Diaz recovering from his injuries and Noah still in a coma was taking a toll on him. And listening to Ashley plead with him to bring her son back alive had twisted him up into knots. All he needed was for Lenora to stand in front of him, holding their daughter Lauren in her arms, begging him not to leave. Connor sighed and dismissed that last thought. He meant what he'd said about having absolute faith in Sean, but he hoped he'd never have to tell Ashley that her son wasn't coming home. He'd do everything in his power to make sure that never happened.

Connor left the medical center and decided to take a walk. There were gray skies over Sanctuary, but he needed to stretch his legs and be alone for a while. He had people waiting for him at the CDF base, and there were even more people waiting for him at Sierra. The list could go on and on. Sometimes it seemed as if *everybody* was waiting for him—as if he had some way to protect the entire colony from an enemy they were only beginning to understand. What little they'd learned only reinforced the fact that they needed to know more. *He* needed to know more.

He'd been walking for about a half hour and was by the Colonial Research Institute when Dash came out of the entrance. His eyes widened when he saw Connor.

"I was just coming to find you," Dash said.

"Today that's pretty easy, apparently. I just came from the medical center."

Dash nodded. "I heard what happened. Lenora just told me some of the things, anyway."

Connor didn't want to talk about it anymore, so he switched the subject. "Did you ever find the NEIIS medicinals?"

Dash walked next to him and they kept going. "The medicinals they had stored were long dead, but I was just talking with some people inside who're going to try to extract the DNA to reconstruct it. We should know in a few days."

Then Dash told him about Lars and the clash between the people working with Lars and the CDF. "I know the CDF isn't supposed to become involved with colonial affairs that deal with other colonists, but it was a close thing. They had us pinned down. Lars let us go."

"You did what you had to do. It sounds like you kept a level head and helped defuse the situation. I'd call that a win in my book, and you might've found a way to stop what's happening to the NEIIS."

"When you put it like that, it sounds great. Doesn't feel like a win, though. Lars is still out there, and he has a lot of help," Dash said, glancing around. "I almost feel that there are a lot of people who support what Lars is doing. There's not much trust where the NEIIS are concerned."

"No, there isn't, but we need them, and they need us."

"I wish I could've done more. I wish I could've caught Lars."

"We'll keep looking for him," Connor said

Dash nodded. "I know, but Lars talked about knowing something about the NEIIS again—something he believes the rest of us don't know. I've been studying the NEIIS for a long time, and I keep wondering what Lars could have found that we haven't already discovered."

"What does Lenora think of all this?" Connor asked and glanced down the road ahead of them. He heard Dash begin to reply but then stopped what he was saying. A giant bear of a man was walking toward them from down the street. He was dressed in civilian clothes, but his muscles pushed against his shirt. He had short-cropped hair unlike when Connor had last seen him. The scraggly beard was gone, and for a moment Connor was reminded of a time before he'd come to the colony.

"Who is *that*?" Dash asked.

"Used to be an old friend," Connor said.

The man walked directly towards them. There was still a wildness to his gaze, something just along the edge that could be revealed or exposed at the slightest provocation, but somehow he seemed a little bit different now.

"General," Samson said, "I heard you had a few open slots on your team."

Connor regarded the former Ghost for a moment. "That depends. I only work with the best. Do you think you have what it takes?"

Samson showed a healthy set of pearly white teeth. "Give me a couple squads and just point me in the right direction."

"We'll still need to qualify you. You might've gotten rusty living out in the forest by yourself. Do you still remember how to handle a rifle?"

Samson arched a dark eyebrow. "I thought we covered hand-to-hand combat the last time we met."

"That we did," Connor replied, remembering when he and Diaz had gone to find Samson. "I hope you're ready to work because we've got a lot to do."

They continued walking ahead, and Connor introduced Dash to Samson. He hadn't been joking about qualifying Samson for the CDF. He expected Samson wouldn't have any problems when it came to weapons qualifications—he was a specialist in that regard—but the psychological tests were another matter. Samson was a soldier to his core, but he'd left the colony and lived in isolation. Connor had hated knowing he was alone, away from people, living like some kind of animal. He'd lost a lot of people along the road that had brought him where he was, but sometimes they came back. He hoped it would be that way for Samson, and he also hoped it would be that way for Sean.

38

THE SURVIVING ships of the CDF Battle Group Trident were huddled together like some form of interstellar life raft. It'd taken nearly twenty-four hours to transfer the surviving crew off the *Douglass* and give them temporary homes on the other ships, including the *Vigilant*. With the exception of the *Yorktown*, no ship had escaped unscathed. Sean had kept their carrier ship away from the fighting, and it had been the first through the space gate. Damage reports, repairing critical systems, and search and rescue had become the top priorities, and Sean had authorized the use of stimulants to keep the crew working. The *Dutchman* and the *Ajax* were still unaccounted for, and the general assumption was that they'd been lost.

Sean kept wondering how the hell their mission had gone to shit so damn fast. One moment they'd achieved their objective, taking out two enemy ships and disabling a third, and he'd been about to order the Talon-V Stormers to board the enemy ship. Sean shook his head. He was standing in his ready room near the bridge. Compared to the cacophony of the past twenty-four hours, the silence there was almost unnerving yet welcoming at the same time. He had multiple wallscreens active, and Gabriel had the status reports showing for each ship in the battle group. He stared at it all, but he couldn't read any of it. His brain refused to process any more information. He'd reached his limit, and he almost wished he could get someone else to deal with all of it. He was just so damn tired. One single clash with the enemy, which should have been a straight-shot operation, had unraveled so disastrously that they'd almost all been killed. The list of casualties was in the hundreds, and the nausea he felt at the back of his throat and the tightness in his stomach had become the norm.

Sean closed his eyes for a moment and then opened them again. The wallscreens with their critically important data pushed in all around, smothering him. He drew in a deep breath that sounded like a snarl and held it in a half-strangled choke. Then the wallscreens flickered off all at once, plunging the room into visual silence. Even the buzzing in the back of his head lessened.

"Colonel Quinn," Gabriel said, his baritone voice coming through the speakers in the ready room, "your heart rate is extremely elevated. Stress levels are rising. Shall I contact Dr. Grady?"

Sean blew out the breath he'd been holding and shook his head. "No." Even the damn AI was worried about him. He took a few more breaths, pacing back and forth for a few moments before continuing. "Not necessary, Gabriel."

Sean swung his gaze around his completely well-ordered office and wanted to smash everything. It was stupid and he knew it, but he wanted to do it anyway. He'd been to the med bay to check on the injured soldiers and the medical staff there. The soldiers who'd lived largely had broken bones, but there were a few burn victims. They offered a brief respite from the crew who had died.

He tapped his leg absently and shook his head. He hadn't felt this wrung out since the end of the Vemus War, but at least back then he'd been planet-side, and opportunities to blow off some steam had been plentiful. Operating like they were made everything—the risks, the intensity, the stakes—just more. Sean exhaled a long breath. He needed to get back out there. There was so much more to be done.

"Dr. Evans is outside your door. Shall I let her in?" Gabriel asked.

Without waiting for Sean's reply, the door opened and Oriana stood outside. Appearing startled for a moment by the unexpected opening of the door, she just looked at him, but then her eyes slipped into a quick assessment as if she were debating whether to speak to him.

"You might as well just give me the bad news. There's never going to be a good time," Sean said and gestured for her to come in.

Oriana stepped through the door and tilted her head ever so slightly to the side. It reminded him of his mother's look of borderline disapproval when his attitude wasn't what she'd deemed appropriate—not that any of his thoughts of Oriana coincided with thoughts of his mother. It was probably just a woman thing.

Sean looked away from her and squeezed his eyes shut. "I'm sorry, it's just been a hell of a day."

"Has anyone ever told you that you have a knack for understatement?"

A tired smile struggled to lift Sean's lips. "I've been called worse," he said and took a few steps toward his desk, leaning back to rest on the edge and gesturing next to him so Oriana could sit. She had faint smudge marks on her cheek left over from a quick rinse, but her sweetly angelic face seemed untarnished by all that had happened—her face maybe, but not her eyes. The luminous depths of her gaze held the tension of the past twenty-four hours.

Sean swallowed hard.

"There are several gate cube matrices that are unaccounted for, and over half of them have sustained damage that we're still trying to assess. Bottom line is that we're not going anywhere anytime soon. I thought you ought to know so you could..." She paused. Sean had reached out and placed his hand over hers. He hadn't thought about it; he'd just done it. Her eyes widened a little. "Sean," she said softly.

He closed his eyes, unable to look at anything right then. "It feels... nice. Doesn't it?" he asked, not wanting her to pull her hand away. Not now.

She was going to slap him.

Instead, Sean felt her other hand rubbing the top of his. Her hands were smooth and warm and perfect. He sighed and felt some of the tension just melt away from the depths of his core. The skin around his eyes tightened and they began to ache. He gritted his teeth. "I'm sorry. I know this isn't... professional," he said and looked at her.

"No," Oriana said gently, "but it's fine."

Sean's throat thickened. "I just couldn't—I can't—I want to..." he began, but then shook his head. "We're in the shit now. God, we are so far in it now." Oriana didn't say anything. She was never one to fill a moment of time with idle chitchat. He liked that about her. "Thanks," he said.

"Good," she said. "As pleasant as holding your hand is, I think we ought to get back to work."

She eased her hands away from his and they stood up. Sean didn't know why, but he felt a renewed sense of vigor. He arched an eyebrow towards her. "So you liked it?"

Oriana frowned.

"I just wanted to confirm that you liked it when I held your hand."

Her expression was a mix between annoyance and amusement, and he was pretty sure she was thinking of another word to call him at that moment—shout it more likely. Instead, she met his gaze and leaned toward him. "I think you enjoyed it more than I did," she said and started heading toward the door.

He thought he saw more of a swing of her hips and grinned. "Well, it's not every day I can say that I held hands with the illustrious and beautiful Dr. Oriana Evans. Do you know how many other men would—" He stopped talking when her expression registered.

"Go on, finish what you were saying."

Sean smiled. "I was going to say ... be fortunate to have you as a friend."

Oriana opened the door and then paused for a moment, as if considering what she wanted to say. Then she looked at him in such a way that he felt like some unseen force was pushing on his chest. "Well, the way *you* handle things, friends is all we'll ever be."

She left the room and Sean quickly followed her. She was making a beeline to the bridge and he caught up to her. Just as the door was beginning to open, he said, "We'll see about that."

She heard him. She had to have heard him, but the door to the bridge opened, and Sean stepped inside, walking toward the command area. Their situation hadn't improved in the slightest, but he felt like he could take it on now. What a difference a few moments alone made. He glanced at Oriana as she came to sit at the workstation next to the command chair. No, not alone, but in the right company. The right woman.

"Colonel Quinn," Specialist Sansky said, "I just received an update from the *Dutchman*. The ship is intact but heavily damaged."

"Good news. Where are they?"

"Captain Martinez says the *Ajax* was destroyed before they went through the Krake space gate. He reports that they have minimal engines and have been using maneuvering thrusters to nudge the ship away from the gate. He's not sure where they are."

"Open a comlink to my personal holoscreen," Sean said. A

moment later there was a subspace communication comlink on his holoscreen. A timer appeared in the upper right-hand corner. He had five minutes or less. "It's good to hear from you, Captain."

"Colonel, you're a sight for sore eyes. I thought the battle group was a goner."

"We almost were, but let's get you sorted out first. I was told that you have limited engine capacity and that you're using maneuvering thrusters to help get underway."

"Yes, Colonel. It's slow going, and I don't know where you are. We have limited use of our scanner array and have done only a passive scan. We might've detected a few Krake installations farther in system, but they don't seem to have been alerted to our presence."

"Understood. Do you have any combat shuttles available?"

Martinez frowned for a moment. "Yes, we do, Colonel."

"If they're flight worthy, use them to give you an extra boost. As soon as we're done here, I'm going to send you a set of coordinates. Slow and steady, and we'll get you back safely."

Martinez blew out a breath. "Colonel, I'm so glad you're here. The crew and I... Well, you know."

"I understand. We're not out of the woods. We've all been beat up, and it's going to take a while for us to make repairs. Stand by for data package transfer," Sean said.

The timer on the subspace communication session ran out.

"Tactical, send a retrieval data package to the *Dutchman*," Sean said.

"Yes, Colonel, will do," Lieutenant Russo said, smiling.

On Sean's personal holoscreen, he saw that the casualty list had just become a little shorter. It didn't make up for the lives that had been lost, but he was thankful that at least some of them had been spared.

AUTHOR NOTE

Thank you for reading one of my books! This is the 18th book I've written since 2013. It took me years to write that first book, mostly because I couldn't get out of my own way. I worked in IT security for 20 years. However, in 2013 I set a goal to finish a story I'd begun writing a long time ago.

So what happened in 2013? It was simple. I decided that I wanted to change careers. I'd just finished getting a masters degree, which required a lot of work outside my normal day job. Why not put that effort into something I really wanted to do. I wanted to become a writer.

Quitting my job to give this whole writing thing a shot wasn't a serious option for me. I have a family and all the responsibilities that go along with it. I've always been an avid reader. I wrote a few short stories, and I had a book that I'd started. I spent years occasionally revising the first one hundred pages, kidding myself that if I got them perfect the rest of the story would just flow. That didn't work for me at all. In 2013 I started over and finished the entire book in about six months. This was a fantasy book about a guy from Earth who discovers that his family is from another world. This became a four book series called the Safanarion Order, which I've described as a science fiction story disguised as a fantasy. A true mashup that crosses genres.

I learned a lot writing that series. I didn't go through the time-honored tradition of acquiring a stack of rejection letters from publishers. What I did get instead was validation from readers that they enjoyed my work and encouraged me to keep writing. I wasn't one of those overnight successes that you might have heard about. My first royalty payment paid for the heating oil delivery to my house, which was awesome.

After I finished the Safanarion Order series, I wrote down an idea that involved the New Horizons spacecraft that had recently gone to Pluto. What if those pictures had included an alien structure on Pluto. What if aliens were watching us? Monitoring our progress. What would we do? What if they sent us a warning? This idea became the Ascension series. I think I learned more about the solar system writing the Star Shroud than I have writing any other book to date.

While writing the Ascension series, I worked to improve my craft. Ascension was my first science fiction series. It was fun and readers seem to really like it. I released Star Shroud in 2016 and wrote two more books in the Ascension series that year. The series was doing well enough to garner the attention of a few audiobook publishers. Later that year those books were released in audiobook format. This was pretty exciting and I was getting close to earning enough from book sales to replace my current salary.

2017 turned out to be a rough year for me. A major set back. More on that in a minute.

I periodically write down ideas for stories and then keep them on the back-burner for a while. I don't have a set schedule for it; I just do it. One of those ideas became the First Colony series. I wanted to write a story set a few hundred years in the future. I wanted to go to a new world. What if things went really bad for people on Earth while a colony ship was traveling to a new star system? So bad in fact that they modified the navigation system on the ship to change colony destination. Sending them much farther away than originally anticipated. I had a new world to explore which had remnants of a previous civilization (the good stuff), but what if whatever happened to Earth eventually caught up with the colony? What if the main character wasn't supposed to be on that colony ship in the first place? This was the premise for the First Colony series. I had no idea that so many people would come to enjoy the story so much. I wanted to tell a colonization story with elements of a military science fiction. Thus, Connor Gates was born.

Since you've read this book and assuming you've read the previous books in the series, you've come along for what I hope was a fun escape from everyday life. First Colony is my most popular series of books. I am immensely grateful for all the support and kind words people have sent me about it. The First Colony series allowed me to become a full-time writer. After four and a half years of setting goals and improving my craft, I achieved my dream. I still work very hard to improve my craft and I don't think I will ever stop. When I write a story, I have a vision in my head and I want to be able to deliver it masterfully. My goal now, aside from paying my bills, is to be a great writer and storyteller. My journey is far from over. When other writers ask me what it's like to be a full-time author, I describe it as a labor of love. I don't think a person would really enjoy doing this unless they loved it.

Back to 2017. A lot of things happened to me that year before I started writing the First Colony series. As I said before, 2017 was a tough year for me. I released a book called Haven of Shadows, which was the 1st book of a spinoff series from the Safanarion Order. It flopped. For whatever reason, that book has never really found its audience. I wrote and released two more books in the Ascension series (Infinity's Edge - Book 4 & Rising Force - Book 5), however interest in the series was waning. During the time between releasing these two books, I'd found out from my employer that I was going to be laid off in about six months. I'd worked for them for over ten years. Anyone who's ever gone through a layoff knows how difficult and unsettling news like that can be. It's shocking. My boss hated giving me the news probably as much as I hated receiving it. Both my kids are in high school, but I didn't tell them for a long time. They didn't need to worry about that. I did tell my wife of course, and despite the lackluster year of book sales it had been so far, I was seriously considering making a go at becoming a full-time author. She was scared and rightfully so. Up to that point, I'd released ten books, and I had about four years worth of steadily increasing book sales, so the numbers were generally going in the right direction despite the recent setbacks. However, I was not earning enough to quit my job at that time. I had six months to prepare. So I freaked out a little bit. Alright, more than a little. I'll be honest, I was terrified. I was being pushed out of my comfort zone. Could I go from being a hobbyist-with-potential to a full-time author? I mentioned earlier that I worked in IT security. Technology aside, IT security is mostly about reducing risk. I needed a plan, so I wrote out a business plan. Sexy right? Actually...it depends, but it was necessary. Having a well thought out plan with clearly defined goals made both me and my wife feel a little bit better about changing careers, but I had a lot of work to do. This was April 2017.

Over the next six months until my last day at work, I took the premise for the First Colony series and wrote two books. I got up early in the morning (4AM) and wrote before I had to work (8am) and then on lunchtime and in the evenings. Part of the weekends too. It was crunch time. I put my blinders on and got to work. I started a daily journal at that time, which I continue to write in. What can I say, writers are going to write. I've gone back and re-

read all those journal entries. It was interesting for me to look back and see the transition in myself that was occurring.

I still remember the day I published Genesis – First Colony book 1 in September 2017. On the whiteboard in my home office, I wrote, Sink or Swim with a big question mark. My last day at work came at the beginning of September. I took a day off for that and then got back to work. The clock was ticking. I said a few prayers right before I published Genesis and I started writing the third book in the First Colony series. I remember thinking I really hoped people liked this story.

Within a month after I published Genesis, the book skyrocketed to the top of the charts and stayed there. I was awestruck. In December 2017, I finally came up for air. Life certainly hadn't stopped because I had decided to change careers. I had a lot going on aside from changing careers and I think my brain simply said you need a break, Ken. So I slowed down just a little bit. I went from working insane hours to working a more regular schedule.

In 2018 I continued to write and release books along with asking myself how long can this last? Was the success of the First Colony series some kind of mistake? I don't doubt my abilities as a writer. I'd proven that I could write a story, but was I good enough to keep going for the long haul? This is a question that most writers I've met have thought about. I plan to be around for a long time writing books. We'll just have to wait and see if I'm still around five, ten, or twenty years from now.

Why put all this at the end of the book? It's simple really. I wanted you to know a little bit about who I am. The person behind the stories.

If you're a reader reading this, then you have my profound thanks. You read one of my books and I sincerely hope you've enjoyed it.

If you're a writer reading this, then I hope you've gleaned some useful information and possibly some inspiration for your own journey. For me, the secret sauce was hard work and dedication. While overnight success stories are extremely inspiring, it's also nice to know that success is something you can work toward one step at a time.

Again, thank you for reading one of my books. If you wouldn't mind, please consider leaving a review for this book. Reviews really do help even if it's just a few words to say that you really like this book.

I do have a Facebook group called **Ken Lozito's SF readers**. If you're on Facebook and you'd like to stop by, please search for it on Facebook.

Not everyone is on Facebook. I get it, but I also have a blog if you'd like to stop by there. My blog is more of a monthly check-in as to the status of what I'm working on. Please stop by and say hello, I'd love to hear from you.

Visit www.kenlozito.com

THANK YOU FOR READING VIGILANCE - FIRST COLONY - BOOK SEVEN.

If you loved this book, please consider leaving a review. Comments and reviews allow readers to discover authors, so if you want others to enjoy *Vigilance* as you have, please leave a short note.

The series will continue with the **8th book.** If you would like to be notified when my next book is released please visit kenlozito.com and sign up to get a heads up.

I've created a special **Facebook Group** specifically for readers to come together and share their interests, especially regarding my books. Check it out and join the discussion by searching for **Ken Lozito's SF Worlds.**

ABOUT THE AUTHOR

Ken Lozito is the author of multiple science fiction and fantasy series. I've been reading both genres for a long time. Books were my way to escape everyday life of a teenager to my current ripe old(?) age. What started out as a love of stories has turned into a full-blown passion for writing them. My ultimate intent for writing stories is to provide fun escapism for readers. I write stories that I would like to read and I hope you enjoy them as well.

If you have questions or comments about any of my works I would love to hear from you, even if its only to drop by to say hello at KenLozito.com

Thanks again for reading *First Colony - Vigilance*

Don't be shy about emails, I love getting them, and try to respond to everyone.

ALSO BY KEN LOZITO

Haven of Shadows

CPSIA information can be obtained
at www.ICGtesting.com
Printed in the USA
LVHW091336240419
615387LV00001B/236/P